THE
BURGLAR
IN THE RYE

Other Books by Lawrence Block

THE
BURGLAR
IN THE RYE

LAWRENCE BLOCK

NO EXIT PRESS

This edition published in 2001 by No Exit Press
18 Coleswood Road, Harpenden, Herts, AL5 1EQ

www.noexit.co.uk

A CIP catalogue record for this book is available from the British Library.

ISBN 1-84243-030-0 The Burglar in the Rye

2 4 6 8 10 9 7 5 3 1

Printed by Omnia Books, Glasgow

this one's for JOE PITTMAN

The author is pleased to acknowledge his gratitude to the crew and passengers of the clipper ship *Star Flyer*, where much of the writing of this book was done en route from Phuket to Athens.

ONE

The lobby was a bit the worse for wear. The large oriental carpet had seen better days, lots of them. The facing Lawson sofas sagged invitingly and, like the rest of the furniture, showed the effects of long use. They were in use now; two women sat in animated conversation, and, a few yards away, a man with a long oval face and a high forehead sat reading a copy of *GQ*. He wore sunglasses, which made him look dapper and sly. I don't know how they made the magazine look. Dark, I suppose.

While the lobby may have been the least bit down at the heels, the overall impression was not so much of shabbiness as of comfort. The glow of a fire in the fireplace, a welcome sight on a brisk October day, put everything in the best possible light. And, centered above the fireplace mantel, painted with such œil-tromping realism you wanted to reach out and pick him up and hug him, was the hotel's namesake.

He was a bear, of course, but not the sort whose predilection for sylvan defecation is as proverbial as the Holy Father's Catholicism. This bear, one saw at a glance, had never been to the woods, let alone behaved irresponsibly there. He was wearing a little red jacket, and he had a floppy royal blue rain hat on his head, and his legs ended in a pair of Wellington boots the color of a canary, and every bit as cheerful. He was perched on a shelf between a battered Gladstone grip and a shopping bag from Harrods, and a stenciled sign overhead proclaimed, "Left Luggage," and . . .

But I don't need to go on, do I? If you didn't have such a bear yourself, surely you knew someone who did. For this was Paddington Bear himself, and who else should it be? Who better to grace the lobby of the legendary Paddington Hotel?

And legendary was the word for it. The Paddington, seven stories of red brick and black ironwork, stands at the corner of Madison Avenue and East Twenty-fifth Street, across from Madison Square and not far from the site of Stanford White's Madison Square Garden. (That was the *second* Madison Square Garden, as opposed to Garden #3, the one your father remembers at Eighth Avenue and Fiftieth Street, or the current entry, Garden #4, above Penn Station. White's Garden was an architectural masterpiece, but then so was the original Penn Station. Sic transit damn near everything.)

But not the Paddington, which had gone up before the Garden and had lived to tell the tale. Built around the turn of the century, it had watched the neighborhood (and the city, and the world) reinvent itself continually over the years. For all that, the old hotel remained essentially the same. It had never been terribly grand, had always had more permanent residents than transient guests, and had from its earliest days drawn persons in the arts. Brass plaques flanking the entrance recorded some of the Paddington's more prominent tenants, including the writers Stephen Crane and Theodore Dreiser and the Shakespearean actor Reginald French. John Steinbeck had spent a month there during a period of marital disharmony, and Robert Henri, the Ashcan School artist, had stayed at the Paddington before relocating a few blocks south and east at Gramercy Park.

More recently, the hotel had drawn touring British rock stars, who seemed less inclined to destroy rooms here than in other American hotels, either out of respect for its traditions or from a sense that the damage they did might go unnoticed. Two of them had died on the premises, one murdered by a drifter he'd brought back to his room, the other more conventionally of a heroin overdose.

Classical music was represented as well, by at least two of the permanent residents, and the occasional performer on tour. An octogenarian pianist, Alfred Hertel, whose annual Christmas concert at Carnegie Hall was always sold out, had occupied an apartment on the top floor for over forty years. At the opposite end of the same floor lived the aging diva Sonia Brigandi, whose legendary temperament survived the decline of her legendary soprano voice. Once in a while one or both of them would leave their doors open, and one would play what the other would sing, thrilling (or annoying) the other residents with something from Puccini or Verdi or Wagner.

Other than that they didn't speak. Rumors abounded—that they'd had an affair, that they'd been rivals for some other tenant's affections. He was said to be gay, although he'd been married twice and had children and grandchildren. She had never married and was said to have had lovers of both sexes. And both of them were supposed to have slept with Edgar Lee Horvath, who'd never slept with anyone. Except for his bears, of course.

It was Horvath, the founder of Pop Realism, who had painted the Paddington Bear over the lobby fireplace. He'd taken rooms in the hotel in the mid-sixties, shortly after the success of his first one-man show, and had lived there until his death in 1979. The painting had been a gift to the hotel, given early in his stay, and, with the sharp increase in value of Horvath's works since his death, it was probably worth close to a million dollars. And there it was, hanging right there in plain sight, in an essentially unguarded lobby.

Of course a person would have to be crazy to steal it. Edgar Horvath had painted a whole series of teddy bears, from bedraggled early Stieff creations to contemporary plush creatures, and a teddy bear of one sort or another was invariably present in his portraits and landscapes and interiors. His desert landscapes, done during a brief stay in Taos, show bears sprawled at the foot of an enormous cactus, or straddling a fence rail, or propped up against an adobe wall.

But, as far as anyone knew, he'd only painted Paddington once. And that painting hung famously in the hotel's famously threadbare lobby. It was there for the taking, but so what? If you hooked that painting, how and to whom would you sell it?

I knew all that. But old habits die hard, and I've never been able to look at something of great value without trying to figure out a way to rescue it from its rightful owner. The painting was in a massive frame of gilded wood, and I pondered the relative merits of cutting it out of its frame as opposed to lifting it, frame and all.

I was busy contemplating grand larceny when the desk clerk asked if he could help me.

"Sorry," I said. "I was looking at the painting."

"Our mascot," he said. He was a man about fifty, wearing a dark green silk shirt with a flowing collar and a string tie with a turquoise slide. His hair was Just for Men black, and his sideburns were longer than fashion would have them. He was clean-shaven, but he looked as though he ought to have a mustache, and as though it ought to be waxed.

"Poor Eddie Horvath painted him," he said. "Such a loss when he died, and so ironic."

"He died in a restaurant, didn't he?"

"Right around the corner. Eddie had the world's worst diet, he lived on cheeseburgers and Coca-Cola and Hostess cupcakes. And then some doctor convinced him to change his ways, and overnight he became a health-food fanatic."

"And it didn't agree with him?"

"I didn't notice any difference," he said, "except that he became a bit of a bore on the subject, as converts will do in the early days of their conversion. I'm sure he'd have outgrown it, but he never had the chance. He died at the dinner table, choked to death on a piece of tofu."

"How awful."

"Awful enough to eat it," he said. "Hideous to die of it. But Eddie's painting linked us forever to Paddington Bear, to the point where people think we're named for him."

"The hotel came first, didn't it?"

"By a good many years. Michael Bond's book about the brave little bear in the Left Luggage isn't much more than thirty years old, while we go back to the turn of the century. I can't say for certain if we were named for Paddington Station or its immediate environs. The neighborhood's not the best in London, I'm sorry to say, but it's not the worst, either. Cheap hotels and Asian restaurants. The Welsh take rooms there, fresh off the trains that pull into Paddington Station. And there's a tube stop there as well, but I can't believe this hotel was named after a tube stop."

"I'm sure it wasn't."

"And I'm sure you're terribly polite, letting me natter on this way. Now how may I help you?"

The nattering had changed the way he sounded, I noted; talking about London had given him an English accent. I told him I had a reservation, and he asked my name.

"Peter Jeffries," I said.

"Jeffries," he said, thumbing a stack of cards. "I don't seem to . . . oh, for heaven's sake. Someone's written it down as Jeffrey Peters."

I said it was a natural mistake, fairly certain as I spoke that the mistake was mine. I'd somehow managed to screw up my own alias. Inverting the first and last names was a natural consequence of picking an alias consisting of two first names, which in turn is something amateurs tend to do all the time.

And that was more dismaying than the mistake itself. For what was I if not a professional? And *where* was I if I started behaving like an amateur?

I filled out the card—an address in San Francisco, a departure date three days off—and said I'd be paying cash. Three nights at $155 a night plus tax, and a deposit for the phone, came to somewhere around $575. I counted out six hundreds and the fellow ran a finger over his upper lip, grooming the mustache he didn't have, and asked me if I would be wanting a bear.

"A bear?"

He nodded at a trio of Paddington Bears, perched atop a filing cabinet and looking quite like the bear over the fireplace. "You may think this is all too cute for words," he said, the English accent gone now, "and perhaps you'd be right. It started after Eddie's painting brought the hotel a new burst of fame. He collected teddy bears, you know, and after he died his collection brought ridiculous prices at Sotheby's. A Horvath Collection pedigree is for a bear what a few hours around Jackie O's neck is for a string of cultured pearls."

"And these three bears were his?"

"On, no, not at all. They're ours, I'm afraid, purchased by the management from FAO Schwartz or Bears R Us. I don't really know where we get them. Any guest who wants can have the company of a bear during his stay. There's no charge."

"Really."

"You needn't think it's sheer altruism on our part. A surprising number of guests decide they'd rather take Paddington home with them than get their deposit back. Not everyone takes a bear upstairs in the first place, but of those who do, few want to give them up."

"I'll take a bear," I said recklessly.

"And I'll take a fifty-dollar deposit, cheerfully refunded on checkout, unless you want him to share your life forever."

I counted out a few more bills and he wrote out a receipt and handed over the key to Room 415, then scooped up the trio of Paddingtons and invited me to select one.

They all looked the same to me, so I did what I do in such circumstances. I took the one on the left.

"A good choice," he said, the way the waiter does when you say you'll have the rack of lamb with new potatoes. What, I often wonder, are the bad choices? If they're so awful, what are they doing on the menu?

"He's a cute little fellow," I started to say, and in midsentence the cute little fellow slipped out of my arms and landed on the floor. I bent over and came up with him in one hand and a purple envelope in the other. ANTHEA LANDAU, it said, in block capitals, and that was all it said. "This was on the floor," I told the clerk. "I'm afraid I've stepped on it."

He curled his lip, then took a Kleenex from a box on the ledge behind the desk and wiped at the mark my shoe had left. "Someone must have left it on the counter," he said, rubbing briskly, "and someone else must have knocked it off. No harm done."

"Paddington seems to have survived the experience."

"Oh, he's a durable chap," he said. "But I must say you surprised me. I didn't really think you'd take a bear. I play a little game with myself, trying to guess who will and who won't, and I ought to give it up because I'm not very good at it. Almost anyone's apt to take a bear, or not to take a bear. Men on business trips are least likely to be bear people, but they'll surprise you. There's one gentleman from Chicago who's here twice a month for four days at a time. He always has a bear and never takes the little fellow home. And he doesn't seem to care if it's the same bear every time. They're not identical, you know. They vary in size, and in the color of their hats and coats and wellies. Most of the wellies are black, but the pair in the picture are yellow."

"I noticed."

"Tourists tend to take bears, and to want to keep them as

souvenirs. Especially honeymoon couples. Except one couple—the woman wanted to take Paddington home, and the husband wanted his deposit back. I don't have much hope for that marriage."

"Did they keep the bear?"

"They did, and he'll probably wind up fighting her for custody of it when they divorce. For most couples, though, it's never a question. They want the bear. Europeans, except for the English, don't generally take the bears in the first place. Japanese always take bears to their room, sometimes more than one. And they always pay for them and take them home."

"And take pictures of them," I ventured.

"Oh, you have no idea! Pictures of themselves, holding their bears. Pictures of *me*, with or without the bears. Pictures of them and their bears on the street in front of the hotel, and posed in front of poor Eddie's painting, and in their rooms, and in front of the various rooms where some of our more famous guests lived or died. What do you suppose they do with all the pictures? When can they possibly find the time to look at them?"

"Maybe there's no film in the camera."

"Why, Mr. Peters!" he said. "What a devious mind you have."

He had no idea.

Bear or no bear, Room 415 didn't look like $155 a night plus tax. The maroon carpet was threadbare, the dresser top scarred here and there by neglected cigarettes, and the one window looked out on an airshaft. And, as any member of the Friars Club would be quick to tell you, the room was so small you had to go out to the hall to change your mind.

But I hadn't expected anything different. The Paddington was a great deal for its permanent residents, who paid less for a month in a spacious one-bedroom apartment than a transient paid for a week-long stay in a room like mine. There was,

I suppose, a trade-off; the transients paid a premium to bask in the painter-writer-musician glamour of the place, and sub-sidized the artists who lived there year-round and provided the glamour.

I wasn't too sure how the little chap in the floppy blue hat fit into the equation. Charming or twee, as you prefer, it made good marketing sense, giving the hotel a human (well, ursine) face while constituting a small profit center in its own right. If half the guests took bears, and if half of those decided they couldn't part with their bears, and if the per-bear markup was a conservative fifty percent, well, it would come to enough an-nually to pay the light bill, or a good chunk of it, anyway. Enough, at the very least, to make the operation cost-effective.

There was a mantelpiece above a fireplace that had long since been bricked up and plastered over, and that's where I placed Paddington, where he could have a good look around and make sure that everything was all right. "I'd let you look out the window," I told him, "but there's nothing to see out there. Just a brick wall, and a window with the shade down. And maybe that's a good idea, drawing the shade. What do you think?"

He didn't say. I drew the shade, tossed my small suitcase onto the bed, popped the catches, and opened it. I put my shirts and socks and underwear in the dresser, hung a pair of khakis in the tiny closet, closed the suitcase, and stood it against a wall.

I looked at my watch. It was time I got out of there. I had a business to run.

I said goodbye to the bear, who paid about as much atten-tion as my cat does when I say goodbye to him. I pulled the door shut. That was enough to engage the snap lock, but I double-locked the door with my key before taking the elevator to the lobby.

The pair of women had ended their conversation, or at least taken it somewhere else. The guy with the long face and high forehead and horn-rimmed shades had put down *GQ* and picked up a paperback. I walked over and dropped my key at the desk. It was an actual brass key, unlike the computerized plastic key cards the newer hotels use, and it had a heavy brass fob attached, designed to punish you for walking off with it by ripping a hole in your pocket. I was happy to leave it, glad of an excuse to pass the desk and have a quick look at the triple row of guest mailboxes.

That purple envelope I'd found on the floor was in Box 602.

I slapped down my key, gave the fellow with the too-black hair a nod and a smile, and watched a tall and elegant older gentleman enter the lobby from the street, looking as though he could have stepped out of the pages of the long-faced guy's *GQ*. He was wearing a beautifully tailored sport jacket and slacks and escorting a much younger woman.

Our eyes met. His widened in recognition. I couldn't see mine, but they may have done the same. I recognized him, even as he clearly recognized me. And we did what gentlemen do when they encounter one another in a hotel lobby. We passed each other without a word.

TWO

The business is Barnegat Books, an antiquarian bookstore on East Eleventh Street between University Place and Broadway. The Paddington is fourteen blocks north of my shop, and north-south blocks in Manhattan run twenty to the mile, and I'll leave it to you to do the mathematics. I wanted to open up by two, as the sign on my door promised, but a few minutes one way or the other wouldn't matter, and it was too nice a day for a cab or a subway. I'd come up by taxi, suitcase in tow, but I could walk back, and did.

I cut through Madison Square, paying my respects to the statue of Chester Alan Arthur, twenty-first President of the United States and a man with even more first names than Jeffrey Peters. I walked down Broadway, trying to remember what I knew about Chester Alan Arthur, and once I got the store open and dragged the bargain table ("Your Choice @ 3 for $5") out front, I browsed through my own stock until I found *The Lives of the Presidents*, by William Fortescue. It had been published in 1925, and only went as far as Warren Gamaliel Harding (one first name, one last name, and one that was essentially a toss-up). The book was evidently written with a teenage audience in mind, though I couldn't think of too many teenagers who'd rush to turn off MTV and check out what Fortescue had to say about Franklin Pierce and Rutherford Birchard Hayes (who could boast, you'll notice, not a single first name between them).

Fortescue's volume had had a long shelf life at Barnegat Books, having been part of the original stock when I bought the place from old Mr. Litzauer some years ago. I didn't expect to sell it anytime soon either, but that didn't mean it was destined for the bargain table. It was a worthy volume, the sort of book you liked to have around a bookshop, and this wasn't the first time I had consulted it. I'd let Fortescue fill me in a few months ago on Zachary Taylor, although I can't remember much of what I read, or why I'd been interested in the first place. Still, he'd come in handy then—Fortescue, I mean, not Taylor—and he was handy now.

I kept the book on the counter and dipped into it during slow periods, of which there are an abundance in the life of an antiquarian bookman. I did have some traffic that afternoon, and I did do some buying and selling. A regular customer found some mysteries she hadn't read, along with an out-of-print Fredric Brown she figured she must have read, but wouldn't mind reading again. I'd had the same thought myself, and was sorry to see the book go before I had another crack at it, but that's part of the game.

A stout gentleman with a droopy mustache spent a lot of time browsing a six-volume half-leather edition of Oman's *History of Britain Before the Norman Conquest.* I had it tagged at $125, and allowed I would probably take a little less than sticker price for the set, but not a great deal less.

"I'll be back," he said finally, and left. And perhaps he would, but I wasn't counting on it. Customers (or more accurately, noncustomers) use that as an exit line, handing it out to tradesmen the way men tell women, "I'll call you." Maybe they will, and then again maybe they won't, and there's no point sitting by the phone waiting.

My next customer brought in a book from the bargain table, paid his two bucks for it, and asked if he could browse a bit. I told him to feel free, but that it was a dangerous pastime. You never knew when you'd find something you felt compelled to buy.

"I'll risk it," he said, and disappeared into the stacks. He'd been around a couple of times in the course of the past week, looking quite presentable if the slightest bit down at the heels and smelling faintly and not disagreeably of whiskey. He was somewhere around sixty, about the same age as the man I'd seen at the Paddington, with a deep suntan and a carefully trimmed little beard and mustache. The beard was V-shaped and came to a precise point, and it was silver in hue, as were his eyebrows and the hair on his head, or at least as much of it as showed out from under his tan beret.

This was the first time he'd bought anything, and I had a hunch he thought of the two dollars as an admission charge. Some people just like to hang out in bookstores—I did, before I bought one of my own—and Mr. Silver Beard struck me as a fellow who didn't have anything much to do or anyplace to do it. He wasn't homeless, he was too well groomed for that, but he looked to be biding his time.

If he'd gone on biding it until six o'clock I'd have gotten him to give me a hand closing up. But he was long gone by then. The phone rang around five-thirty, and it was Alice Cottrell. "I've got a room," I said. I didn't mention the bear.

"And tonight?"

"If all goes well," I said. "If not, the room's mine for two more nights. But I figure the sooner the better."

And then we said the things a man and a woman will say when they've been rather more to each other than bookseller and customer. I dropped my voice to say them, and I kept it low even after Mr. Silver Beard had given me a wave and departed. She said goodbye after we'd done a reasonable amount of billing and cooing, and not too long after that I brought in the bargain table all by myself. That done, I put fresh water in Raffles's water bowl, replenished the dry food in his dish, and made sure the bathroom door was open in case he needed to use the toilet. Then I locked up for the night and went over to the Bum Rap.

The Bum Rap, where Carolyn Kaiser and I meet almost every evening for a Thank God It's Over drink, is a neighborhood saloon with an eclectic juke box and a bartender who can't make a gin and tonic without looking it up first in his Old Mr. Boston manual. We have our usual table, although it's no big deal if it's taken and we have to sit somewhere else. It was taken this evening, I noticed. There were two women sitting there. Then I looked again and saw that one of them was Carolyn.

The other was Erica Darby, who'd come into Carolyn's life recently in a big way. Erica did something at a cable TV company. I wasn't too clear on what it was, but I was sure it was important, and probably glamorous. You sensed that about Erica. She was smart and polished and great-looking, with long chestnut hair and bright blue eyes and a figure I had the good sense not to notice.

"Hey, Bernie," she said. "How's the book biz?"

"Leisurely," I said.

"That's great," she said. "When my business is leisurely, that means we're about to be driven out of it." She pushed back her chair, got to her feet. "Gotta run, kiddies." She leaned over, kissed Carolyn on the mouth. "See ya."

She swept out. I sat down. Carolyn had a tall glass of ruby liquid in front of her, and I asked if it was cranberry juice.

"Campari and soda. You wanna taste it, Bern?"

"It seems to me I had it once," I said, "and it seems to me once was enough. Anyway, it has alcohol in it, doesn't it?"

"They claim it does," she said, "but you couldn't prove it by me."

"Well, I'll take their word for it," I said, and motioned for Maxine. When she came over I ordered a Perrier.

"You're working tonight," Carolyn said.

"I checked in this afternoon."

"How's your room?"

"Small, but who cares? It's just a place to put my bear."

"Huh?"

I explained about the loaner bears the hotel furnished, and Carolyn raised an eyebrow. "I'm not sure why I took the bear," I went on. "Maybe I didn't want it to feel rejected."

"That's a good reason."

"Anyway, I get the deposit back when I check out."

"Unless you keep the bear."

"Why would I keep the bear?"

"To keep it from feeling rejected," she said, "and it would be a more serious rejection now, after all the two of you have been to each other. Bern, I know what your problem is."

"You do?"

"Uh-huh. You're too tense. You need to loosen up. I'd tell Maxine to bring you a scotch, but you wouldn't drink it, would you?"

I shook my head. "I'm not positive I'll pull it off tonight," I said, "but I've got a shot. I paid cash at the Paddington for three nights—"

"Not to mention a bear, Bern."

"So don't mention it. Anyway, if I can get in and out in one night I won't complain. And I know the room number, so that's taken care of."

"You're staying in a room and you know the number? I guess you're not losing your edge after all, Bern."

"I know Anthea Landau's room number," I said. "You knew that's what I meant, didn't you?"

"Well, yeah." She picked up her glass of Campari, made the

face people don't usually make until they've had a sip of the stuff, and put it down untasted. "So you're sticking to Perrier," she said.

"Right."

"That's what I figured," she said, and waved a hand for the waitress's attention. "Hey, Max," she called out, "bring Bernie here a drink, will you? Rye whiskey, and you might as well make it a double."

"I just said . . ."

"I heard you, Bern. And I get the message. Tonight's a working night, and you don't drink when you work. Aside from soda water and fruit juice and coffee and other things that don't count. I know all that."

"Then why . . ."

"I understand your no-alcohol policy," she went on, "even if it does strike me as the least bit extreme. And I certainly wouldn't do anything to sabotage it."

"But you just ordered me a drink."

"I did," she said, "and I made it rye whiskey, because you seemed to enjoy it the other night. What do you know, here it comes. Thanks, Maxine, and why don't you take this and pour it back in the Lavoris bottle?" She handed Maxine the unfinished Campari. "Here's mud in your eye, Bern."

And she picked up my drink and drank it down. "It's this deal I've got with Erica," she explained. "She's not much of a drinker herself, and she doesn't really get it, you know? She ordered the Campari for me because it's real easy to stop at one."

"There's a recommendation. 'Order a Campari—you'll never want another.' "

"The point is, she's concerned about how much I drink."

"You don't drink all that much."

"I know," she said, "and if I ordered girly-girly drinks with fruit salad and little umbrellas, or if I put away a couple of bottles of chardonnay with dinner, why, she wouldn't think twice about it. But because I happen to drink like a man, she's all set to race off to an Al-Anon meeting and tell them all what a raging drunk I am."

"You're occasionally drunk," I allowed, "but you hardly ever rage."

"My point exactly. Anyway, she's concerned that I celebrate a little too enthusiastically every time I get through one more day of dog washing. She wanted me to quit coming to the Bum Rap altogether. I told her that wasn't negotiable. 'Bernie's my best friend in all the world, and I'm not going to force the man to drink alone. So get that right out of your pretty little head.' And she really is pretty, Bern. Don't you think?"

"Very pretty."

"And what's neat," she said, tossing her head, "is she thinks *I'm* pretty. Isn't that a hoot?"

I think so, too, though it's not something I tend to dwell on. Carolyn Kaiser is a couple of inches shorter than the five-two she claims to be, which leaves her not much taller than some of the dogs she grooms at the Poodle Factory just two doors down the street (or up the street, depending which way you're headed) from Barnegat Books. We lunch together during the week, at her place or mine, and we unwind after work at the Bum Rap, and she is my best friend and occasional henchperson. If she didn't happen to be a lesbian (or, by the same token, if I didn't happen to be a guy) we'd probably have a romance, as people do, and it would run its course, as romances do, and that would be that. But this way we can be best friends forever, and I honestly think we will. (It got a little complicated once when we were both sleeping with the same girl, but we got over that with no damage done.)

So yes, she's pretty, with dark hair and a round face and big eyes, and sometimes I'll compliment her on what she's wearing, the way I might say something nice about a male friend's necktie. But it doesn't happen very often, because I don't notice very often.

"She's right," I said now. "In fact, there's something different about you. You're letting your hair grow, aren't you?"

"Everybody does, Bern. Between haircuts. It's not like shaving. You don't have to do it every day."

"It looks longer than usual," I said. As long as I've known Carolyn she's worn her hair Dutch-boy style, perhaps in unconscious tribute to the resourceful lad who saved Holland from flooding by putting his finger where it would do the most good. "The bangs are the same as always, but it's longer in back."

"So I'm trying something a little different," she said, "just to see how it looks."

"Well, it looks nice."

"That's what Erica said. In fact it was her idea."

"It's becoming," I said. "It's sort of . . ."

"Finish the thought, Bern."

"It's just different, that's all."

" 'Softer, more feminine.' That's what you were gonna say, Bern. Right?"

"Well . . ."

"Pretty soon guys'll be holding doors open for me, and I'll be sipping Sambucca instead of Johnnie Walker Red, and I'll lose my edge and turn into Rebecca of Sunnybrook Farm. Is that what you were going to say?"

"Actually, I was going to say something about Chester Alan Arthur."

"Why, for God's sake?"

"To change the subject," I said, "and because I saw his statue in Madison Square and spent the afternoon reading about him. He got the Vice-Presidential nomination in 1880 as a sop to Roscoe Conkling, the Republican boss of New York State. He was Garfield's running mate, and—"

"You don't mean John Garfield, do you?"

"No, or Brian, either. James Abram Garfield, and the ticket won, and Garfield was inaugurated in March, and—"

"Not in January?"

"No, it took them longer in those days. Garfield was inaugurated in March, and in June he met up with Charles Guiteau. 'My name is Charles Guiteau, my name I'll never deny.' Remember that song?"

"No, Bern, but I don't remember a whole lot of songs from 1881."

"Some folksinger recorded it a few years ago. I thought you might have heard it."

"I must have been too busy listening to Anita O'Day and Billie Holiday. They didn't play songs about Charles Guiteau in Paula's or the Duchess. They might have in Swing Rendezvous, but that was before my time. Who was Charles Guiteau and why sing a song about him?"

"He was a disappointed office-seeker. He shot Garfield because he couldn't get a job, and a month later Garfield died."

"I guess dying took longer then, too."

"It didn't take long for Guiteau. They hanged him, and Chester Alan Arthur was President of the United States of America. And Roscoe Conkling thought he had the keys to Fort Knox, but it didn't work out that way. Arthur wound up pushing for the Civil Service System, which eliminated most of the federal patronage and left the bosses with fewer jobs to hand out."

"I guess that's one way to cut down on disappointed office-seekers," she said, "but you can't win, can you? This way you're up to your neck in disgruntled postal employees. What happened to Arthur? Was he considered a hero?"

I shook my head. "Conkling was pissed off, and the party didn't nominate him in '84. They ran James G. Blaine instead, and Grover Cleveland beat him, and Chester Alan Arthur returned to the obscurity most people figure he richly deserved."

"But at least he got a statue in the park."

"So did Conkling," I said. "The same park, but the other end of it. The two of them stare across Madison Square at each other. It seems to me they both look disappointed."

"That's a sad story," she said. "It shows what happens when a person tries to do the right thing." She waved a hand. "Maxine," she called out, "Bernie just told me a sad story. You better bring the poor guy another double."

She drank my drink, and I had another Perrier to keep her company. We raised our glasses to Chester Alan Arthur, and I wondered how long it had been since anyone had drunk the man's health. Probably a long time, I decided. Possibly forever.

"That's better," Carolyn said, setting her glass down empty. "I'll tell you, it's no hardship limiting myself to a glass of that mouthwash as long as I've got you across the table from me. I'll be seeing Erica later, and she probably won't say anything, but if she does I can just tell the truth. 'I just had the one Campari,' I'll say, 'while I kept Bernie company.' "

"I suppose there are people who would call that a lie of omission," I said.

"I suppose there are, Bern, and I say the hell with them." She peered at me. "I know what you're thinking. You'd like to order one more for the road, but I'm not going to let you do it. I'm going to show a little restraint, even if you don't."

"If it weren't for you," I said, "I'd probably be rolling in the gutter."

"Instead of heading off to commit a felony." She signaled for the check, then waved me off when I reached for my wallet. "Get out of here," she said. "You didn't have anything but H_2O and CO_2. The least I can do is pick up the tab."

"If I get it," I said, "I can call it a business expense. It's a small price to pay for a clear head on a working night."

"You figure tonight's the night, Bern?"

"Well, the sooner the better."

"Haste makes waste," she said sagely, "and you've got to look before you leap." She frowned. "On the other hand, you've got to strike while the iron is hot, and he who hesitates is lost."

"That's helpful," I said.

"I hope so," she said, "because it's confusing the hell out of me. Maybe you shouldn't have had that last drink. It went right to my head."

"I'll try to restrain myself next time."

"Anyway," she said, "this is on me. You've already got a lot invested in this business, haven't you?"

"Six hundred and change."

"All to get into the hotel."

"In and out whenever I want," I said, "just like a legitimate guest, which is what I am. It's the one foolproof way to get past hotel security. Take a room, pay for it, and you've got the run of the place. Of course, you're not entitled to break into the other guests' rooms, but how are they going to stop you?"

"Your whole face glows when you talk about it, Bern. It's something to see."

"Well, it's exciting," I said. "A hotel is like a cafeteria for a thief, or a smorgasbord table. But instead of seeing everything all laid out for you, it's all tucked away behind closed doors. And you never know what you'll find." I smiled at a memory. "One time," I said, "I checked into the old Hotel Astor. It was early in my career and late in the life of the hotel, but we had that one brief moment together."

"You make it sound like a romance."

"I got my key," I said, "and it took me an hour or two to do this, but I filed it and buffed it until I'd turned it into a master key for every lock in the hotel. I'm pretty quick picking a lock, but I'm even faster when I've got the key. I must have hit fifty rooms that night. I came up empty in a lot of them, but it still added up to a profitable night's work."

"You won't hit fifty rooms at the Paddington, will you, Bern?"

"One should be plenty."

"And you really think you'll find what you're looking for?"

"I don't know."

"If you do, the six hundred dollars is a good investment. If not, it's a lot of money down the drain."

"I'll get fifty bucks back," I said, "when I return the bear. And there's a deposit for the phone, and I don't expect to be making any calls, so I'll get that back too."

"You really think you'll be able to get the bear deposit back, Bern?"

"Not if I have to leave in a hurry. But otherwise, sure, they'll give me the money back. As long as I return old Paddy in good condition."

"That's not what I meant."

"It's not?"

"Not exactly. What I meant was, will you be able to part with him? I used to have a Paddington Bear when I was a kid, and I never would have given him up for fifty dollars, or even five hundred. He was my little buddy."

"Mine's a perfectly good bear," I said, "but I don't foresee a whole lot of separation anxiety. We haven't had enough time to bond, and if all goes well I'll be out of there before we're all that deeply attached to one another."

"Maybe."

"You sound dubious."

"Well, it took me about ten seconds to fall in love with my own Paddington Bear, Bern. Of course I was younger then. I don't commit that quickly these days."

"You're older."

"Right."

"Seasoned. More mature."

"You bet."

"How long did it take you to flip over Erica?"

"About ten seconds," she said, "but that's different. All I had to do was look at her. She's beautiful, isn't she, Bern?"

"She's very good-looking."

"You could go for her yourself, right?"

"I wouldn't," I said, "for all the usual reasons. But as a hypothetical question, well, sure. She's an attractive woman."

"Beauty's only skin deep," she said, "but unless you're a radiologist, I figure that's plenty. Bern, you're staring at me. You've been sneaking stares all night and you're doing it again."

"Sorry."

"Maybe you need another drink. But I'm not so sure that's a good idea."

"Neither am I. Carolyn, you look different. That's why I've been staring."

"I guess it's the hair."

"That's what I thought, but there's something else, isn't there? What is it?"

"You're seeing things, Bern."

"It's lipstick," I said. "Carolyn, you're wearing lipstick!"

"Not so loud! What's the matter with you, Bern?"

"Sorry, but—"

"How would you like it? 'Hey, Bern, what's with the blusher and mascara?' And next thing you know the whole room's gawking at you."

"I said I was sorry. You took me by surprise, that's all."

"Yeah, it was a real sneak attack. We've been sitting here for close to an hour, and I just now snuck up and ambushed you."

"Lipstick," I said.

"Cut it out, Bern. It's not such a big deal."

"Long hair and lipstick."

"Not *long* hair. Longer, that's all. And the lipstick's just to add a little color."

"Why else would anyone wear it? That's all it ever does, it adds color."

"Right. So don't make a federal case out of it, okay?"

"Lipstick," I marveled. "My best friend is turning into a lipstick lesbian."

"Bern . . ."

"So long, L. L. Bean," I said. "Hello, Victoria's Secret."

"Some secret. You know how many of those catalogs they mail out every month? They don't make money on me, Bern. All I like to do is look at the pictures."

"If you say so."

"It's not like I've got a closet full of flannel shirts, you know. I've never dressed all that butch. A blazer and slacks doesn't make me a diesel dyke, does it?"

"Far from it."

"And it's just a touch of lipstick. You sat across the table from me for a whole hour without noticing it."

"I noticed it," I said. "I just didn't know what I was noticing."

"My point exactly. It's not blatant. Just a subtle touch."

"Of femininity."

"Of youth," she said. "If I were a teenager I wouldn't need it, but I'm old enough so nature can use a little help. Don't look at me like that, Bern."

"Like what?"

"Like that. All *right*, dammit. It was Erica's idea. Are you happy now?"

"I was already happy."

"She's a genuine lipstick lesbian," she said, "and that's something I've never objected to, Bern, philosophically or aesthetically. I like lipstick lesbians. I think they're hot." She shrugged. "I just never thought I was going to be one, that's all. I didn't think I was cut out for it."

"But now you've changed your mind?"

"Erica thinks it's low self-esteem, and not feeling confident about my looks. And she thinks a softer hairstyle and a little lipstick will change my self-image, and I have to say I think she's right. Anyway, she likes me this way."

"Can't argue with results."

"That's what I figure."

"And you look nice," I said. "I'll tell you, I can't wait to see how you look in a dress."

"Cut it out, Bern."

"Something low-cut, with lace trimming. That's always nice. Or one of those scoop-necked peasant blouses, the gypsy look. That might work for you."

She rolled her eyes.

"Or a dirndl," I went on. "What's a dirndl, anyway? What does it look like?"

"To me," she said, "it always looks like a typographical error. Beyond that I don't know what it is, and I don't plan on knowing. Could we talk about something else, Bern?"

"Earrings," I suggested. "Gold hoops would be good with the peasant blouse, but how will they look with the dirndl?"

"Keep going, Bern. What are we gonna talk about next? Panty hose? High heels?"

"And perfume," I said, and sat up and sniffed the air. "You're wearing perfume!"

"It's a cologne," she said, "and I've been keeping a bottle at the Poodle Factory for years. I splash on a little after work sometimes to counteract the doggie smell."

"Oh."

"Don't look so disappointed. Listen, I can't tell you how much I'm enjoying this conversation, and I'm glad you let me buy you those drinks. They really loosened you up, even if I was the one who drank them."

"Well . . ."

"But all good things have to end," she went on, "including this sparkling conversation. It's time we got out of here. I've got a late date with a beautiful woman. And you've got a date with a bear."

THREE

Since I'd missed lunch, you could say that I'd had two double shots of rye on an empty stomach. Thanks to Carolyn, I wasn't feeling their effects. Still, I figured I'd better eat something, and on my way back to the Paddington I stopped at a West African place I'd been meaning to try. I ordered a stew of vegetables and groundnuts because it sounded exotic, only to find out that "groundnut" is another name for our old friend the peanut. Still, it tasted exotic, and the waiters were cheerful. I ordered a glass of baobab juice, which sounded even more exotic than the groundnuts, but don't ask me what that tasted like, because they were out of it. I had lemonade instead, and it tasted like lemonade.

I walked the rest of the way to the hotel, and didn't recognize any old friends in the lobby, unless you count the desk clerk, the same fellow who'd checked me in almost eight hours earlier. I went to collect my key and mentioned that he seemed to be working a long shift.

"Noon to midnight," he said. "I'd be getting off at eight, but Paula's got a show tonight. She's a magician, and she's working a bachelor party this evening."

"A magician at a bachelor party?"

"She performs nude."

"Oh," I said.

"She's covered for me when I've had auditions, and I'm glad to return the favor. I just hope she shows up at midnight, or I could be stuck here until Richard comes on at four."

"And then you start in again tomorrow at noon?"

He nodded, then leaned forward and propped an elbow on the counter. There was a limp, boneless quality to him that reminded me of Plastic Man in the comics. "Yes, but I'll be off at eight, so it won't be that bad." He frowned. "I know you're on the fourth floor but I can't remember the room number."

"Four-fifteen."

"That's one of the smaller rooms. I hope it's all right."

"It's fine."

"I could probably put you in something larger in a day or two."

"I'll be fine," I said. "I'm only going to be here for a few nights."

"That's what I said myself, and that was over twenty years ago." He smoothed an eyebrow with a fingertip. "And I've been here ever since. I'd been living here for, oh, seven years or so when Mr. Oliphant needed someone to fill in behind the desk, and he'd been awfully good about my rent, in which I was three or four months behind. So I filled in, and continue to do as time permits. I'm an actor, you see."

He'd mentioned auditions, so this didn't come as a surprise. And it explained why he'd shifted in and out of an English accent earlier.

"My name's Carl Pillsbury," he said. "You may have seen me onstage."

"I was thinking that you looked familiar."

He told me some plays he'd been in, all off-Broadway, then said that I wouldn't have seen them, as I was from out of town. "But you might have seen me on television," he suggested. "I was the airlines ticket agent in the Excedrin commercial a couple of years ago. And I've had small parts in *Law & Order*. Of course, you know what they say. There are no small parts, only small salaries."

"That's funny," I said.

"Do you think so? It's my own line, and *I* like it, but not everybody seems to get it. It may be my delivery. I had a stand-up routine that I tried at the comedy clubs, and the material was okay, but I have to say it fell flat most of the time. I just don't think I'm particularly funny. Funny peculiar, maybe, but not funny ha-ha."

Funny peculiar for sure. I kept up my end of the conversation with a few words now and then, which was all that was required of me, and he did the rest. He talked largely about himself, which was enough to erase any doubts I might have had about his really being an actor, but he also talked a little about the hotel and how living and working there was like being a member of a large loving family, albeit a dysfunctional one filled with wacky aunts and eccentric uncles.

He had me wondering if I too might turn into a permanent resident, extending my three days to as many decades. Maybe I'd wind up taking the occasional turn behind the desk myself, telling transient guests how I was only doing this as a stopgap while I waited for something to open up in my true line of work, breaking and entering.

By the time I got away from him, I had learned more than I had to know about the Hotel Paddington, and more than anybody needed to know about Carl Pillsbury. He wished me a good night's sleep, and I told him I hoped his relief showed up on time, and I scooped up my key and headed for the elevator.

The purple envelope, I had noticed, was no longer in the box for Room 602.

My room was as I'd left it, with the bear on the mantelpiece. I gave him a nod. I wasn't quite prepared to talk to the creature, but I couldn't bring myself to cut him altogether.

What did I know about Anthea Landau? Well, I knew she was a literary agent. She'd been one for half a century, and for all of that time she'd occupied a suite at the Paddington, where she'd read manuscripts, conducted her business by mail and telephone, and met the odd client. In recent years she'd become increasingly reclusive, and these days she rarely ventured out. And, because of my little trick with the purple envelope, I knew the number of her suite. If I wanted to find her, the place to look was 602.

But I didn't want to find her. I wanted to find her room, and I wanted to find it empty.

Some burglars don't mind if the householder's at home when they come calling. Indeed, one chap of my acquaintance never went in unless he could assure himself that the residents were home and asleep. That way, he explained, you didn't have to worry about them coming home and catching you in the act.

We were both the guests of the state when he told me this, so his advice needs to be assessed accordingly. (He was a nice enough fellow, if limited conversationally, but in the main the lads you meet in prison are an oafish and mean-spirited lot, and I was as glad to get away from them as from the institution itself. When I made parole they warned me against associating with known criminals, and I didn't really need to be told.)

For my own part, I'd much rather pay my visit when there's nobody home. I suppose you could say I'm solitary by nature. I've gone in, by mistake or out of necessity, when the householder was home and asleep, and I have to say I hate all that pussyfooting around. I never make a lot of noise, and I always try to leave a place as neat as I found it, but while I'm there I like to feel at home. How can you do that with someone sleeping in the next room?

But I might not have a choice. From what I'd heard, Anthea Landau didn't get out much. It was her reputation as a stay-at-home, after all, that had led me to pay over six hundred dollars for a room key. If I'd been likely to find her gone during the day, I'd have been inclined to take my chances with hotel security. It's not all that hard to slip past a desk clerk during the late morning or early afternoon. There are all sorts of impromptu stratagems to render one invisible, or make one look as though one belongs. I have, on various occasions, posed as a deliveryman, arranged an appointment with another guest, or merely walked in carrying a clipboard and looking official.

The one thing you don't want is to look furtive. Slink and the world slinks after you, and soon enough the long arm of the law reaches out and takes you by the collar. But if you look as though you're doing what you're supposed to be doing, why, they'll hand you the key to the front door and the combination to the safe.

I was guided in this matter by my Uncle Hi. A man of unblemished reputation, Hi was on his way home from a business trip when he saw, hanging over the check-in desk at a flight gate, an electrified sign advertising the airline. (It was Braniff, so you know this didn't happen a week ago. I was in high school at the time. I won't tell you who was President.)

Hi's son, my cousin Sheldon, collected signs and decorated his room with them. I remember one from Planters Peanuts, with old Mr. Peanut leaning against a wall and grinning like something Stephen King would write about. (In West Africa I suppose they call him Mr. Groundnut.) This sign, though, showed a plane and a palm tree, and touted Braniff's flights to the Caribbean, and Uncle Hi thought it would look great in Shelly's room.

So he walked around the corner to his own flight lounge, where he set down his valise, took off his tie and jacket, and rolled up his sleeves.

Then he went back to the Braniff counter, pocket notebook in hand. There was a line, but he walked right up to the front of it, where a young woman was handling check-ins and issuing boarding passes.

"This the sign?" he demanded.

She looked blank or begged his pardon or stammered. Whatever.

"This here," he said, pointing. "Is this the sign?"

"Uh, I guess so."

"Yeah," Hi said. "This is the one." And he unhooked it from its moorings, with the young woman interrupting her own chores to give him a hand. He tucked it under his arm and went back to where he'd left his jacket and luggage. It was undisturbed, as he'd assumed it would be. (An honest man himself, Hi took honesty for granted in others, and was rarely disappointed.) He stowed the sign in his valise, unrolled his shirtsleeves, tied his tie, put on his suit jacket, and waited for them to call his flight.

The sign did in fact look splendid in my cousin Shelly's room, and when he got old enough to redecorate, replacing Mr. Peanut and his friends with *Playboy* centerfolds, the Braniff sign remained. It sort of fit, Shelly said, because you could just picture those babes under that palm tree, sipping piña coladas and showing off their full-body suntans. You could even imagine them as Braniff stewardesses, offering you your choice of coffee, tea, or milk, and a whole lot more.

Well, that was years ago. Shelly's a doctor now, and the sign in his waiting room is all about medical insurance, and no one on earth would ever want to steal it. Uncle Hi's retired and living in Pompano Beach, Florida, clipping coupons and playing golf and adding stamps to his collection. I never steal a stamp collection without thinking of Hi. He collects British Commonwealth, and now and then over the years I'll run across something I think he can use, some scarce Victorian provisionals or Edward VII high-values, and I'll send them along with a note explaining that I found them tucked between the pages of an old volume of *Martin Chuzzlewit*. If Hi suspects the stamps might have a less wholesome provenance, he's too much of a gentleman to mention it, and too ardent a collector to send them back.

I'm the family's sole black sheep, and I sometimes wonder what went wrong. With upstanding role models on both the Rhodenbarr and the Grimes sides of my family, why did I wind up with a lifelong penchant for skulking and stealing?

A bad gene in the woodpile, I sometimes think. A chromosome gone haywire. But then I'll think of my Uncle Hi, and I'll find myself wondering. Look at his life and you see an honest businessman, ethical and law-abiding. But one afternoon in an airport he'd shown that he had the resourceful imagination of a con artist and the guts of a second-story man. Who's to say how he might have turned out if circumstances early on had given him a nudge in the wrong direction?

Oh, I don't suppose he'd have had my natural talent with locks. That's a gift. But anyone with a little training can learn all you absolutely need to know about locks and how to get around them.

If Hi could manipulate a pair of stamp tongs, he could handle lockpicking tools. And Shelly was a surgeon, certainly capable of applying those same skills to the creations of Rabson and Segal and Fichet and Poulard. If they'd taken a hard left turn a while back, any of my relatives could have turned out wrong. And, if they'd taken up burglary, I bet they'd have been damn good at it.

Instead, they were all leading exemplary lives, and I was getting ready to break into an old lady's hotel room.

Go figure.

Anthea Landau was listed in the Yellow Pages, under Literary Agents. I got an outside line and had her number half-dialed when I caught myself and broke the connection. If I dialed her private line there'd be a record of the call, and did I want that?

I dialed 7, then 602. I let the phone ring half a dozen times before hanging up.

Could it be that easy? Could I be that lucky? Was she really out somewhere, having dinner or seeing a play or visiting an old friend?

It seemed possible. The envelope I'd left for her had disappeared from her mailbox, suggesting that she might have come down and retrieved it. (It was equally possible that Carl or another hotel employee brought her mail to her door, a not unlikely service for a reclusive tenant.)

Even if she'd gone for the mail herself, that didn't mean she hadn't turned around and returned directly to her room. But she hadn't answered her phone now, and that meant something, didn't it?

Maybe it meant she was sound asleep. It was not quite nine o'clock, too early to be bedtime for most of the people I know, but how did I know what hours Anthea Landau kept? Maybe she took naps. Maybe she slept in the early evening and stayed up all night. Older people are typically light sleepers, and might be roused by a ringing telephone, but who could say with assurance that Ms. Landau wasn't an exception? Maybe she welcomed Morpheus with a cocktail of Smirnoff's and Seconal, and slept so soundly an earthquake wouldn't wake her.

Maybe she was in the bathroom when the phone rang and couldn't get to it in time. Maybe she was watching TV and never picked up the phone during *Seinfeld*.

Maybe I should try her again. I reached for the phone, caught myself in time, put my hand back in my lap before it could get me in trouble. I had called her number once and nobody answered. What was I doing, stalling to get my three nights' worth out of the hotel? I couldn't wait for some sort of guarantee that she wasn't home and that I could get in and out undetected. If I wanted guarantees, I was in the wrong business.

It was time to get to work.

FOUR

The Paddington had a single stairwell, and the fire door giving access to it had a sign on it explaining that it was the reverse of a Roach Motel. Guests could get out, but they couldn't get back in again, not without walking clear down to the lobby.

Yeah, right.

I let myself out and walked up two flights of stairs. At the fifth-floor landing there was a wall-mounted firehose with a massive dull brass nozzle, and I figured they'd picked the right spot for it, because the stairwell reeked of cigarette smoke. Evidently one or more of the hotel employees was in the habit of ducking onto the stairs for a quick smoke, and if there'd been anything flammable on hand, it probably would have long since caught fire. But there was nothing but the metal stairs and the plaster walls, unless you counted the firehose itself, and you never hear of them burning, do you?

At the sixth floor I put my ear to the door, and when I didn't hear anything but the beating of my own heart I took out my tools and put them to work. There was really nothing to it. A little strip of spring steel snicked back the spring lock and I stepped out into the sixth-floor hallway, confidence and self-assurance oozing from every other pore, and ran head-on into the appraising gaze of a woman who stood waiting for the elevator.

"Good evening," she said.

"Good evening."

Well, it had been, up to then. And in ordinary circumstances the sight of her would have done nothing to detract from it. She was tall and slender, with skin the color of coffee with plenty of cream and sugar. She had a high forehead and a long narrow nose and prominent cheekbones and a pointed chin, and her hair was in cornrows, which often looks hokey to me, but which now looked quite perfect. She was wearing what I think you call a bolero jacket over what I'm pretty sure you call a skirt and blouse. The jacket was scarlet and the blouse was canary yellow and the skirt was royal blue, and that sounds as though it should have been garish, but somehow it wasn't. In fact there was something reassuringly familiar about the color scheme, although I couldn't think what it was.

"I don't believe we've met," she said. "My name is Isis Gauthier."

"I'm Peter Jeffries."

Shit, I thought. That was the second time I'd got it wrong. I was Jeffrey Peters, not Peter Jeffries. Why couldn't I remember a simple thing like my own goddam name?

"I could have sworn," she said, "that you just now came through the door from the stairs."

"Is that right?"

"Yes," she said. I'd seen her in the lobby that afternoon, but I hadn't looked twice at her. I couldn't remember what she'd been wearing, but I was sure it was less colorful than what she wore now. And I hadn't even noticed her eyes then. They were cornflower blue, I noted now, which meant either contact lenses or a genetic anomaly. Either way the effect was startling. She was as striking a woman as I'd seen in years, and I wished to God the elevator would come along and take her the hell out of my life.

"And those doors lock automatically," she went on. "You can open them from the hall, but not from the staircase."

"Gauthier," I said, thoughtfully. "That's French, isn't it?"

"It is."

"There was a writer, Théophile Gauthier. *Mademoiselle de Maupin*. That was one of his books. I don't suppose he's any relation?"

"I'm sure he was," she said, "to someone. But not to me. How did you manage to get in from the stairs, Mr. Jeffries?"

"I stepped out," I said, "and before I let the door close I wedged some paper in the lock. That way I could get back in again."

"And is the paper still wedged in the lock?"

"No, I took it out just now, so that the door would function the way it's supposed to."

"That was considerate," she said, and smiled warmly. Her teeth were gleaming white, her lips full, and did I mention that her voice was pitched low, and a little husky? She was just about perfect, and I couldn't wait to see the last of her.

"Why," she had to ask, "did you want to use the stairs, Mr. Jeffries?"

"Let's not be so formal," I said. "Call me Peter."

And you must call me Isis, she was supposed to say. But all she did was repeat the question. At least by then I had an answer for it.

"I wanted a cigarette," I said. "My room's nonsmoking, and I didn't want to break the rule, so I ducked into the stairwell for a smoke."

"That's what I want," she said. "A cigarette. Do you have one, Peter?"

"I just smoked my last one."

"Oh, that's a pity. I suppose you smoke one of those ultra-low-tar brands."

Where was she going with this?

"Because you don't smell of tobacco smoke at all, you see."

Oh.

"So I don't think you ducked into the stairwell for a cigarette." She sniffed the air. "In fact," she said, "I doubt you've had a cigarette in years."

"You've caught me," I said, smiling disarmingly.

She was about as easily disarmed as the Michigan Militia. "Indeed," she said, "but in what? What were you doing on the stairs, Mr. Jeffries?"

Damn, I thought. We were back to Mr. Jeffries again, after having so recently reached a first-name basis.

"I was visiting someone," I said.

"Oh?"

"Someone who lives on another floor. I wanted to be discreet, because my friend wouldn't want it known that I'd paid a visit."

"And that's why you used the stairs."

"Yes."

"Because if you were to take the elevator . . ."

"Carl downstairs might see me on the closed-circuit monitor."

"Unlikely," she said. "And so what if he did?"

"Or I might run into someone in the elevator," I said.

"Instead you ran into me."

"So I did."

"In the hallway."

"Yes." Waiting for the bloody elevator, I thought, which had evidently stopped running altogether, because where the hell was it?

"What's your friend's name?"

"Oh, I couldn't say."

"Well, that's good," she said. "You're a gentleman, and they're rare these days. Male or female?"

"I should think that's fairly obvious," I said. "You just called me a gentleman, and I told you my name, so of course I'm a man . . . Oh, you mean my friend."

"Good thinking."

"My friend's a woman," I said, "and I'm afraid that's all I'm prepared to tell you about her. Oh, look. Your elevator's come."

"And about time," she said, making no move to get on it. "Sometimes it takes forever. Is she a permanent resident? Or a transient?"

"What possible difference can it make to you?"

"She'd have to be a resident," she said, "or you'd probably be sharing a room. And she probably lives alone, or the two of you would be meeting in your room, not in hers."

"Let me ask you a question," I said.

"Actually, you already did. You asked me what possible difference it could make to me whether your friend was a resident or a transient. No difference, I suppose."

"Here's another question," I said. "What do you do for a living? Because you'd probably make a pretty good private detective if you put your mind to it."

"I never thought of that," she said. "It's an interesting idea. Good night, Peter." And she stepped onto the elevator and the doors closed.

So she never did answer my question, and I still didn't know what she did for a living, or anything else about her. But at least we were back on a first-name basis.

No light showed beneath the door of 602.

All that told me for sure was that the light was out, and I made doubly sure by stooping for a squint through the keyhole. The light was out and the phone had rung unanswered, and what did that mean? Either she was out or she was deep in sleep. Or she'd been in the tub when I phoned earlier, and now she was sitting in the dark, alone with her memories of writers she'd discovered and editors she'd outsmarted.

Abort the mission, urged an inner voice. *Cut your losses and pull the plug. Hoist anchor, haul ass, and escape while there's still time.*

I listened hard to that still small voice, and what it said made good sense to me. Why not heed what it had to say?

Why not? Anthea Landau would keep. She wasn't going anywhere, and neither was her collected correspondence. Why not take the night off?

Why not? another voice countered. *I'll tell you why not. Because that's how it starts, with the postponement of a simple act of burglary. The next thing you know, you'll leave the store unopened on a sunny morning, not wanting to waste the day in a bookstore. Or it'll rain, and you won't want to leave the house. Procrastination is the thief of time, and what's more it's a dangerous habit, and so is self-indulgence, and if you give either one of them an inch they'll take an ell, whatever that is, and the next thing you know you'll be drinking on work nights, and breaking into apartments on an impulse, and looking at five-to-fifteen in a hotel with no room service, and no teddy bears, either.*

Does that sound overstated? Well, that's a conscience for you. Mine has never maintained a sense of proportion, or learned the art of wearing the world as a loose garment. It's an uptight conscience, a shrill small voice within, and I'm scared to tell it to shut up.

I knocked, not too loud, on Anthea Landau's door. When it drew no response I knocked again, and when my second knock went unanswered I took a quick look around. No Isis, thank God, and nobody else, either.

I could have tried my own room key. There's always some duplication—a hotel with a thousand rooms doesn't have a thousand different keys—but I didn't waste seconds trying it. My picks worked, and almost as quickly.

The door eased open on silent hinges. Within, the room was dark and still. I slipped in, shut the door behind me, and stood for a moment, letting my eyes accustom themselves to the darkness. And I suppose they did just that, but it was hard to tell, because I still couldn't see a damn thing. Evidently the place had blackout curtains, and evidently she'd drawn them, and evidently the moths hadn't gotten into them, because the only light I could spot was the narrow line at the bottom of the door.

I got out my pocket flashlight and played its narrow beam around the room, starting with the door I'd just breached. There was a chain lock, I was pleased to see, and its presence, unfastened, was further suggestion that I was alone. She'd probably have engaged it before turning in, and that would have sent me back to Room 415 for the night. (Not that a chain lock's much of a barrier. A forceful burglar snaps it with a good shove, or goes through it with a bolt cutter; an artful burglar slips the catch free of its moorings, doing no damage, leaving no trace.)

I had a pair of Pliofilm gloves in my back pocket, and I put them on now, before I touched a thing. Then I turned the bolt, fastened the chain lock, and took a good look around, or as good a look as I could with a pocket flash. I was in a combined office and living room, with two walls lined with bookcases and a third with filing cabinets. The bookcases ran clear to the ceiling, while over the filing cabinets I saw a few dozen photos and letters in plain black frames.

So this was where Anthea Landau conducted business. I could see her at the desk, smoking cigarettes (the ashtray was piled high with butts), drinking coffee (Give Me a Break, it said on her twelve-ounce mug), and burning up the telephone lines. And I could picture her in the Queen Anne wing chair, with her feet up on the matching ottoman and the good reading light switched on behind her, turning the pages of manuscripts. Including, I supposed, the early works of Gulliver Fairborn, from his astonishing debut, *Nobody's Baby*, to the last of his books she'd represented, *A Talent for Sacrifice*.

I'll tell you, it gave me a thrill. But then it always does, whenever I let myself into another's residence or place of business, getting past all the devices aimed at keeping me out. Burglary pays the rent and keeps Raffles in cat food, but it's always been more than a livelihood to me. It's a vocation, a sacred calling. The thrill I got in my early teens when I first wriggled through a neighbor's milk chute has never entirely gone away, and I recapture the rapture every time I break and enter. I'm a born burglar, God help me, and I love it. I always have and I'm afraid I always will.

But this room would have thrilled me if I'd visited it legitimately, with its door opened for me by its tenant herself. Like every other secretive and half-literate American adolescent, I'd been caught up in and utterly transported by *Nobody's Baby*, sure that its tortured protagonist, Archer Manwaring, was a lifelong friend I'd somehow never met before, and that he was drawling his story right into my ear.

Right here, in this room, a much younger Anthea Landau had read the opening pages of *Nobody's Baby* and at once recognized a new and important voice in American fiction. She read the book at one sitting, pausing halfway through to call a publisher and tell him she had something he had to read.

And the rest was publishing history, and it all started here, in this room.

This smoke-filled room. So many people have quit smoking, and the pastime is off-limits in so many public and private spaces, that I'm not much used to smelling cigarette smoke. Oh, I'll get a whiff of somebody's cigarette on the street, and there are always a few people puffing away in the Bum Rap, but this was different. Anthea Landau had lit up a cigarette when she first moved into these rooms, and she'd kept at it ever since. And she never ducked into the stairwell, either. She stayed home and smoked like a chimney.

If I ran into Isis Gauthier again, God forbid, she wouldn't be able to dilate her nostrils and tell that I wasn't a smoker. I couldn't tell how much of the odor my clothes were picking up, not while I was standing there in the midst of it, but I could hardly expect to escape unscathed.

There was another smell, too, along with the cigarette smell. It was distinct from it and yet somehow akin to it, and I recognized it but couldn't place it.

And why was I standing here drinking in odors, like a dog with his head out a car window? Burglary's thrilling, all right, but it's a lot less satisfying if you get caught in the act.

I went straight to the top drawer of the second file cabinet, the one marked F–G. It was unlocked. I held my flashlight in one hand and riffled file folders with the other. There were a couple of overflow E files—Ewing, J. Foster, and Exley, Oliver—and then came Fadiman, Gordon P., and Faffner, Julian. If these were writers, I thought, they weren't notable success stories, because I hadn't heard of any of them. Then came Farmer, Robert Crane, and I'd heard of him, and had put a book of his on my bargain table. Unless someone had bought or stolen it, it was still there.

I kept going, on the chance that Fairborn, Gulliver, was present but slightly misplaced, but it was no go, and I was not much surprised. Nothing's quite that easy, is it?

It was going to take a more intensive search to turn up Gully Fairborn's file, and first I did what I probably should have done right away, before checking the file cabinet. I found my way to the bedroom to make sure I was alone in the apartment.

The bedroom door was a few inches ajar. I eased it open and went in. The curtains were drawn in here, too, and with my flashlight switched off the place was as dark as the inside of a cow. And, like the rest of the place, it stank of cigarette smoke.

The smell of smoke masked other smells, a base of sleep and face powder and eau de cologne. And there was that other top note to the scent, even more noticeable in here. I wrinkled my nose at it, still unable to say just what it was.

Maybe the Fairborn file was on the bedside table. The wish, I'm sure, was father to the thought—I wanted to scoop it up and get the hell out of there—but it seemed more than remotely possible. Landau could sit up in bed sipping a hot chocolate and poring over the letters from her most remarkable client. She could warm herself with the memories, or with the thought of all the money those letters were going to bring.

I was pretty sure the place was empty—I didn't hear breathing, didn't have the sense of another person's presence—but even so I shaded my flashlight with my free hand before I switched it on.

And switched it off in a hurry when I saw a white-haired head on the pillow.

I stood still and held my breath, alert for any sound to indicate I'd disturbed her sleep. I couldn't hear a thing, and I backed to and through the bedroom door, taking little steps on tiptoe, careful not to make a sound. If that file was on her nightstand—and I hadn't seen it, hadn't even noticed if she had a nightstand—if it was there, then it could stay there. I wasn't going to risk waking the woman. If she opened her eyes and saw me, it might scare her to death. If she let out a scream, it might scare *me* to death.

Back in the other room, I went to the desk and went to work on the drawers. There were seven of them, three on each side and one center drawer. I opened and closed them one after the other until I found the locked one. The drawer that's worth locking generally turns out to be the one worth unlocking.

The locks on desk drawers are never much of a challenge. It's a little trickier when the light's not good and you're wearing gloves and trying not to make any noise, but it's still easy work.

I hoped there wouldn't be a gun in there. The locked desk drawer is where you generally find a handgun, if there's one to be found. That way, if the householder needs to protect himself, he can start by trying to remember where he put the key.

I've never liked guns, and I especially dislike the guns you find in desk drawers. They're there so that people can shoot burglars, and I'm opposed to that. I hate the very idea of it.

I opened the drawer, and I didn't find a gun in it, but neither did I find the Fairborn file. I closed the drawer, and if I had all the time in the world I'd have locked up after myself, but I didn't. I opened and closed the other drawers, just taking time for a quick glance within, and I didn't find Gully Fairborn's letters, and I didn't find any guns, either, and—

Gunpowder.

That's what I'd smelled. Gunpowder, cordite, call it what you will. I'd smelled what you smell in a room where a gun's been fired. And I could smell it now, and that's definitely what it was, and it had been stronger in the bedroom, and I hadn't heard any breathing, and the way she smoked you'd think her breathing would be a pretty audible affair, and—

I went back to the bedroom. I was more concerned with speed and less with stealth this time around, and I walked right up to the side of the bed. I still couldn't hear any breathing, and at this range that meant there wasn't any to hear.

I reached out a hand and touched her forehead.

She was dead. She wasn't up there at 98.6, but she wasn't all the way down to room temperature, either. She hadn't been dead long, but then I'd guessed that much before I laid a hand on her. If she'd been dead any length of time, I'd have smelled more than cordite and cigarette smoke in that little room.

Didn't I tell you? nagged an inner voice. *Didn't I say to abort the mission? Didn't I tell you to pull the plug? But did you listen? Do you ever listen?*

I was listening now, but not to inner voices. I was listening to sounds outside the apartment, sounds in the hallway. I could hear footsteps, and it took a lot of feet to make that sort of sound, and flat feet at that. I heard voices, too, and I heard men knocking on doors and calling out. I couldn't make out what they were saying, but I didn't think it was anything I wanted to hear.

And now someone was pounding on my door—well, Ms. Landau's door—and calling out "Police!" and "Open up in there!" I knew it was the police, and opening up was the last thing I wanted to do.

I drew the curtains, looked out the window. No fire escape, and the street was a long way down.

I heard a key in the lock, Carl's passkey, and the lock turned. By the time the door opened a crack I was in the bedroom, and the chain lock kept them out while I fumbled behind the drawn curtains. I flung open the window, and, thank God and St. Dismas, there was a fire escape out there.

I climbed out onto it, and I was just shutting the window behind me when I heard them crashing through the door.

FIVE

I didn't bide my time on the fire escape. I passed nothing but lighted windows on the fourth and fifth floors. A lighted room is not necessarily an occupied room, but I didn't want to waste time on a closer look. I kept going until I found a dark room on the third floor. The window was closed but not locked, and I opened it and clambered over the sill and pulled it shut behind me.

I drew the curtain, turned on the light, and took a moment to catch my breath. The room had been rented—to either a woman or a male transvestite, judging from the array of cosmetics on the dresser top—and whoever it was had gone out for a night on the town. Unless a sudden fit of homesickness sent her straight to the airport, she'd be back sooner or later. So I couldn't stay indefinitely, but for the time being I was perfectly safe.

Perfectly safe, and in somebody else's abode. Under such circumstances it's second nature for me to look around for something to steal. I had entered the premises illegally. I was where I clearly did not belong. While I was there, why not take something?

The necklace and earrings, for example.

If I wasn't supposed to take them, what the hell were they

doing out in plain sight? I mean, there they were, in a palm-sized jewelry case tucked underneath the bras and panties in the second drawer of the dresser. Well, maybe that's not exactly in plain sight, but still . . .

Each earring sported a ruby of about a carat, ringed with diamond chips. The necklace's ruby was larger—three or four carats, at a guess. There are, alas, a lot of fake rubies around, and I didn't have a jeweler's loupe with me, or time for a good look, but my guess was that these were the real thing. Good color, no obvious inclusions. And the settings were gold, at least eighteen-karat and probably twenty-two.

If they were fakes, they'd be larger. And who'd set fake rubies in solid twenty-two-karat gold? They looked real to me, and if so they were worth enough to put the evening in the plus column.

After all, I had an investment to protect. I was out better than six hundred dollars for my room. Gully Fairborn's letters were gone. Someone else had beat me to them, and killed a woman to get them. I'd had a bad night, and it wasn't over yet, and why not grab at an opportunity to turn a small profit?

Still, I was going to be walking through a lobby crawling with cops. I was a registered guest, and there was nothing inherently suspicious in my dropping the key at the desk and walking out of the lobby. My belongings could stay in Room 415 until the chambermaid collected them and cleaned up after me. I'd probably left a few fingerprints there, along with my socks and underwear, but so what? No one was going to bother dusting an empty room for prints. Given the Paddington's casual approach to housekeeping, they'd probably find a whole collection, all the way back to Stephen Crane.

So what was I supposed to do? Just put the rubies back where I'd found them? Just abandon them?

I took a last look at them, sighed, and closed the case with a snap. It was the sort of case that would slip right into your pocket, and wasn't that a sign?

I thought so.

* * *

I went out the door to a blissfully empty hallway, then passed up the elevator in favor of the stairs. At the bottom of the last flight I walked through an unlocked door into a lobby full of people, a good number of them wearing blue uniforms. Others were citizens, trying to loiter long enough to determine what all the fuss was about, while some of the uniforms urged them to get on about their business. And that's what I was planning to do, and the business I planned to get on about was escape.

I didn't slink and I didn't scamper. I did my best to saunter, room key in hand, passing the desk on my way out, and—

"That's him!"

The last time I'd heard that voice, low-pitched and husky, it had been at once irritating and inviting. Now it was considerably elevated in volume, and urgent in tone. And the voice's owner, a vision in bold primary colors, was just a few yards away, and she was pointing a finger and the finger was aimed at me.

"He's the man I saw," she went on. "He was prowling around on the sixth floor, and he'd just come through a locked door, and he couldn't give a good account of himself. He told one lie after another."

And you walked into the lobby this afternoon, I thought, *with a man old enough to be your father, though I have reason to believe he wasn't. But did I say anything?*

Her blue eyes flashed. "His name is Peter Jeffries," she said. "At least that's what he told me. I rather doubt that's his real name."

"It's close," Carl Pillsbury said. He had a faint Southern accent I hadn't noticed before, and I realized he'd put it on for the occasion, as if he was playing a part. "He's a registered guest," he continued, the accent quite convincing, and by no means overdone. "He's in Room 415, and his name is Jeffrey Peters."

You dye your hair, I thought, *and it couldn't be more obvious. But do I say a word?*

"You're both wrong," said a voice I recognized. "This here's somebody else altogether, an' if he's registered here it's suspicious all by itself, on account of he's got a perfectly good place of his own on West End Avenue. This here is nobody but Mrs. Rhodenbarr's son Bernard. What's the matter with you, Bernie? Aren't you gonna say hello?"

"Hello, Ray."

" 'Hello, Ray.' Say it like you mean it, why don't you?"

"I did."

"Yeah, well, I guess you did at that. You can't be too happy to see me, an' I can understand that, but better me than someone who doesn't know you in the first place. We'll go downtown an' book you an' print you, an' you can call up Wally Hemphill to come down an' bail you out, an' sooner or later we'll get things sorted out. We always do, don't we?"

"Ray," I said. "You've got no reason to take me downtown."

"You gotta be kiddin', Bern."

"Miss Gauthier says I didn't give a good account of myself," I said. "Well, no law says I have to, not to her. I didn't ask her what she was doing on the sixth floor, so what gave her the right to ask me?"

"I live there," Isis said.

There was something familiar about the color scheme of her outfit, beyond the fact that I'd seen it a little while ago in the sixth-floor hallway. I realized what it was when I glanced at the Horvath painting over the fireplace. Her skirt was the same blue as his hat, and her bolero jacket matched his little jacket, and her blouse was as brilliantly yellow as his Wellington boots. It was uncanny, and while her skin tone was not the exact tan of his fur, it was close.

"Because of my past history," I said, "and because you've never been able to believe I've changed my ways—"

"Which you haven't," Ray said, "not for a minute."

"—you think I was prowling around looking for something to steal. Well, even if that was what I had in mind, you can't hang a man for his thoughts, or jail him, either. I didn't take anything, and I'm not carrying burglar's tools. You don't have to take my word for it. You can search me."

"We will," he said, "once we get you downtown. You can count on that, Bern."

"When you do," I said, "you won't find anything, and that's something *you* can count on. So what have you got? I was on the premises of a hotel in which I happened to be a registered guest. Where's the crime in that?"

"You registered under a false name."

"So? That's only a crime if it's done with the presumed intent to defraud the innkeeper. I paid cash in advance, Ray. If you're planning to skip out on a hotel bill, you don't generally pay it ahead of time. I'm in the clear on this."

"You know," he said, "you can really shovel the stuff out, Bernie. It's a hell of a talent. If all we had was the report of a prowler, an' if you're really not carryin' lockpicks an' stolen goods on your person, I'd probably have to cut you loose. But there's a dead woman in a room on the sixth floor, an' it looks like she had help gettin' that way, an' you were spotted on Six, an' what does that look like?"

"It looks like sheer coincidence to me," I said. "Whatever happened, I had nothing to do with it. And now what I'd like to do is go home. You've got no reason to hold me, and I know my rights."

"I'm sure you do," he said. "You ought to by now. You've heard 'em enough times. But just in case your memory's rusty, here's how they go. You have the right to remain silent. Do you understand?"

"Ray, I—"

"Yeah, you understand. You have the right to an attorney. Do you understand? Yeah, you understand that, too . . ."

SIX

I suppose I should begin at the beginning.

It started the week before, on as perfect an autumn afternoon as anyone could wish for. New York had suffered through a long hot summer, capped with a truly brutal heat wave, and now the heat had broken with the arrival of some cool clean air from Canada, where it's evidently a local specialty.

My shop's air-conditioned, of course, so it's not a bad place to be even on a hellishly hot day. But heat can dull a person's enthusiasm for browsing in a bookstore, even if the store itself is comfortable enough, and business had been off for the last week or so.

The cool weather brought the browsers back. The store had people in it from the minute I opened up, and every once in a while someone actually bought a book. I was pleased when they did, but I can't say I really minded if they didn't, because in a sense I wasn't really there at all. I was thousands of miles away, in the jungles of Venezuela with the intrepid Redmond O'Hanlon.

Specifically, I was reading about the candiru, the toothpick fish, a tiny catfish adapted for a parasitic life in the gills and cloaca of bigger fish. I'd read O'Hanlon's earlier book, *Into the Heart of Borneo*, and when a copy of *In Trouble Again* turned up in a bag of books, I'd set it aside to read before shelving.

And I was reading it now, in what I thought was the companionable silence suited to a bookshop, when I felt a hand on my arm. I looked at the person attached to the hand. It was a woman—slim, dark-haired, late twenties—and her long oval face was a mask of concern.

"I didn't want to disturb you," she said, "but are you all right?"

"Yes," I said. She didn't seem reassured, and I could understand why. Even I could tell that my voice lacked conviction.

"You seem . . . anxious," she said. "Unnerved."

"What makes you say that?"

"The sounds you were making."

"I was making sounds? I hadn't realized it. Like talking in one's sleep, I suppose, except I wasn't sleeping."

"No."

"I was caught up in my book, and maybe that amounts to more or less the same thing. What sort of sounds was I making?"

She cocked her head. She was, I saw, a very attractive woman, a few years older than I'd thought. Early thirties, say. She was dressed in tight jeans and a man's white dress shirt, and her brown hair was drawn back in a ponytail, and thus at first glance she looked younger than her years.

"Troubled sounds," she said.

"Troubled sounds?"

"I can't think how else to describe them. 'Arrrghhh,' you said."

"Arrrghhh?"

"Yes, but more like this: *'Arrrghhh!'* As if you were trying to get the word out before you strangled."

"Oh."

"You said that two or three times. And once you said, 'Oh my God!' As if consumed with horror."

"Well," I said, "I remember thinking both those things, *arrghhh* and *Oh my God*. But I had no idea I was saying them out loud."

"I see."

But I could tell she didn't. She was still looking at me with clinical interest, and she was far too attractive for me to let her think there was something wrong with me. "Here," I said, shoving O'Hanlon at her. "Here, where I'm pointing. Read this."

"Read it?"

"Please."

"Well, all right." She cleared her throat. " 'In the Amazon, should you have too much to drink, say, and inadvertently urinate as you swim, any homeless candiru—' Candiru?"

I nodded. I'd meant for her to read the paragraph to herself, not out loud, but I couldn't think of a graceful way to tell her so. And she was a good reader, with volume and presence. My other customers, already alerted by the sounds I'd been making and our subsequent conversation, had stopped what they were doing in order to hear her out.

" 'Any homeless candiru'—I hope I'm pronouncing it correctly—'attracted by the smell, will take you for a big fish and swim excitedly up your stream of uric acid, enter your urethra like a worm into its burrow, and, raising its gill covers, stick out a set of retrorse spines' . . . retrorse? 'Nothing can be done. The pain apparently is spectacular. You must get to a hospital before your bladder bursts; you must ask a surgeon to cut off your penis.' "

She closed the book, looking troubled herself, and placed it on the counter between us. Even as she did so, all my other customers began drifting out of my store. One man actually cupped a hand over his groin. The others looked less defensive, but just as determined to get away from the very thought of such a thing.

"That's awful," she said.

"It doesn't make one want to grab the next plane to the Amazon."

"Or go into any river at all," she said. "Or step into a bathtub."

"It could put a person off water entirely," I agreed. "I may quit drinking the stuff."

"I don't blame you. What does that word mean, anyway?"

"Uh . . ."

"Not 'penis,' silly. 'A set of retrorse spines.' What does 'retrorse' mean? It's not a word I've ever seen before."

"I think it's like the barbs on a fishhook," I said. "Meaning it can't go back out the way it came in, because of the direction the spines are pointing."

"That's what I assumed, but the word's a new one to me. The whole thought ties you up in knots, doesn't it? You just now got a real arrrghhh look on your face."

"Did I? I'm not surprised. It's a pretty arrrghhh concept."

"I'll say. I suppose it's every man's worst nightmare. I wonder what it's like for girls?"

"Girls?"

"Did I say something wrong? Do you prefer women?"

"To almost anything," I said, "which is one reason I never want to meet a candiru. But I wasn't being politically correct. Whatever you call them, girls or women, I wouldn't think they'd have anything to fear from the candiru."

"This one wouldn't," she said, "because she has no intention of placing herself on the same continent with the horrid thing. But girls swim, too, the same as men. And I hope it won't shatter any illusions to tell you that sometimes we piddle in the pool."

"I'm shocked."

"Well, welcome to the world, Mr. . . . I don't know your name. Is it Barnegat?"

"It's Rhodenbarr. Bernie Rhodenbarr."

"And is Bernie short for Barnegat?"

"It's shorter *than* Barnegat," I said, "but what it's short for is Bernard. Barnegat Light is a place on the Jersey shore where Mr. Litzauer used to spend his vacations, so when he opened a bookstore he used the name."

"And this is his store?"

"Not anymore. He sold it to me a few years ago."

"And your name is Bernie Rhodenbarr, and mine is Alice Cottrell. Where were we?"

"You were welcoming me to the world, and telling me that you pee in the pool."

"Never again," she vowed. "I won't even dip a toe in the pool, for fear that there might be a candiru in it. Who's to say it couldn't happen? I gather it's some sort of fish."

"The toothpick fish. It's a kind of catfish, according to O'Hanlon."

"People bring in fish from South America," she said. "Tropical fish, for people to keep in their aquariums. Aquaria?"

"Whatever."

"And it's possible someone could fly in some candiru, mixed in with a shipment of neon tetras and opaline gouramis."

"Gouramis come from Asia."

"Neon tetras, then. Are you sure gouramis come from Asia?"

"Positive."

"Do you keep tropical fish?" I shook my head. "Then how do you happen to know an arcane factoid like that?"

"I own a bookstore, and I pick books up and read them, and odd facts lodge in my mind."

"Like the candiru in one's urethra," she said. "Which could arrive in a shipment of fish for the hobby market, and could wind up in someone's aquarium or outdoor pool, and could get released into the wild. The water's probably too cold for them up here, but suppose they were released in Florida?"

"I'm convinced," I said. "I'll never go swimming again, and I'll steer clear of Florida forever. But where's the danger for girls—or women either, for that matter? I realize you pee, although I understand you have to sit down to do it—"

"Not when we're swimming."

"But you don't have penises, so what's the problem?"

"You're saying there's nothing for the surgeon to cut off."

"Right."

"You should see your face. You don't even like to talk about the surgeon, do you?"

"Not especially, no."

"We don't have penises," she said, "but we do pee, and we do have urethras. And a toothpick fish could swim in there, and find a place he'd care to call home, and then what's a girl to do? No point running to the surgeon. 'Cut it off! Please, cut it off before my bladder bursts!' 'Sorry, can't do that, as you haven't got one.'"

"Oh."

"You see what I mean?"

"I'll make you a deal," I said. "Let's never go to the surgeon."

"All right."

"And we won't go to Jones Beach, either."

"That's all right, too."

"And we won't talk about this anymore."

"That's even better."

There was the trace of a smile on her lips, an impish light in her brown eyes. You don't expect a conversation centered on something as horrible as the candiru to be what you would call flirtatious, but ours was, just the same. It might not be evident in the words we spoke, but a transcript of our conversation wouldn't include the sidelong glances and raised eyebrows, the subtle nuance of a stressed syllable here and a bit of body language there. It was a flirtation, and I didn't want it to end.

"But we ought to talk about something," I went on. "Forget my book. What about your book?"

"Actually," she said, "this one's your book as well. I took it off the shelf, and I haven't bought it yet."

"You can, of course. If you can't bring yourself to part with it."

She put it on the counter, and I recognized it right off. It was a hardcover copy of *Nobody's Baby*, by Gulliver Fairborn.

"That just came in a month or so ago," I said. "I'm not sure what it's marked. Thirty dollars?"

"It's marked thirty-five."

"If you want it," I said, "you could probably talk me down to thirty."

"If I really worked at it."

"That's right."

"It's not a first, is it?"

"For thirty dollars, or even thirty-five? Not hardly."

"But that's a high price for a book that's not a first, isn't it? If I just wanted to read it, I could buy a paperback. It's available in paperback, isn't it?"

"Abundantly. It's never been out of print since the day it was published."

"How nice for Mr. Fairborn."

"I don't know how many copies it sells annually," I said, "or what kind of royalty he gets, but I'd say it's nice for him, all right. But he deserves it, don't you think? It's a wonderful book."

"It changed my life."

"A lot of people feel that way. I read it when I was seventeen, and I would have sworn at the time that it changed my life. And for all I know, maybe it did."

"It changed mine," she said flatly, and tapped the book with her forefinger. "No dust jacket," she said.

"No."

"And it still brings thirty-five dollars?"

"Well, it hasn't yet," I said, "but I live in hope. If it had a jacket, I'd remove it, and wait until a first comes in without one. Or sell it separately. The jacket's worth two hundred dollars, maybe a little more. That's the difference in price between a first with and without a jacket."

"That much?"

"It would be more," I said, "but for all the jackets from later printings like this one. The jacket's identical, at least through the first ten printings or so. Then they started putting review quotes on the back. But what you want to know is why this book costs as much as it does, and that's because it's a later printing of the original edition, and that makes it collectible for someone who'd like to have a first but can't afford one. After all, the only difference between this copy and a first edition is that this one doesn't say 'First Edition' on the copyright page. Instead it says 'Third Printing,' or whatever it says."

" 'Fifth printing,' actually."

I flipped to the page in question. "So it does. If you just want to read the book, well, Shakespeare and Company's a few blocks down Broadway, and they've got the paperback for five ninety-nine. But if you want something closer to a first and don't want to pay a fortune for it . . ."

"How large a fortune?"

"For a first edition of *Nobody's Baby*? I had a copy show up shortly after I took over the shop. It came in with a load of stuff, and I thanked my lucky stars when I realized what it was. I priced it at two hundred dollars, which was much too low even then, and I sold it within the week to the first person who spotted it. He got a bargain."

"That doesn't answer my question."

"No, it doesn't. What's a first of Gulliver Fairborn's first book worth? It depends on condition, of course, and the presence or absence of a jacket, and—"

"A very fine copy," she said. "With an intact jacket, also in very fine condition."

"The last catalog listing I saw was fifteen hundred dollars,"

I said, "and that sounds about right. For a really nice copy in a really nice dust jacket."

"And if it's inscribed?"

"Signed by the author, you mean? Because an inscription that reads 'To Timmy on his seventeenth birthday, with love from Aunt Nedra' doesn't add anything to the book's value. Quite the reverse."

"I'll tell Aunt Nedra to keep her good wishes to herself."

"Or write them very lightly in pencil," I said. "Gulliver Fairborn's signature is rare, which is a rarity itself in this age of mass public book-signings. But you won't see Fairborn hawking signed copies on QVC, or jetting around the country with pen in hand. In fact you won't see him at all, and I for one wouldn't recognize him if I did. He's never given an interview or allowed himself to be photographed. Nobody knows where he lives or what he looks like, and a few books ago you started hearing rumors that he'd died, and that the recent books were the work of a ghostwriter. V. C. Andrews, no doubt."

"Not Elliott Roosevelt?"

"Always a possibility. Anyway, someone did a computerized textual analysis, the same kind that reporter did to prove Joe Klein wrote *Primary Colors*, and established that Fairborn was writing his own books. But he hasn't been signing them."

"Suppose he signed one."

"Well, how sure could we be that he really did the signing? It's not terribly difficult to scribble 'Gulliver Fairborn' on a flyleaf, especially when hardly anyone has seen an authentic signature."

"Suppose the signature's authentic," she said. "And suppose it's what I originally asked you about, not just a signed copy but an inscribed one."

"Saying something about Timmy and his birthday?"

"Saying something like 'To Tiny Alice—Rye can do more than Milt or Malt / To let us know it's not our fault. Love always, Gully.' "

"Gully," I said.

"Yes."

"And I guess you'd be Tiny Alice."

"You're very quick."

"Everybody tells me that. So your question's not hypothetical. You've got the book, and you're in a position to be sure of the signature."

"Yes."

"Tell me the inscription again." She did, and I nodded. "He's paraphrasing Housman, isn't he? 'Malt can do more than Milton can to justify God's ways to man.' A friend of mine used to recite that couplet just before he drank the fourth beer of the evening. Unfortunately he did it again with beers five through twelve, and one grew a little weary of it. 'Rye can do more than Milt or Malt'—why rye, do you suppose?"

"It's all he drinks."

"You'd think he could find something better to drink, wouldn't you? What with *Nobody's Baby* still in print after . . . how many years?"

She answered before I could consult the copyright page. "About forty. He was in his mid-twenties when he wrote it. He's in his early sixties now."

"If the computer analysis is right, and he's still alive."

"He's alive."

"And you . . . know him?"

"I used to."

"And he inscribed a book to you. Well, as far as the value's concerned, all I could do is guess. If the copy came into my hands, I'd call a few specialists and see what I could find out. I'd get the handwriting authenticated. And then I'd probably consign the book to an auction gallery and let it find its own price, which I'd be hard put to guess at. Over two thousand, certainly, and possibly as much as five. It would depend who wanted it and how avid they were."

"And if you had a few of them bidding against each other."

"Exactly. And it wouldn't hurt if you were somebody famous. Alice Walker, say, or Alice Hoffman, or even Alice Roosevelt Longworth. That would make it an association copy, and would render it a little more special for a collector."

"I see."

"On the other hand, the inscription's interesting in and of itself. How did he come to sign it? For that matter, how did you happen to meet him? And, uh . . ."

"What?"

"Well, this may be a stupid question, but are you sure the man who signed your book was who he claimed to be? Because if no photos of the man exist, and if nobody knows where he lives or what he looks like . . ."

She smiled a knowing smile. "Oh, it was Gully."

"How can you be sure?"

"Well, I didn't just run into him at a bookstore," she said. "I lived with him for three years."

"You lived with him?"

"For three years. Do you suppose that makes my book an association copy? Because you could say we had an association."

"When did this happen?"

"Years ago," she said. "I moved in twenty-three years ago, and—"

"But you would have been a child," I said. "What did he do, adopt you?"

"I was fourteen."

"You're thirty-seven now? I'd have said early thirties."

"And you'd have been sweet to say it. I'm thirty-seven, and I was fourteen when I met Gully Fairborn, and seventeen when we parted company."

"And you were, uh . . ."

"We were."

"No kidding," I said. "How did you meet?"

"He wrote to me."

"You wrote him and he wrote back? That's remarkable in and of itself. For thirty-some years every sensitive seventeen-year-old in America has read *Nobody's Baby*. Half of them write letters to Fairborn, and they never get an answer. He's famous for never answering a letter."

"I know."

"But he answered yours? You must write a hell of a letter."

"I do. But he wrote to me first."

"Huh?"

"I was precocious," she said.

"I can believe that," I said. "But how would Gulliver Fairborn know of your precocity, or even of your existence? And what would move him to write you a letter?"

"He read something I wrote. And it wasn't a letter."

"Oh?"

"I read *Nobody's Baby*," she said, "but I wasn't seventeen when I read it. I was thirteen."

"Well, you already said you were precocious."

"It makes an impression on most people, especially the ones who read it at an impressionable age. It certainly made an impression on me. There was a point when I was certain Gulliver Fairborn wrote the book with me in mind, and I thought of writing him a letter, but I didn't do it.

"Instead, a couple of months later, I wrote an article. I handed it in for a school assignment and my teacher was over the moon about it. It's not hard to understand why. The best anybody else managed was two or three ungrammatical pages, 'How I Spent My Summer Vacation,' di dah di dah di dah. I turned in a closely reasoned seven-thousand-word essay full of half-baked philosophy and sophomoric soul-searching."

"And your teacher sent it to Fairborn?"

"I'm sure that never occurred to her. She did something far more outrageous. She sent it to *The New Yorker*."

"Don't tell me."

"I'm afraid I must. They accepted it, incredibly enough. I'd called it 'How I Didn't Spend My Summer Vacation,' which made a kind of ironic sense, but only in context. They changed the title to 'A Ninth-Grader Looks at the World.' "

"My God," I said. "You're Alice Cottrell."

The essay was a sensation, and won the young author a good deal of attention. She had her fifteen minutes of fame, about which Edgar Lee Horvath had then only recently expounded, and was every op-ed writer's flavor of the month. And then, just as the fuss was winding down, she got a letter in a purple envelope.

It was typed on paper of the same hue, and ran to three single-spaced pages. It began as a response to her essay, a sort of essay in reply, but by the middle of the second page it had wandered far afield and overflowed with its middle-aged author's musings on life and the Universe.

She knew almost from the first sentence who its author was, but even so the signature left her breathless. *Gulliver Fairborn*, in beautiful flowing script, and, beneath it, an address on a rural route in Tesuque, New Mexico. She looked it up in the atlas, and it turned out to be just north of Santa Fe.

She wrote back, careful not to gush, and his response came by return mail. He was living for the time being, he told her, in a three-room cottage outside Tesuque, which in fact was a small Indian pueblo. His residence was an adobe shack, thrown up in an unplanned fashion. But it was cozy, he wrote, and weren't the best things often ones that just happened on their own, without preplanning? He'd written *Nobody's Baby* without an outline, without any real clue, really, of what he was doing or where it was going, and it had turned out better than he could have planned.

His letter just ended, without the invitation that seemed to be implicit in it. She wrote back immediately, telling him his little house sounded perfectly charming. If she ever were to see it, she wrote, she was sure it would look familiar to her, as if she had lived there in a dimly recalled past life.

This time his reply was a little longer in coming. The letter itself, barely filling a single page, made no reference to anything either of them had previously written. Instead, he reported on a neighbor of his, who had two mixed-breed dogs. They were inseparable, he noted, though their temperaments were quite different, with one of them considerably more venturesome than the other. When she finished the letter, she wasn't even sure if the dogs existed, or if they were characters in some fiction crafted for the occasion, a little parable with its point unclear. This letter, like the others, was typed on purple paper, and came in a purple envelope. And it included an airline ticket from New York to Albuquerque.

Four days later she was on a plane. When it landed he was at the gate. Neither had seen a photograph of the other, but they recognized each other the instant their eyes met. He was tall and slender, darkly handsome. They waited for her suitcase to show up on the baggage carousel. She pointed it out, and he carried it to his car.

On the drive to Tesuque, he told her he'd foreseen all of this when he read her essay. "I knew I wanted you to come to me," he said, "and I knew you would."

The shack, overlooking an arroyo, was just as she'd pictured it, and every bit as comfortable as he'd claimed. They lived in it for the next three years.

"What I don't get," I said, "is where he got the nerve to write you, and where you got the nerve to accept. Did he know you were only fourteen years old?"

"He knew I was in the ninth grade in school. If I was much older than fourteen, I'd have to be retarded."

"Didn't it occur to him that your parents would try to find you? And that he might wind up facing criminal charges?"

"I don't think any of that ever entered his mind," she said. "Gully's not reckless, but I don't think he spends much time considering the consequences of his actions. He may not really believe that actions necessarily have consequences. You read *Nobody's Baby.*"

"Yes."

"So you know what he says about synchronicity. Anyway, he knew there wouldn't be a problem. The same way he knew I would use the airline ticket."

"And your parents?"

"They were a couple of old hippies," she said. "My father was in Nepal at the time, staying stoned in Katmandu. My mom was back home in Greenwich, Connecticut, living on a trust fund and volunteering three days a week at that organization lobbying to legalize marijuana. NORML, though it and she were anything but."

"So she didn't object?"

"She drove me to the airport. Gully didn't have a phone, but I called her a few days later from down the road and told her I would probably stay awhile. She thought that was cool."

"And you were fourteen."

"I used to say I had an old soul. I don't know that I believe that, but I wasn't your average fourteen-year-old, either. And I never felt as though I was in over my head. I was right where I belonged."

She told me some of this at the bookstore, with Raffles purring on her lap and other customers staying away in droves, as if they somehow sensed they would be intruding. She told me more at the Cedar Tavern on University Place, where we went after I closed for the day, and where she asked the waiter if they had rye whiskey. He came back to report that they had Old Overholt, and she ordered a double shot with water back.

I said I'd have the same, but on the rocks with a splash of soda. I asked her if it was good that way. She said it was better straight up, and I changed the order—double rye, straight up, water back.

We had two rounds of drinks at the Cedar, then walked a

couple of blocks to an Italian place I know that doesn't look like much on the outside. The interior's not too impressive either, but the food makes up for it. We ate osso buco and drank a bottle of Valpolicella, and the waiter brought us complimentary glasses of Strega with our espresso. The meal might have been better at a little trattoria in Florence, but I can't imagine how.

She told me more while we ate and drank, and on the pavement outside the restaurant, in the wine-warmed cool of the evening, we gazed into one another's eyes even as she and Fairborn had done in the Albuquerque airport, and she answered my question before I could ask it.

"Your place," she said.

I held up a hand and a cab appeared. It was that kind of evening.

SEVEN

"So this is rye," Carolyn said. "It tastes a little sweet to me, Bern. Compared to scotch."

"I know."

"But it's not bad. The taste's kind of interesting, once you get past the sweetness. There's a real depth to the flavor, though you couldn't put it in the same class with Glen Drumnadrochit."

Glen Drumnadrochit is a rare single-malt scotch that we sampled on a weekend in the Berkshires, and it's in a class by itself. You couldn't compare anything to it, except perhaps whatever Bacchus was pouring for the heavy hitters on Mount Olympus.

"I thought rye was what you called a cheap blend," she went on. "You know, one of those whiskeys with numbers."

"Numbers?"

"Like Three Feathers, Bern. Or Four Roses."

"Five Gold Rings," I offered, and motioned to Maxine to bring us another round.

"Six Swans a-Swimming," she said. "Seven Lords a-Leaping. When I was growing up, rye and ginger ale was what most of my aunts would have before family dinners, and that meant Three Feathers or Four Roses. Or Schenley's, or something like that."

"Blended whiskey," I said. "Mostly grain neutral spirits. A lot of people call that rye, but properly speaking it's not. Real rye is a straight whiskey, like scotch or bourbon, except that it's made from a different grain. Scotch is made from barley and bourbon is made from corn."

"And rye?"

"Rye is made from rye."

"Who would have guessed it? Thanks, Maxine." She raised her glass. "Here's to crime, Bern."

We were, as you've likely guessed, at the Bum Rap. I'd called Carolyn to cancel our usual after-work drink the night before, and then she'd called in the morning to cancel our usual lunch, so we were making up for lost time.

"It seems to me," she said judiciously, "that this stuff gets better as you go along. That's the test of a good whiskey, wouldn't you say?"

"I think that just proves there's alcohol in it."

"Well, maybe *that's* the test of a good whiskey. Rye, huh? That's a grain?"

"Ever hear of rye bread?"

"Of course I have. But this stuff doesn't taste anything like those little seeds."

"Those are caraway seeds, for flavoring. Rye is what they make the flour out of."

"And what they don't bake into bread they turn into whiskey?"

I nodded. "And it's the only thing Gully Fairborn drinks, and he evidently drinks a lot of it."

"Well, more power to him. And it's what she drinks, too? Alice Cottrell?"

"She also managed to put away some wine with dinner and a glass of Strega afterward. And I didn't have any rye at my apartment, and she seemed to find my scotch perfectly acceptable. But rye's what she drinks. That's one lingering effect of three years with Fairborn."

"And now you're drinking rye," she said, "and, come to think of it, so am I. You think there's a trend forming here, Bern? You figure it's going to sweep the country?"

"Probably not."

" 'If rye whiskey don't kill me, I'll live till I die.' You know that song, Bern?"

"I don't think so."

"Well, I'd sing it, but it'd take three or four more of these to get me in the mood. It goes 'Jack of Diamonds, Jack of Diamonds, Jack of Diamonds I cry, If rye whiskey don't kill me, I'll live till I die.' "

"Why Jack of Diamonds?"

"How do I know, Bern?"

"And what kind of sense does it make, anyway? Everybody lives until they die, whiskey or no whiskey."

"Bern, it's a folk song, for God's sake. 'Go tell Aunt Rhody the old gray goose is dead.' Does that make any sense? Who's Aunt Rhody? What does she care about a goose, gray or otherwise? Folk songs aren't supposed to make any sense. That's why they're written by ordinary people and not by Cole Porter."

"Oh."

"I can't believe you don't know the song. Didn't you ever have an affair with a folksinger?"

"No, and when did you . . . Oh, of course. Mindy Sea Gull."

"Née Siegel. Remember her?"

"The guitar player."

"I wouldn't exactly call her a guitar player, Bern. She only knew three chords and they all sounded the same. She just strummed the guitar to accompany herself when she sang." She shrugged. "She didn't have much of a voice either, as far as that goes."

"She had a nice little body, though."

"That's a hell of a thing to say, Bern."

"Don't tell me it was a sexist remark, because you were just about to make it yourself. 'She didn't have much of a voice, but she had a nifty little body.' Isn't that what you were going to say?"

"It's different if I say it. You're not supposed to notice what kind of a body she had."

"Mindy Sea Gull? Who could miss noticing a pair of wings like those?"

"Bern . . ."

"And what do you mean, I'm not supposed to notice? Because she's gay? You notice straight women. You even hit on them, and sometimes you get lucky."

"Short-term lucky, Bern. Long-term miserable. And not because Mindy was gay. You weren't supposed to notice her neat little body because she was my girlfriend."

"Oh."

"But she's not anymore," she said, drinking her drink, "and you're right, she had a set of wings on her that could fly you to the moon, so the hell with it. How about you?"

"No wings to speak of."

"I meant how about you and Alice Blue Gown. You get lucky?"

I lowered my eyes.

"Bern?"

"A gentleman never tells," I said.

"I know, Bern. That's why I picked you to ask instead of Prince Philip. So? How'd you make out?"

When a woman invites herself to your place, a flop in the feathers seems like a foregone conclusion. But I wasn't about to jump to it. We'd spent most of the evening talking about her affair with another man, a man who just happened to be a legendary figure of mystery and romance, and what kind of prelude is that for a game of slap and tickle?

So, when I picked out music to play, I left my Mel Tormé record on the shelf. It's got an amazing track record, but in this instance I wasn't sure it was appropriate.

While Coltrane played for us, she told me some more about Gulliver Fairborn. How he would reinvent himself every couple of years, taking a new name, adopting a new lifestyle, moving to a new part of the country. It was easy for him to remain undiscovered, she explained, because nobody knew what he looked like, and thus no one would be able to recognize him at the gas station or the supermarket. He paid cash for most of his purchases, and when he had to write a check, it was in whatever name he was using at the time, and he'd have a wallet full of ID to back it up.

And he didn't socialize, didn't make friends. "We kept to ourselves," she said. "It was easy enough, living out in the country like that. He'd get up first, before daybreak, and he'd get the day's writing done before breakfast, which he always cooked for us. Then we'd hang out. We took a lot of long walks, we went for drives, we paid a few visits to different Indian pueblos. He got very interested in San Ildefonso pottery and found out who was the best potter in the pueblo. We spent a couple of hours with her and he wound up buying a little round bowl that her mother had made. We brought it home to Tesuque and he put it on a table and recited the Wallace Stevens poem about placing a jar on a hill in Tennessee. You know the poem?"

I nodded. "But I'm not sure I know what it means."

"Neither do I, but it seems to me I did then. I still have the bowl, or jar, or whatever you want to call it."

"He bought it for you?"

"He left it for me. The day I moved in he told me he wanted me to stay as long as I wanted, and that he hoped I would never leave him. But that he would leave me."

"He told you that?"

"He stated it as a fact. The sky is blue, ontogeny recapitulates phylogeny, and the day will come when you'll wake up and I'll be gone."

"It could be a country song," I said, "except that ontogeny recapitulates phylogeny would be tough for Garth Brooks to sing with real conviction."

"And then one morning I woke up," she said, "and he was gone."

"Just like that? You never saw it coming?"

"Maybe I should have, but I can't say I did. In fact at first I didn't know he was gone. He'd left the car and all but the clothes on his back. He'd mailed off the manuscript of his book just a couple of weeks earlier. I thought he'd gone for a walk before breakfast—he did that sometimes. Then I found the note."

" 'It's been great fun, but it was just one of those things.' "

"Actually, that's close. It was from Swinburne. 'One love grows green, one love turns gray. Tomorrow has no more to say to yesterday.' "

"That's a lot clearer than Wallace Stevens."

"It didn't leave me wondering. And there was a PS, which I used to know by heart, but I got over it. He said to stay as long as I wanted, and that the rent was paid through the end of June, which was about six weeks off. There was some cash in the top dresser drawer along with a ticket to New York; I could use the ticket or cash it and go somewhere else. I could do what I wanted with everything in the house. He'd signed the car registration over to me, and the title was in the glove compartment, so I could drive it or sell it, whatever I wanted."

"Could you drive? Last I heard you were fourteen."

"I was seventeen by this point, but no, I hadn't gotten around to learning. I was going to ask a neighbor to drive it to a dealer so I could sell it, but in the end I just left it there, along with just about everything else. I packed the suitcase I'd brought from Greenwich, and I took the black San Ildefonso pot, wrapping it in my clothes so it wouldn't break. And it didn't. I still have it."

"And you flew back to New York?"

"Almost. I took a bus to the airport and got a boarding pass. Then when they called my flight I didn't get on it. I just picked up my bag and walked out of the terminal. I suppose there was a way to cash in my ticket, but it just felt like too much of a hassle. I had enough money left for a ticket to San Francisco on Greyhound, and that's where I went."

"With your clothes and your black bowl."

"I got a room in the Tenderloin. I put my clothes in the closet and I put the bowl on the dresser. I didn't recite any poems."

"You were seventeen."

"I was seventeen. I was a published writer, and I'd spent three years with a famous novelist who'd given me daily lectures on writing, but I hadn't written a word since I left Connecticut. And I was still a virgin."

Coltrane had finished, and what we were listening to now was Chet Baker.

I said, "A virgin. Do you mean that metaphorically or . . ."

"Literally. *Virga intacta*, or however it goes in Latin."

"He, uh, wasn't interested?"

"He was vitally interested. We had sex just about every day."

I thought about it. "He'd been to the Amazon," I suggested, "and he went skinny-dipping and ran into a candiru."

She shook her head. "No surgery," she said, "and no performance problems. He just wouldn't put the usual protrusion into the usual orifice. He did all manner of other things, but the girl who went to San Francisco was still technically a virgin."

"How come?"

"He never said. Gully wasn't much on explaining himself. It may have had something to do with my age, or my being a virgin. Or he may have been the same with other women. He may have had a morbid fear of fathering children. Or it may just have been an experiment of his, or a stage he was going through. I tried not to ask questions I sensed he didn't want to answer. He'd just get this disappointed look on his face, and he'd never answer anyway, so I learned not to ask."

"So it was something you didn't talk about."

"One of many things we didn't talk about. You get so you take it for granted. And there were plenty of other things we *did* talk about. And it's not as though my sexual education was being neglected, because there were plenty of things we did."

And she commenced to tell me about some of them. She sat a little closer to me on the sofa, and she settled her head on my shoulder and she talked about the things she'd done twenty years ago with a man old enough to be her father.

"Bernie? Where are you going?"

"I'll be right back," I told her. "I want to put a record on. I hope you like Mel Tormé."

"Well," I said a little later, "you're not a virgin now."

"Silly. I stopped being a virgin my second week in San Francisco. And the only reason I lasted that long was that every cute guy I met turned out to be gay."

"Well, San Francisco."

She'd stayed in San Francisco for a year and a half, which was how long it took her to write a first draft of a novel. When she was done she set it aside for a week. Then she read it and decided it was terrible. She would have burned it in the fireplace, but she didn't have a fireplace. Instead she tore it up, tore all the pages in half and then in half again, and let the garbage men take it away.

She'd been supporting herself by waiting tables in a coffeehouse, but she was sick of that, and sick of San Francisco. She moved, San Ildefonso pot and all, to Portland, and then to Seattle. She found a room off Pioneer Square, got a job in a bookstore, and wrote a short story. She sent it to *The New Yorker*, and when it came back she sent it to Anthea Landau, the only agent she knew of. Fairborn had written to Landau occasionally and got occasional letters from her, sent to him at General Delivery in Santa Fe.

"She sent the story back," she said, "along with a letter saying it struck her as derivative and unconvincing, though skillfully crafted. And she said she was no longer representing Gulliver Fairborn, and I gathered that mentioning his name might have been a strategic error."

She reread the story and decided that the agent was right. She tore it up, and a day or two later she came home from the bookstore with a Harlequin romance in her purse. She read it that night, and another the next night, and five more over the weekend. Then she sat down at the typewriter and within a month she had a book written. She sent it directly to the publisher and they sent her a check and a contract.

She used the pen name Melissa Manwaring. The Manwaring came from *Nobody's Baby*, of course, and Melissa just seemed to go well with it. She quit her bookstore job when she was halfway through with the second book. Later on she began writing Regency romances for another publisher, with period dialogue and dastardly male characters, and her pen name for these was Virginia Furlong. She changed cities every couple of years, and friends and lovers a little more frequently than that, and she turned out a book often enough that money was never a problem, but not so often that she had to worry about burning out.

Every now and then, say eight or ten times in twenty years, she'd get a purple envelope in the mail with her current address typed on it. And a letter inside from Gulliver Fairborn.

"He wouldn't have needed to hire detectives," she said. "I wasn't hiding from the world the way he was. Each time I moved I sent a change-of-address to the post office. I never paid extra for an unlisted telephone number. Still, he had to make an effort to find me."

The first letter showed up a few months after Melissa Manwaring's first novel hit the bookstores. Maybe the pen name caught his eye. In any event, he'd spotted her style right away, and took the time to read the book through and comment on it. That was flattering. He included a return address—General Delivery, Joplin, Missouri, with a false name to address it to. She dashed off a long letter, tore it up, wrote a short one, and sent it off—and heard nothing further, until two years later and a thousand miles away when another purple envelope turned up, this one postmarked Augusta, Maine.

And so it went. She got a letter from him shortly after she was married, and another, two years later, shortly after her divorce. They both kept moving around the country, and occasionally out of it. Their paths never crossed, but she never went more than a couple of years without hearing from him. The purple envelopes always took her by surprise, and she would take them up with a mixture of excitement and dread. He remained, she had to admit, the most important man in her life. Sometimes she cursed him for it, but it was true.

And now, just weeks ago, she'd heard from him after a silence of almost three years.

"Here in New York?"

But no, she'd been living in Charlottesville, Virginia, had moved there in the spring, subletting an apartment a short walk from the University of Virginia campus. She got to share a rose garden with the building's three other tenants, and she took his letter out to the garden and read it there, on a warm afternoon with a scented breeze blowing.

He was very agitated. That was unusual, as his letters were typically laid-back. What, he wanted to know, had she done with the letters he had sent her? Had she destroyed them? Would she please do so, either that or return them to him?

She wrote back at once, saying that she had kept all of his letters from the very beginning. She traveled light, she kept little, she didn't even have copies of all of her own books, but she still owned the copy of *Nobody's Baby* he'd inscribed to her, and she still had his letters. And she wanted to keep them. Why on earth did he want her to destroy them?

For answer he sent her—by return mail!—a photocopy of an article that had run in the *New York Times*. Anthea Landau, his erstwhile agent, had made arrangements with Sotheby's for the sale of all the letters he'd sent her over the years.

He'd called the woman up, outraged, and had made the tactical error of letting phrases like "bloodsucker" and "money-grubbing vampire" and "ten percent of my soul" creep into his conversation. Landau hung up on him and wouldn't pick up the phone when he called back. He wrote her a letter, arguing his case more diplomatically, stressing that his letters had been written for her eyes only and that it was important to him that he get them back. He offered to pay for them, and invited her to set a price. She wouldn't have to pay a commission, he said, or report the sale to the IRS, and she would be doing the right thing, too.

She never responded. He wrote a second letter, and had no sooner dropped it in the mail than he realized she could add these letters to the auction. The idea infuriated him, and he didn't write again.

"And there was nothing he could do," I told Carolyn. "The law's very clear when it comes to letters. They belong to the recipient. If I send you a letter, it's yours. You can keep it, you can tear it up, you can sell it to somebody else."

"First I'd have to find someone who wanted it, Bern."

"Well, if I was Gully Fairborn, you wouldn't have a lot of trouble. He's an important writer, and he's such a man of mystery that his letters are particularly desirable. So you could sell them if you wanted. About the only thing you couldn't do is publish them."

"Why not, if they belong to me?"

"The letters as physical property belong to the recipient. As literary property, title remains with the sender. He owns the copyright."

"Wait a minute. I know Fairborn's a couple of beads off

plumb, Bern, but don't tell me he sent his letters to the Library of Congress to have them copyrighted."

"He doesn't have to. Anything you write is automatically protected by copyright, whether or not you register it in Washington. Fairborn retains the copyright to his letters, and he can keep them from being published. In fact he did just that a couple of years ago."

"Anthea Landau tried to publish his letters?"

"No, but there was a fellow who wrote a biography of Fairborn—an unauthorized biography, obviously. There were a few people around who'd received purple envelopes over the years, and some of them were willing to let the writer read them. He was going to quote at length from them in his book, until Fairborn went to court and put a stop to it."

"The guy couldn't even quote excerpts from the letters?"

"The court ruled that he could report on their contents, because that was a matter of fact, but he couldn't quote without infringing on Fairborn's copyright. He could paraphrase, but not in great detail, and the upshot of it all was that he couldn't write the book he'd set out to write, and the one he wound up with wasn't one too many people wanted to read."

She thought about it. "If nobody can publish his letters," she said, "what does Fairborn care who owns them? What difference does it make to him if they sit in Anthea Landau's files or in some collector's library? If they can't be published . . ."

"But they can. Sort of."

"You just said . . ."

"I know what I said. You couldn't quote them in a book, or even paraphrase them in great detail. But you could quote from them and give a detailed description of their contents in an auction catalog."

"How come?"

"Because you've got a right to furnish a description of goods offered for sale. And you've also got a right to show the goods to prospective buyers, so anyone who wanted could turn up at

Sotheby's the week before the auction and read through Fairborn's letters. And the press could report on their contents."

"Would they bother?"

"With all the mystery surrounding Fairborn, and with all the interest in the letters? I think they might. They'd certainly cover the sale and report on the selling price."

"More publicity for Fairborn."

"And he's the one author in America who doesn't want it. He makes B. Traven look like a media slut, and now his private correspondence is up for grabs to the highest bidder. And sooner or later it'll be published in full."

"When the copyright runs out?"

"When Fairborn dies. It'll still be protected, but his heirs would have to go to court, and who knows if they'll bother? Even if they do, the courts are less impressed with the need to protect a man's privacy when he's not around to notice one way or the other. The only way Fairborn can be positive those letters won't be published is if he gets hold of them and burns them."

"So why doesn't he go to the auction and buy them himself?"

"He's not one to show his face in public."

"Why not, if nobody knows what he looks like? But he wouldn't have to show up in person. He could deputize someone to bid for him. A lawyer, say."

"He could do that," I allowed. "If he could afford it."

"How much money are we talking about, Bern?"

I shrugged. "I couldn't even tell Alice how much her inscribed first of *Nobody's Baby* is worth. I couldn't begin to guess what a hundred letters would bring."

"A hundred letters?"

"Well, she was his agent for four or five books. Some of the letters are probably cut-and-dried—here's the manuscript, where's the check?—but there are probably longer letters that shed light on his creative process and provide personal glimpses of the man behind the books."

"Ballpark it for me, Bern."

"I really can't," I said. "I haven't seen the letters and I don't know just how revealing they'll turn out to be. And I've got no way of knowing who might show up the day of the sale. I'm sure there'll be a couple of university libraries bidding. If the right private collectors come around, and if their pockets are deep enough, the prices could go through the roof. And don't ask me how far through the roof, or even where the roof's located, because I don't know. I can't imagine they'll bring less than ten thousand dollars, or more than a million, but that doesn't really narrow it down."

"And Fairborn's not rich?"

"Not as rich as you'd think. *Nobody's Baby* made a lot of money, and still earns steady royalties, but none of his books since then have amounted to much in sales. He keeps trying new things and won't write the same book twice, or even the same kind of book. He always gets published, because how can you not publish Gulliver Fairborn? But his recent books haven't made money, for him or his publishers."

"Are the new books any good, Bern?"

"I've read most of them," I said, "although I've missed a few along the way. And they're not bad, and they may even be better novels than *Nobody's Baby*. They're certainly more mature work. But they don't grab you the way that first book did. According to Alice, Fairborn doesn't care how the books sell, or if they sell. He barely cares if they're published, just so he can get up each morning and write what he wants to write."

"He could make money if he wanted to, couldn't he?"

"Sure. He could write *Nobody's Toddler* or *Nobody's Adolescent*. He could go on tour with it and give readings on college campuses. Or he could sit back and sell film rights to *Nobody's Baby*, which he's always refused to consider. There are lot of things he could do, but not if he wants to live his life in peace and privacy."

"So he can't buy the letters back."

"He tried to, remember? Landau didn't even answer his letter. And he can't afford to pay what they'll bring at auction."

"I get the picture," she said. "And I guess that's where you come into it, huh, Bern?"

"It's really a shame," I'd told Alice. "You would think lawyers could do something, wouldn't you? I guess the best he can do is hope the letters wind up with someone who'll keep the public away from him."

"There would still be the auction catalog."

"True."

"And the newspaper stories."

"It'll blow over eventually," I said, "but so will a tornado, and your trailer park never looks the same afterward. There ought to be something somebody can do."

"Perhaps there is."

"Oh?"

"If someone were a burglar," she said, not looking at me, "one could get hold of the letters before they got into Sotheby's hands, let alone into their catalog. Isn't that the sort of thing a skilled and resourceful burglar could do?"

"I suppose I should have seen it coming," I told Carolyn. "I bought the bookstore thinking that it might be a good place to meet girls, and every once in a while it is. People do wander in, and some of them are female, and some of them are attractive. And it's natural enough to fall into conversation, about books if nothing else, and sometimes it's a conversation that can be continued over drinks and even dinner."

"And once in a while it's not over until Mel Tormé sings."

"Once in a while," I agreed. "Once in a great while. But I should have seen it coming all the same. I mean, it's not as if I was irresistible that afternoon. All I could talk about was the candiru. That's some icebreaker."

"Well, it gets your attention."

"She's living in Virginia when she hears from Fairborn," I said, "and a couple of weeks later she walks into my store, picks a fifth printing of his book off the shelf, and asks what an inscribed first edition would be worth. She'd owned the book for twenty years. Don't you think she'd have a better idea of its value than I would?"

"It was a way to start a conversation, Bern, and a better one than the candiru. It was a coincidence, her needing a burglar and you happening to be one, but the thing about coincidences is they happen. Look at Erica."

"I'd better not," I said. "I looked at Mindy Sea Gull, and I got bawled out for it."

"I'm talking about coincidence," she said. "Erica came into my life when I just happened to be in the mood for romance and open to the possibility of a relationship. Wouldn't you call that a coincidence?"

"Not really."

"No? Why the hell not?"

"You're generally in the mood for romance," I said, "and whenever you see somebody cute, you're ready to start picking out drapes together."

"Our eyes met across a crowded room, Bern. How often does that happen?"

"You're right," I agreed. "It was a remarkable coincidence, and it means the two of you are made for each other. But it wasn't a coincidence with Alice. She'd managed to learn about me, and maybe that's not as hard to do as I'd like to think. Sit down at a computer, punch in *books* and *burglar*, and whose name is going to pop up?"

"It's true you've had your name in the papers a few times."

"That's the trouble with getting arrested," I said. "All the publicity. If Fairborn wants to find out what invasion of privacy is all about, let him stick up a liquor store. 'No mug shots, please. I never allow photographs.' Lots of luck, Gully."

"I guess that means he'd better not go after the letters himself."

"I should have seen it coming," I said again, "and maybe I would have, but Mel Tormé was singing his heart out, and . . ."

"I understand, Bern. You're gonna do it, aren't you? You're gonna steal the letters."

"I'd have to be nuts," I said. "There's no money in it. The letters may be worth a small fortune, but I'd be returning them to the man who wrote them, and he can't pay enough to make it worthwhile. And she lives in a hotel, and that's always tricky. The Paddington's not Fort Knox, but it's still risky and there's no pot of gold at the end of the rainbow. The only pot is one made out of black clay, and he already gave it to Alice. I'd have to be out of my mind to do it."

"What did you tell her, Bern?"

"I told her yes," I said, and picked up my drink. "I must be out of my mind."

EIGHT

Gulliver Fairborn would have hated it.

They took me to the precinct in handcuffs, which is just plain undignified, and they took my fingerprints and made me pose for pictures, full-face and profile. That's a clear-cut invasion of privacy, but try telling that to a couple of cops at the end of a long shift. Then they strip-searched me, and then they tossed me in a holding cell, and that's where I spent what was left of the night.

I'd have slept better at home, or on the office couch at the store, or in Room 415 at the Paddington. As it was I barely slept at all, and I was groggy and grubby when Wally Hemphill showed up first thing in the morning and bailed me out.

"I told them they had nothing," he said. "You were in a hotel where a woman died. Where's the crime in that? They said a witness could place you on the floor where the murder took place, and where you had no reason to be. And you were registered under a false name, and you have a sheet with a whole lot of arrests on it."

"But only one conviction," I pointed out.

"A judge hears that," he said, "it's like telling him you only

put the tip in. What I stressed was you're an established re-
tailer with your own store, and there's no chance you're going
to cut and run. I tried for Own Recognizance, but the papers
teed off on the last judge who let a murderer out without bail,
and—"

"I'm not a murderer, Wally."

"I know that," he said, "and anyway it's beside the point,
which is that I got bail knocked down to a manageable fifty
K."

"Manageable?"

"You're out, aren't you? You can thank me, for cutting my
run short and coming down bright and early." Wally was training for the New York Marathon, upping his weekly mileage
as the race approached. Law was his profession, but running
was his passion. "And you can thank your friend Marty
Gilmartin," he added. "He put up the dough."

"Marty Gilmartin," I said.

"Why are you frowning, Bernie? You remember him, don't
you?"

Of course I did. I'd met Martin Gilmartin a while back, after
I'd been arrested for stealing his collection of baseball cards. I
hadn't done it, but my alibi would have been that I was crack-
ing an apartment across town at the time, and I figured I was
better off keeping my mouth shut. It all worked out, and Marty
and I wound up having a mutually profitable association,
breaking effortlessly into houses of friends of his who wanted
to collect on their insurance. We each had a good chunk of
cash by the time we were done, and mine was enough to buy
the building that housed the bookstore. Now I don't have to
worry about grasping landlords, since I've had the good fortune to become one myself. You know how they say crime
doesn't pay? They don't know what they're talking about.

"I remember him," I said, "as if I'd seen him only yesterday.
If I was frowning it's because I'd meant to tell you to call him.
But I didn't, did I?"

"No," Wally said, "and *I* didn't, either. Call him, I mean."

"He called you."

"Right. Said he'd heard you were in trouble, and what would it take to get you out? I said it would probably take an act of God to get you out of trouble, but all it would take to get you out of jail was ten percent of the bond, which is to say five large. He sent a messenger with fifty hundred-dollar bills in an envelope, which ought to earn him an invitation to your Christmas party. And here you are."

"Here I am," I agreed.

"You're charged with murder," Wally went on, "but I don't think they're serious about it. They can't possibly make it stick. Of course, life would get a lot simpler if they found the person who actually did kill the Landau woman."

"If I knew," I said, "I'd be happy to tell them. Meanwhile I'd better go open the store. I've got a cat who hates to miss a meal."

"I know how he feels, Bernie. But swing past your apartment first, why don't you." His nose wrinkled. "You might want to get under the shower."

"It's cigarette smoke," I said. "I was in the kind of smoke-filled room where they decided to nominate Harding for President."

"That was a little before my time," Wally said, "and that's not just cigarette smoke."

"You're a runner," I said. "I didn't figure you would mind the smell of good clean sweat."

"Good clean sweat is one thing," he said. "Jailhouse sweat is something else. Go on home, Bernie. Take a shower, put on some clean clothes. You got an incinerator in your building?"

"A compactor."

"Whatever. The clothes you got on? Toss 'em down the chute."

People talk about burning their clothes, but does any sensible middle-class person ever actually do it? I bundled mine up and ran them over to the laundry around the corner.

My apartment's on West End and Seventy-first. I'd cabbed there from the Thirteenth Precinct ("the one-three," as the TV cops would say) on East Twenty-first, and, after a shower and a shave and a change of clothes, I cabbed back down to the store. I usually take subways—they're usually faster, they've got more legroom, and you don't have to listen to Jackie Mason's recorded voice urging you to wear a seatbelt. But there's nothing like a night in a cell to make a man appreciate life's little refinements, even if there's precious little refined about them.

It was around eleven by the time I got to the store, and Raffles made it clear that he was glad to see me, rubbing himself against my ankles in the fashion of his tribe. I'm happy you're here, he was saying, and I'll be happier when you feed me. I did and he was, and as soon as I had the place up and running I looked up Marty Gilmartin's number and dialed it.

"I wanted to thank you," I said.

"It's nothing."

"If you'd ever spent a night in a cell," I said, "you wouldn't say that."

"No, I don't suppose I would. So let me just say that you're welcome, and that I was glad for the chance to do you a service. It's been a long time, Bernard."

"It has," I agreed. "I haven't seen you in ages, except for a quick glimpse now and then."

"Quite. I'm tied up for lunch, dammit, but do you suppose you could drop over to the club sometime this afternoon? Say half past three?"

That would mean closing early, but without his help I wouldn't be open at all. I told him half past three would be fine, then hung up and waited for the world to beat a path to my door. First of the path-beaters was a fellow in his late thirties, wearing navy slacks and a sportshirt he'd buttoned wrong. He was skinny, with knobby wrists and a prominent Adam's apple, and his straw-colored hair looked as though it had been cut at the barber college, and by one of their less-promising students. He squinted through rimless eyeglasses at Raffles, who had made short work of his breakfast and was on his way back to the sunny spot in the front window. When the animal had plopped himself down without turning around three times, thus proving conclusively that he wasn't a dog, the geeky-looking guy turned his pale blue eyes on me.

"He doesn't have a tail," he said.

"Neither do you," I said, "but I wasn't going to mention it. He's a Manx."

"I've heard of them," he said. "They don't have tails, do they?"

"They've outgrown them," I said, "even as you and I. When you come right down to it, what does a cat in this day and age need with a tail?"

I'd offered this by way of small talk, but he took it seriously, creasing his high forehead in thought. "I wonder," he said. "Doesn't it play a role in keeping the animal balanced?"

"He sees a therapist once a week," I said, "and when he has a problem we talk about it."

"Physically, I meant."

Duh. I let him speculate on the role of the feline caudal appendage in maintaining the animal's equilibrium and the possible evolutionary advantage of taillessness on the Isle of Man, the breed's ancestral home, but I didn't contribute much to the conversation myself beyond the occasional nod or grunt. I didn't want to waste wit on him, since he didn't seem to know what it was, nor did I want to inquire too closely into Raffles's origins.

Because, when you come right down to it, I've never been entirely certain that Raffles *is* a Manx. He doesn't look a lot like any photos I've seen of Manx cats, nor does he have the breed's characteristic hopping gait. What he looks like, really, is a garden-variety gray tabby who lost his tail in some unrecorded accident, and who has learned to live without it.

He'd learned, God knows, to live without any number of other things to which he was once presumably attached. Although he still seeks to sharpen them on the furniture, his claws are but a memory, surgically removed before Fate (and Carolyn Kaiser) brought him into my life. And, although he is in attitude and temperament an outstanding example of feline masculinity, two emblems of his maleness have, alas, had similar surgical alteration.

Since this last point makes breeding him out of the question, it renders his bloodlines largely academic. As far as I'm concerned, he's a Manx, and a fine one in the bargain. How he got that way is no concern of mine.

". . . Gulliver Fairborn," my visitor was saying.

That got my attention, which he'd hitherto succeeded in losing. I looked up and there he was, eyes wide, waiting for me to answer a question of which I'd heard only the last two words. I tried to look blank, and I have to say it comes easy to me.

"Let me explain," he said.

"Perhaps that would be best."

"All I need," he said, "are photocopies. Do whatever you want with the originals. It's not the letters I'm interested in. It's their contents, it's knowing what they say."

I could have told him the letters were as hard to trace as Raffles's tail, but what was my hurry? He was a lot more interesting now than when he'd been discussing my cat. "I don't think I got your name," I said. "Mine is—"

"Rhodenbarr," he said. "Did I pronounce it correctly?"

The place some people go wrong is the first syllable. The O is long, as in "Row, row, row your boat," and that's how he'd rendered it. "Either you got it right," I said, "or my parents lied to me. And you are . . ."

"Lester Eddington."

I waited for the name to ring a bell. When you own a bookstore, you recognize the names of thousands of authors. They are, after all, quite literally one's stock in trade. I may not know anything about a writer, I may never have read a word he's written, but I tend to know the titles of his books and what shelf to put them on.

I just knew this bird was a writer, but his name was new to me, and I found out why when he explained that he hadn't published anything yet, except for articles in academic journals that I'd been lucky enough to miss. But this didn't mean he hadn't been writing. For almost twenty years he'd been hard at work on a book about a subject that had preoccupied him since he was—surprise!—seventeen years old.

"Gulliver Fairborn," he said. "I read *Nobody's Baby* and it changed my life."

"That's what everybody says."

"But in my case it really did."

"That's the other thing that everybody says."

"In college," he said, "I wrote paper after paper on Gulliver Fairborn. You'd be surprised how many courses you can fit him into besides English Lit. 'Changing Attitudes on Race in America as revealed in the works of Gulliver Fairborn'—that worked fine in freshman sociology. For art history, I discussed the novels as literary reflections of abstract expressionism. I had a little trouble in earth science, but everything else fell into place."

He'd done a master's thesis on Fairborn, of course, and expanded it for his doctorate. And he'd spent his life teaching at one college or another, always on the move, never getting tenure. Wherever he went, he taught a couple of sessions of freshman English, along with a seminar on Guess Who.

"But they don't really want to study him," he said. "They just want to sit around and talk about how great *Nobody's Baby* is, and how it changed their lives. And, of course, what a 'cool dude' Fairborn must be, and how they'd love to call him up late at night and talk about Archer Manwaring and all, but how they can't because he's such a man of mystery. Do you realize how many books he's written since then?"

I nodded. "I have some of them on the shelves."

"Well, you would. You're in the business. But the man has published a new book every three years, forever taking chances, constantly growing as a writer, and hardly anyone pays any attention. The kids don't care. They don't want to read the later work, and judging by the papers they turn in, most of them don't get very far with it."

"But you've read all the books."

"I read everything he writes," he said, "and everything written about him. He's my life's work, Mr. Rhodenbarr. When I'm done, I'll have produced the definitive book on the life and work of Gulliver Fairborn."

"And that's why you want copies of the letters."

"Of course. Anthea Landau was his first agent, the only one with whom he had a close relationship."

"Not too close," I said. "The way I heard it, they never met."

"That's probably true, although the letters may show otherwise. That's only one of the questions they may answer. Did they meet? Were they more to each other than author and agent?" He sighed. "The answer to both of those questions is probably no. Still, she was as close to him as anyone. What did he confide in his letters? What did he say about the books he was working on? About his thoughts and feelings, about his inner and outer life? You see why I need those letters, Mr. Rhodenbarr?"

"I see why you want them," I said. "What I don't see is what you can do with them. Fairborn went to court once to keep his letters from being quoted in print. What makes you think he won't do it again?"

"I'm sure he will. But I can wait as long as I have to. He's almost thirty years older than I am. I don't drink or smoke."

"Good for you," I said. "How about cursing?"

"Oh, I'm not a goody-goody," he said, about as convincingly as one President insisting he wasn't a crook or another claiming he'd never inhaled. "But the vices I have aren't the sort that compromise one's health. I don't know that Fairborn smokes, but I have it on good authority that he drinks."

"Rye whiskey," I said.

"That's what they say, and I gather he drinks quite a good deal of it. Oh, I hope he lives for years and years, Mr. Rhodenbarr. I hope he writes many more books and that I have the chance to read them all. But all men are mortal, even if some of them manage to create immortal work during their lifetime. And, while he could live another thirty years and I could get run over by a bus this afternoon . . ."

"The odds are you'll outlive him."

"That's what any insurance actuary would tell you. I won't even attempt to publish my book during his lifetime. Believe me, I can write with a freer hand if I don't have to worry what he'd think of it. Once he's no longer in the picture, I can publish as I please. For the time being, my only concern is making the book as accurate and as comprehensive as possible." He smiled with all the warmth of an SS officer in a forties film. "And that is where you come in," he said.

"Except it's not."

"I beg your pardon?"

"I don't have the letters," I said.

"Oh?"

"Not even a postcard. It's true I've been charged with burglary in the past, and it's also true I was arrested at Anthea Landau's hotel last night. But I didn't steal her letters."

"His letters, you mean."

"Whatever."

"I suppose you would have to say that."

"So would Pinocchio," I said, "unless he wanted his nose to grow."

"If you don't have them, who does?"

It was a good question, and I wished I knew the answer myself. I told him as much, and his face took on a crafty look. "Suppose they come into your possession," he said. "If they're floating around they have to wind up somewhere, and who's to say it won't be with you?"

"Who indeed?"

"You'd have to consider your options and select the best course open to you. But, if only for your own protection, you'd want to run them through a Xerox machine, wouldn't you?"

"That's what burglars always do," I said.

"Really?"

"We Xerox everything. Furs, jewelry, rare coins . . ."

He nodded, registering as new data what had been an attempt at levity. "Just let me have a set," he urged. "I don't have any money, that must be obvious, but I could manage a few dollars to cover the cost."

"The cost?"

"Of making copies."

"In other words," I said, "you could pay me ten cents a page."

"Well, perhaps a bit more than that. But what I can offer you is something far more important. You'll be helping a scholar with his life's work. And, of course, you'd be listed in the acknowledgments when the book was published."

"Now you're talking," I said. "How often does a humble burglar get that sort of recognition? 'Thanks to Bernard Rhodenbarr'—do you suppose you'd have room for my middle name?"

"I don't see why not."

" 'To Bernard Grimes Rhodenbarr, for sharing with me useful documents stolen from the late Anthea Landau.' Wouldn't that make her proud?"

"Miss Landau?"

"My mother, to see her son get such recognition. Of course, the police might view it differently, but I suppose we could be a shade more circumspect in the wording. And who's to say the statute of limitations on burglary won't run out by the time you're able to publish?"

He agreed it was possible, even likely, and gave me a card with his name on it, Lester Eddington, along with that of a college and a town in Pennsylvania, neither of which I'd ever heard of. I said as much and learned the town was in the western part of the state, near the Ohio border.

"You must be tired," I said. "You had a long drive this morning."

But he'd been in town since the weekend, staying at a hotel. Not the Paddington, by any chance? Nothing so good, he assured me, and named a hotel on Third Avenue which was indeed a step or two down from the Paddington, but not too many steps away from it. He'd come to town to talk to the folks at Sotheby's on the slim chance they could be persuaded to copy the letters for him. And he'd hoped for an audience with Anthea Landau, either to see the letters or to interview her, a request she'd always refused in the past. And he had other leads to pursue as well.

"Well," he said, straightening up. "I've taken up enough of your time. If it turns out that you have those letters . . ."

"I'll keep you in mind."

He'd have liked something a little firmer than that, but I guess he was used to disappointment. He nodded shortly and thrust his hand across the counter in a manner awkward enough to leave me wondering for a moment just what I was supposed to do with it.

I shook it, which was evidently what he'd had in mind. Then I gave it back to him and off he went.

The door had barely closed behind Eddington when the phone rang. It was Carolyn, offering to pick up lunch and bring it over. "I know today's your turn," she said, "but I also know you just opened up, so I thought I could take two turns in a row. Unless you had a late breakfast and want to skip lunch altogether."

"I didn't have any kind of a breakfast," I said, "now that

you mention it. I fed Raffles, which was the only way to get him out from underfoot. The poor guy was starving. So was I, and I still am, so I certainly don't want to skip lunch."

"That pig," she said.

"What pig are we talking about?"

"Your pig of a cat, Bern. Did he eat his breakfast?"

"Every morsel."

"Well, he's two meals ahead of you. I fed him around nine-fifteen, before I opened up. I bet he didn't say a word, did he?"

"He said 'Meow.' Does that count?"

"The animal's a real con artist. Look, I'll see you in a little while. What would you say to some pastrami sandwiches and a couple of bottles of cream soda?"

"Meow," I said.

"That was really sweet of Marty," she said. "Go figure, huh? You start out by stealing a man's baseball cards, and he winds up getting you out of jail."

"I didn't steal his cards."

"Well, he thought you did. My point is the relationship didn't exactly get off on the right foot, and look at it now."

"I'm seeing him in a couple of hours," I said. "At his club."

"I guess it's been a while since you've seen him, huh?"

"Quite a while," I said, and glanced at my watch. "Something like twenty-two hours."

"Where did you—"

"At the Paddington," I said. "Not last night, but earlier in the day. When I was on my way out of the place, he was on his way in."

"What was he doing there?"

"He didn't say," I said, "because we didn't speak. But my guess would be that he was committing adultery."

"Is it that kind of a hotel, Bern?"

"The kind you commit adultery in? What other kind is there?"

"I mean is it crawling with hookers? Because I didn't think it had that kind of reputation."

"It doesn't," I said, "and it wasn't, but you don't need a hooker for adultery. All you need is a partner you're not married to."

"And he had one?"

"Right there on his arm. I got a good look at her, and she was worth looking at. But I don't think she looked at me, or if she did she wasn't paying attention. Because she didn't recognize me."

"She was someone you knew?"

"No."

"Oh. For a minute there I thought . . ."

"Thought what?"

"That you were going to say it was Alice Cottrell."

"Nope."

"Not if you didn't know her. But in that case why would you expect her to recognize you?"

"Not then," I said. "Later."

"Later?"

"When I met her in the sixth-floor hallway," I said. "God knows I remembered her, even if she was dressed up like Paddington Bear this time around. And she remembered me later on in the lobby. 'That's him!' she sang out, the little darling."

"She's the one you saw with Marty?"

"The very same," I said, "and I've got to say I admire the man's taste. Her name's Isis Gauthier and she lives right there at the hotel."

"And she turned you in to the cops, and Marty bailed you out."

"Uh-huh."

"What does it all have to do with the letters?"

"I don't know."

"Or the murder. Is it all connected?"

"Good question."

"There's nothing like pastrami, is there, Bern?"

"Nothing like it."

"And I don't know why cream soda goes with it. It doesn't go with anything else."

"You're right about that."

"Bern, what *happened* last night?"

"I wish I knew," I said, "because I was there when it happened, and I got scooped up in the net, and I'd be a lot happier if I knew what was going on."

I went over it again, from my own arrival at the Paddington the previous evening to my departure a little while later, handcuffs on my wrists and Ray's singular version of the Miranda warning ringing in my ears.

"My mother always told me to wear clean underwear," I said. "In case I got hit by a car."

"Mine told me the same thing, Bern, but she never said why. I just figured it was one of the things decent people did. Anyway, what good would it do? If you got hit by a car, wouldn't your underwear get messed up along with everything else?"

"I never thought of that," I admitted. "But I've taken her advice and put on clean underwear every morning, and in all these years I've never been hit by a car."

"What a waste."

"But what she should have said," I went on, "is to wear clean underwear in case you get strip-searched by the cops."

"Because that's a lot more likely than getting mowed down by a Toyota?"

"It's certainly worked out that way for me. The thing is, though, what would be really embarrassing is if you had dirty drawers when you were being strip-searched. I mean, it's embarrassing enough with clean ones."

"I can imagine."

"But if you got run over by a car, the odds are you'd be unconscious."

"Or dead."

"Either way, you wouldn't even know your underwear was dirty. And if you were awake, would you care? I'd have too much on my mind to be embarrassed about my underwear."

"It was embarrassing last night, huh?"

"Getting searched? I'll tell you, it would have been a lot worse if they'd found anything. And I'm not talking about dirty underwear."

"Good," she said, "because we've talked plenty about it already and it'd be fine with me if we never talked about it again. They didn't find anything, Bern?"

"Not a thing. They didn't find my tools, or they'd have had more charges to bring. And they didn't find Gulliver Fairborn's letters to his agent, which figured, because neither did I. And they also didn't find—"

The door opened.

"—out what happened to the Mets last night," I said innocently. "That young left-hander they just called up from Sarasota was supposed to start last night, but I never heard how he made out."

Carolyn was looking at me as though I'd lost my mind, or at the very least misplaced it. Then she glanced over at the doorway and got the picture.

NINE

It was Ray Kirschmann, wearing a dark blue suit and a red-and-blue-striped tie and, in all likelihood, clean underwear, which I hoped for his sake fit him better than the suit did. He looked at me, shook his head, looked at Carolyn, shook his head again, and came over to lean on my counter.

"I heard they let you out," he said. "I'm sorry I had to lock you up in the first place. I didn't have a whole lotta choice in the matter."

"No," I said, "I don't suppose you did."

"No hard feelin's, Bern?"

"No hard feelings, Ray."

"Glad to hear it. Bern, I gotta tell you, you're gettin' a little old to be creepin' around hotels. That's a young man's game, and you ain't a kid no more. What you are, you're knockin' on the door of middle age."

"If I am," I said, "I'm knocking gently. And if they don't let me in, I'm not going to pick the lock."

"Then it'd be the first one in ages that you didn't," he said. "You were in the old lady's room last night, weren't you?"

"What gives you that idea?"

His expression turned crafty. "Nothin'," he said.

"Nothing?"

"Nothin' at all, Bern. No burglar tools, no wad of cash, no coin collection, no jewelry. What did the English guy say about a dog that never barks?"

What indeed? I've thought about that sentence, and I have to assume the Englishman in question was Sherlock Holmes, and that the dog in question was not the titular Hound of the Baskervilles (a common mistake) but the beast in "Silver Blaze" who remains silent as a basenji. But at the time the only English guy I could think of was Redmond O'Hanlon, who when last I looked had enough on his mind with jaguars and scorpions and biting flies, not to mention our friend the tooth-pick fish. What did he care about dogs?

"I don't know, Ray," I said. "What did he say about the dog?"

"It bites, Bern. An' so does your story, rentin' a hotel room to meet some girl. There's only one reason a guy like you'd shell out good money for a room, an' it goes by the name of grand larceny. You were on those premises lookin' for some-thin' to steal."

"Maybe I was."

"Bern . . ."

"Carolyn," he said, "didn't they learn you not to interrupt?"

"They tried hard to learn me," she said, "but I was always a slow teacher. Bern, he Mirandized you last night, remember? So watch what you say, because it can be used as evidence. He could stand up in court and swear you said it."

"I could anyway," he said reasonably, "whether Bernie here said it or not. A man who's not willin' to stretch a point on the witness stand is a man's got no business bein' a cop. But this ain't about court, Bern. It's about you an' me comin' out of this in good shape. Now do you want me to keep talkin' or should I take a hike?"

"Do I get to vote?"

He glared at Carolyn, and I took a last sip of my cream soda. "Keep talking," I said.

"You were in this hotel," he said, "an' it wasn't romance brought you there. An' you were up on the sixth floor, 'cause that's where you ran into Goat Ear."

"Goat Ear?"

"You forget her already? The black girl, the one that hollered when you tried to sneak out through the lobby."

"Isis Gauthier."

"Right, like I said. Goat Ear."

"I met her in the hall," I said, "and I thought we hit it off reasonably well."

"Let's say you made an impression, Bern. She went straight to the desk clerk and told him to quit puttin' shoe polish on his hair an' call 911, because there's a suspicious person creepin' the place."

"I don't know how she could call me suspicious," I said. "I never suspected a thing."

"What you were," he said, "is cooler than a cucumber, even if it's a dill pickle. Speakin' of which, you gonna eat that one?" I shook my head and he snatched it off my plate, polishing it off in a couple of chomps. "Thanks," he said. "What you did, Bern, you heard about this Landau woman and these letters of hers. You went lookin' for 'em, an' you walked in on a corpse."

"You mean it wasn't me who killed her."

"Of course not, Bern. You ain't a killer. What you are's a burglar, an' you're one of the best, but when it comes to violence you're Mahatma Gandhi rolled into one."

"That's me," I said.

"So there's Landau," he said, "an' she's dead. And you let yourself out an' lock up after yourself, chain bolt an' all, same as you always do. It's a trademark of yours, Bern."

"I'm neat by nature," I admitted, "but—"

"Lemme finish. You let yourself in, find a dead woman, an' let yourself out. An' run smack into a live one."

"Isis Gauthier."

"The black one," he agreed, "with the French name. She's on her way out. Now why don't you hop on the elevator with her an' get away from the crime scene? That way you're home in your own bed by the time the blue uniforms hit the hotel lobby."

"I'm sure you have the answer, Ray."

"Sure," he said. "The dog."

"What dog?"

"The quiet one. We searched you, Bern. Turned you upside down an' turned your room on the fourth floor inside out. An' you know what we came up with?"

"Some socks and underwear," I said. "And a teddy bear, unless one of New York's Finest stole it for himself."

"You got some high opinion of the police, Bern. Nobody stole your teddy bear, which ain't yours in the first place, bein' as it's the property of the hotel. What we came up with was empty hands, an' what we didn't find none of was burglar's tools."

"So?"

"So where were they?"

"Search me."

"We did, remember?"

"Vividly."

"You didn't leave 'em home," he said, "or how would you open Landau's door, or lock up after you left? Anyhow, they're your American Express card. You never leave home without 'em. But you knew you stood a chance of bein' frisked, so you dumped 'em somewhere."

"And if we only knew where they were," I said, "we could use them to break into the Pentagon and steal government secrets."

"If we knew where they were," he said, "we could find more'n a set of burglar's tools. We could find those letters, too. An' don't ask what letters, Bern. You'd know from reading the papers this morning, as if you didn't know in the first place.

Letters from this famous writer I never heard of, so how famous can he be? It's not like you see the guy on the talk shows. How's anybody supposed to know who he is?"

"You could try reading his books."

"If I want to read, I'll stick with Wambaugh and Caunitz and Ed McBain. Guys who know what it's all about, not some jerk who writes all his letters on purple paper. The letters were gone, Bern. We searched her rooms the way you'd expect, it bein' a crime scene an' all. No letters."

"And no burglar's tools."

"Like I just said."

"And no dog," I said. "Ray, you already said I didn't kill her. Remember?"

"Like it was yesterday."

"And it was homicide, wasn't it? Or did she die of natural causes?"

"Somebody hit her over the head," he said, "an' then stuck a knife in her chest, which naturally caused her to die. The killer took the knife along with him. I suppose he coulda left it behind, an' you coulda picked it up an' put it the same place you put the burglar tools an' the letters, but why would he leave it an' why would you pick it up? It don't make no sense."

"Few things do," I said. "I thought she was shot."

"Why'd you think that?"

Because I'd smelled the gunpowder. "I don't know," I said vaguely. "I must have heard it."

"Well, you heard wrong. But even if she was shot, it wasn't you that shot her, on account of we gave you a paraffin test last night an' you passed it with flyin' colors." He tugged at his lower lip. "Of course you coulda worn gloves. Remember how you always used to wear those rubber gloves with the palms cut out for ventilation? Another trademark of yours, like locking up after the horse is stolen."

"I know Bernie," Carolyn said, "and I'll tell you this right now, Ray. He didn't steal a horse."

He gave her a look. "Those rubber gloves wouldn't help you beat a paraffin test," he went on, " 'cause you'd wind up with nitrate particles on your palms. But nowadays you wear those disposable gloves, made of that plastic film." A smile began to form on his lips. "Except you weren't wearing *any* gloves last night, Bern. Were you?"

"Why do you say that?"

"You left a print."

How? I distinctly remembered sliding my hands into my Pliofilm gloves before I turned the bolt to lock myself in Andrea Landau's chambers. And, gloved, I'd promptly wiped the knob and the surfaces of door and jamb I might have touched. The gloves had stayed on my hands until I was out of the apartment altogether. I was on the fire escape, a floor below the crime scene, before I took them off.

"Ain't you gonna ask where, Bern?"

"I would," I said, "but I have the feeling you'll tell me anyway."

"On one of the envelopes."

"Oh," I said, and frowned. "On one of *what* envelopes?"

"Yeah," he said. "I thought so."

"You thought what?"

"That you didn't even know you left 'em behind. Two purple envelopes, both of 'em addressed to Anthea Landau. What kind of a name is Anthea, anyway?"

"A girl's name," Carolyn said.

"Well, so's Carolyn, and what's that prove? They were the same envelopes the letters came in, Bern, an' they got dusted for prints, same as everything else on the scene, an' one of 'em had prints all over it. Some of 'em were smudged, an' plenty of 'em were hers, but one of 'em was clear as a crystal, an' guess whose it was?"

"Something tells me it was mine."

"You didn't worry about handling it," he said, "because you figured on taking it with you, along with the rest of the letters.

But I guess you dropped it. Don't look so down in the mouth, Bern. It puts you on the scene, but I already knew you were there, so it's no big deal."

"If you say so."

"You had the stack of letters. They musta been in an envelope or a file folder, and that'd be what, an inch thick? Two inches? Goat Ear didn't mention you holdin' nothin', so your hands were empty, but that's because your shirt was full."

"My shirt?"

"Under your shirt, that'd be my guess as to where you put the letters. That'd get you past Goat Ear, but a trained observer would spot it, so you had to stash the stuff before you hit the lobby, since you know somebody's been murdered, and you realize you might get spotted."

"By a trained observer."

"Or anyone who happens to recognize you for the encourageable burglar you are."

"Incorrigible."

"You said it. But you didn't dump the stuff in your room, Bern, an' you didn't get out of the hotel with it, an' what's that leave?"

"Since you don't believe I never had it in the first place—"

"Not on your life, Bern."

"—then I must have stashed it somewhere in the hotel."

"Uh-huh. Another room'd be my guess, an' if I was a young hothead I'd be goin' room to room, movin' furniture an' pullin' up the carpet."

"But you're older and wiser."

"You got the idea, Bern. Why make waves when we both get a chance here to do ourselves some good? What you gotta do is tell me where you stashed the stuff, an' I'll go in myself an' get it, an' we'll wait and see."

"We'll wait and see what?"

"How to cash in. That's gonna be the tricky part. The way I hear it, nobody knows what the letters are worth. An' they ain't worth much unless they can be sold right out in the open. You steal a rare book or a valuable coin or a painting, you got these crackpot collectors who'll pay through the nose for it and keep it where nobody ever gets a peek at it. But your college libraries are the big buyers for letters like this Gulliver wrote, an' they won't pay big bucks for something unless they get to brag that they got it."

"They want the publicity."

"Like an old guy with a young girlfriend. Half the fun is showin' her off to his buddies, especially since that's about all he can still do. So this is the kind of deal where you sell the loot back to the insurance company."

"Well, in that case . . ."

"Except it ain't insured. Landau wouldn't take out a floater policy on all her old letters, an' they wouldn't be covered by Sotheby's insurance because Sotheby's didn't have 'em yet. An' Landau can't ransom 'em back, because she's dead, an' unless there's a new will nobody knows about, the estate goes to the Authors Guild for handouts to writers who are up against it, which I guess plenty of 'em are most of the time."

"It's this society of ours, Ray. We don't value the arts sufficiently."

"Yeah, we all of us oughta be ashamed. Thing is, Bern, somebody's gonna offer a reward, or some other way'll open up to make a quiet dollar. An' we'll split."

"Fifty-fifty," I said.

"Only way to avoid hard feelings, Bernie. Half for you an' half for me. Keep it all as even as Steven."

"It seems fair."

"Damn right it does. So? We got a deal?"

"I guess so," I said. "But I'm going to have to retrieve the letters myself."

"How? Your picture's all over the papers, Bern. You'll never get past the front desk. Lemme get 'em. I can walk in like I own the place."

"Just lend me your badge," I said, "and I can do the same."

"Very funny."

"The letters are in a safe place," I said, "and nobody's going to disturb them. I'll get to them as soon as I can, but there's no hurry. And they'd be difficult for you to get to, Ray, even if you knew where they were."

"That don't make sense, Bern."

"Ray," I said, "I could tell you everything I know about those letters and you couldn't find them. Trust me."

"Yeah," he said, "you're as good at hidin' stuff as you are at findin' it. Only thing is I hope you didn't hide it right there in Landau's apartment."

"How could I do that? You must have searched the place from top to bottom."

"We did," he said, "and your room, too. Includin' the bear."

"The bear? Paddington Bear?"

"In your room, sittin' on top of the fireplace."

"And you thought he might have a two-inch-thick file of correspondence? Did he hide it under his little red jacket?"

He shook his head. "Not the letters. But he coulda been holdin' the burglar's tools, or even the gun, if it was a little one."

Carolyn said, "Is that a gun in your paw, or are you just glad to see me? Ray, did you and your buddies cut open Bernie's bear? Because if you did I think he's got the makings of a pretty good lawsuit."

"An' a complaint to the SPCA," Ray said, "but all we did was x-ray him, so put your mind at rest. All in all it was a pretty thorough search, Bernie, your room an' hers, but it ain't like searching for narcotics, where you can go in with dogs. How's a dog gonna help you find letters from a particular person?"

"Maybe you could let him sniff a sample of Gully Fairborn's handwriting."

"Or a purple envelope. I know how cute you are, an' I had a

couple of uniforms go through her files lookin' for anything purple. Perfect place to hide 'em, just stick 'em in the wrong file."

"Like 'The Purloined Letter,' " Carolyn said.

"Whatever. Purloin or sirloin, they came up empty. But we didn't rip the desk apart, or the refrigerator door, so you coulda double-dipped back into Landau's place an' found some tricky spot to leave everything. Only thing, the apartment's sealed off now as a crime scene. You can't get in."

"I don't need to."

"Good," he said. "So it's somewhere else, somewhere you can get to."

"I'd say so."

"An' where I can't."

"Not without creating a disruption," I said, "and attracting more attention than you'd be comfortable with."

"An' who wants that?" He shrugged. "Okay, Bern. We'll play it your way for now. Take your time, but not too much of it, huh? There's a lot of heat, what with a dame bumped off who's supposed to be kind of prominent, even if nobody I know ever heard of her. You wouldn't happen to know who knocked her off, would you?"

"If all this has been an elaborate buildup . . ."

"Naw, I know you didn't kill her. But you beat us to the crime scene, so you might have seen somethin' that gave you an idea. An' even if you didn't, you got a knack for steppin' on your dick an' coming up smellin' like a daffodil. One minute you're under arrest, an' the next minute you're tellin' a roomful of people who the real killer is."

"Well, I'm glad this room's not full of people," I said, "because for a change I'd be tongue-tied."

"That straight, Bern?"

"Absolutely. I haven't got a clue."

"But you might come up with somethin'," he said. "It wouldn't be the first time. If you do, you know where to bring it."

"Sure, Ray. We're partners."

"You bet we are, Bernie. We generally do all right together, don't we? An' I got a good feelin' about this one. I think we're gonna come out of it lookin' real good." He paused at the door. "Been a pleasure, Carolyn. You hardly said a word."

"I never had a chance, Ray."

"Maybe that's the answer. You're a lot less of a pain in the neck when you don't open your mouth."

"Gee," she said, "I wonder if it'd work for you?"

"See? The minute you got that mouth runnin' you're as bad as ever. But when you zip it up you're okay. You know what? You look different."

"Huh?"

"You look different," he said. "Most of the time you look like a dog gettin' ready to bite somebody."

"And now I look like a poodle that's just had a wash and set."

"More like a fluffy little cocker spaniel," he said. "Softer an' gentler, you know?" He opened the door. "Whatever you're doin', keep doin' it. That's my advice."

TEN

Whatever you're doin'," she growled, "*keep doin' it.* Words of advice from the founder of the Raymond Kirschmann Charm School."

"You know Ray."

"I do," she said, "and I never cease to regret it. Daffodils don't have any odor, Bern, so how are you gonna come out smelling like one? That rat."

"Because of what he said about daffodils?"

"Because of what he said about me. He noticed, Bern. He doesn't know what he noticed, but he noticed it all the same."

"It's the longer hair," I said.

"That's just part of it. It's the clothes, too. Look at this blouse."

"What's wrong with it?"

"Could you wear it?"

"Well," I said, "no, not really. But I'm a guy, Carolyn."

"And it's too feminine, right?"

"Well, yeah."

"It's happening, Bern. I'm turning femme. Look at my nails, will you?"

"What's the matter with them?"

"Just look at them."

"So?"

"They look the same to you?"

"They're trimmed short," I said, "and there's no polish on them, at least as far as I can see. Unless you've got some of that colorless polish on to protect them." She shook her head. "Then as far as I can tell," I said, "they're the same."

"Right."

"So what's the problem?"

"The problem," she said, "is inside."

"Under the nails?"

"Under the skin, Bern. They're the same as ever, but for the first time ever they don't look right. To me, I mean. They look short."

"They *are* short. Same as always."

"Up to now," she said, "they didn't look short to me. They just looked right. Now I look at them, and they look too short. Unattractively short."

"Oh."

"Like they ought to be longer."

"Oh."

"Like my hair."

"Oh."

"You see what's happening, Bern?"

"I think so, yeah."

"It's Erica," she said. "She's turning me into a Barbie Doll. What's next, will you tell me that? Painted toenails? Pierced ears? Bern, you'll be sleeping with a teddy and I'll be sleeping *in* one. Rats."

"Well, you still use strong language."

"For now. Next thing you know I'll be saying 'Mice.' Bern, I thought you didn't take the letters."

"I didn't."

"How'd you get your prints on the envelope?"

"That's how I found out Landau's room number. Remember? I pretended to find an envelope with her name on it . . ."

"And the clerk put it in her box. You just happened to pick a purple envelope?"

"I wanted something distinctive. I knew Fairborn always used purple envelopes, and, well . . ."

"What was in the envelope?"

"Just a piece of blank paper."

"Purple paper?"

"What else?"

"What were you trying to do, give her a heart attack? She gets the letter, she thinks it's from him, and then it's blank. If I were her, I'd figure I just got a death threat from a man of few words."

"What I sort of figured," I said, "is she wouldn't get the envelope until I'd gotten away with the letters, and then she'd think Fairborn was going nyah nyah nyah at her."

"That's what you figured, huh?"

"Well, sort of."

"And this was on Perrier, right?"

"Carolyn . . ."

"So you really don't know where they are?"

"Haven't a clue."

"Did you talk to the woman who started the whole thing?"

"Alice Cottrell?" I reached for the phone. "I tried her earlier, but she didn't answer. . . . Still no answer."

"I'm surprised she hasn't tried to reach you."

"So am I, now that you mention it. I'll try her again later."

"And your partnership with Ray . . ."

"Is a fifty-fifty deal," I said. "Every bit as even as Steven. But we don't have anything to sell, and the best offer so far is from a guy who'll reimburse me for the cost of making photocopies. So there's not going to be anything to divide. Unless . . ."

"Unless what?"

"Unless I'm wrong," I said. "We'll see. I wonder what Marty wants."

I was still wondering after she headed back to the Poodle Factory, but I had a stream of visitors to keep me distracted. First through the door was Mary Mason, who I swear buys books from me as an excuse to visit my cat. She made her usual fuss over him, and as usual he took it as his due. Then he hopped onto a high shelf and curled up next to a boxed volume of the letters of Thomas Love Peacock, which I'm afraid I'll own as long as I own the store. I sold Miss Mason reading copies of two or three mysteries—cozies, you'll be astonished to learn—and while I was ringing the sale a man came in on crutches and wanted to know how to find Grace Church.

It's just around the corner on Broadway, and a lot easier to get to than Lourdes. I pointed him in the right direction. He hobbled off, and in came my friend with the long face and the tan beret and the silver beard, smiling wistfully and smelling pleasantly of whiskey. He found his way to the poetry section and got down to the serious business of browsing.

A young woman in bib overalls wanted to know what time it was, and I told her, and a Senegalese, very tall and impossibly thin, wanted to sell me some Rolex watches and Prada handbags. They were, he assured me, genuine fakes, and represented an excellent business opportunity for me. I explained that I was running a bookshop, and consequently dealt exclusively in printed matter, and he went off shaking his head at my lack of enterprise and business acumen. I shook my own head, though I'm not sure what at, and tried Alice Cottrell's number again. No answer.

I made another call, this one to Mowgli. He's a Columbia dropout, a former druggie with just enough brain cells left to make a living as a book scout. I've bought quite a few books from him, and he's bought a few from me, when he's spotted something badly underpriced on my shelves. When he's not otherwise occupied he'll fill in for me behind the counter, and I was hoping he could do that today, while I met with Marty Gilmartin. But he didn't answer, either.

I went back to Redmond O'Hanlon, hoping to be reminded that there were worse jungles than the one I lived in, and the next person to interrupt me was a fat fellow with an under-slung jaw and a head of tightly curled brown hair. He looked like a bulldog with a permanent.

"Rhodenbarr," he said, and shoved a card at me. *Hilliard Moffett*, it read. *Collector*. And beneath that was an address consisting of a post office box in Bellingham, Washington, along with phone and fax numbers and an e-mail address.

Collectors can drive you crazy. They're all a little bit nuts, but the antiquarian book business wouldn't exist without them, because they buy more books than anybody else. They buy books they've already read, and other books they never in-tend to read. They don't really have time to read, anyway. They're too busy poring over book catalogs and rummaging through thrift shops and yard sales and, yes, stores like mine.

I asked him what he collected. He leaned over the counter and lowered his voice to a confidential whisper.

"Fairborn," he said.

What a coincidence.

"I'm a completist," he said, with an air that combined pride and resignation, as if he were at once claiming royal blood and admitting to hemophilia. "I want everything."

"Well, I don't have much," I said. "A few books shelved al-phabetically in the fiction section. I've got *Nobody's Baby*, but it's a fifth printing."

"I have a first."

"I thought you probably did."

"And a tenth," he said. "For the revised jacket. And I have fourteen paperbacks."

"So you can give copies to friends?"

He gaped at the very idea. I don't know which seemed outlandish to him—the idea of having friends, or the thought of giving books to them. Both, probably.

"Fourteen paperbacks," I said. "Oh. One for each printing?"

"Hardly. There have been over sixty printings. What sort of fool would want to collect them all? What I want is a copy of each cover. There have been fourteen different covers among the sixty-plus printings."

"So you have them all."

"I have the first printing in which each appeared. Except in one instance. There was a new cover introduced on the twenty-first printing, but my copy is the twenty-second. I've not yet been able to get my hands on a twenty-first. It's not rare, it's certainly not valuable, but try to find one."

"Well," I said, "I wish I could help you out, but I only get paperbacks when I buy a whole library, and I wholesale them off right away."

"I have my want list with specialists," he said. "That's not what I came here for."

"Oh."

"I just wanted you to understand the scope of my collection."

"You're a true completist."

He nodded. "I have the foreign editions. Almost all of them. I have *Nobody's Baby* in Macedonian. Not Serbo-Croat, Serbo-Croat's common as dirt, but Macedonian. It's not supposed to exist, none of the bibliographies list it, and I don't believe the edition was ever authorized. It must have been pirated. But somebody translated the text, and somebody set type and printed it, and I have a copy. It may be the only copy this side of Skopje, but it exists and I've got it."

"That's impressive."

"When I collect someone, Rhodenbarr, I go all out."

"I can see that."

"I don't just collect the books. I collect the man."

I pictured him with a great butterfly net, running over hill and dale in pursuit of a terrified Gulliver Fairborn.

"I have a copy of his high school yearbook," he said. "There were eighty students in the graduating class, so how many yearbooks could they have printed? And how many do you suppose have survived? It wasn't easy to find a classmate who still had his yearbook handy, and it was harder still to persuade him to sell it."

"But you managed."

"I did, and I can assure you I wouldn't part with it, not for twenty times what it cost me. He was the only senior who didn't have his picture included. There's a blank space opposite his list of accomplishments and activities. He was a hall monitor his junior year, did you know that? He was in the Latin Honor Society, he played trombone in the school band. Did you know that?"

"I know the capital of South Dakota."

"That's neither here nor there."

"It's not here," I said, "but I'm pretty sure it's there."

He gave me a look. "He was camera-shy even then," he said, "the only senior class member unpictured. He signed this particular copy. Where the photo would have been, he wrote, 'When you are old / And sitting still / Remember the fellow / Who wrote uphill.' The handwriting slants."

"Upward," I guessed.

"And he signed his name in full. Gulliver Fairborn."

"A signed photo," I said. "Without the photo."

"His photograph does appear in the book, however. Not in the senior listings, but in the group photos. He's in the band photo, but he's holding the trombone right in front of his face. On purpose, I'm sure."

"What a kidder."

"But he was also in the Latin Honor Society, as I may have mentioned, and they didn't let him hide behind a copy of Caesar's *Commentaries*. He's in the last row, second from the left.

He's half hidden behind another student, and his face is shadowed, so you can't really get much sense of what he looked like. But it's nevertheless a genuine photograph of Gulliver Fairborn."

"And you have it."

"I have the yearbook. I'd like to get the original. The photographer's long dead, and his files were dispersed years ago. The original's lost, probably forever. But I do have an original photograph of Fairborn's boyhood home. The house itself was torn down over twenty years ago. I missed my chance."

"To see it for yourself?"

"To buy it. The state took the property for an expressway extension, but I could have bought the house and moved it to another lot. Imagine housing the world's foremost Gulliver Fairborn collection in the house he grew up in!" He sighed for what might have been. "Over twenty years ago. Even if I'd known about it, I'd have been hard put to afford it. Still, I'd have found a way."

"You're dedicated."

"One has to be. And now I have the means, as well as the dedication. I want those letters."

"If I had them," I said, "what would you pay?"

"Name your price."

"If I had a price," I said, "it would be high."

"Name it, Rhodenbarr."

"The thing is, you're not the only person who wants those letters."

"But I'm the one who wants them the most. Get all the offers you want. Just give me the opportunity to top them. Or set a price yourself and give me the chance to meet it." He leaned forward, his collector madness burning in his dark eyes. "But whatever you do, don't sell those letters without giving me a crack at them."

"The letters," I said carefully, "are not physically in my possession at the moment."

"Quite understandable."

"But that's not to say they won't be."

"And when they are . . ."

"I'll want to contact you. But you're in . . ." I looked at his card. ". . . Bellingham, Washington. That's near Seattle?"

"It is but I'm not. I'm in New York."

"I can see that."

"I flew in the day before yesterday. I thought I might speak to this Landau and see if she'd entertain a preemptive offer as an alternative to public auction. Why wait for her money? Why pay a commission?"

"What did she say?"

"I never spoke to her. I went first to Sotheby's, where I learned they had a signed agreement with the woman. They'd given her an advance and she'd agreed to turn over the entire Fairborn file within the month, so it could be cataloged for sale in January. I urged them to offer it as one lot. I'm sure the University of Texas would prefer it that way, and whatever other institutional bidders turn up."

"And did they agree?"

"They hadn't decided, and won't until they see the material. My hunch is they'll parcel it out. That means bidding lot by lot. I'll do that if I have to, but I'd much rather write one enormous check and be done with it."

Checks, I pointed out, could be a problem. Not for Sotheby's, he said, but in the event of a private sale, entirely off the record, it would be a simple matter to handle the transaction in cash. He told me he was staying at the Mayflower, on Central Park West, and that he'd be there for the next week or so. There were some other dealers he had to see, booksellers and others, and he might get to a few museums and see a show or two. Gulliver Fairborn, while his great passion, was not his only interest.

We shook hands. I expected a sweaty palm, but his hands were dry, his grip firm. He wasn't creepy after all. He was just a collector.

*   *   *

I picked up the phone and tried Alice Cottrell and Mowgli, neither of whom answered. I decided they must be having a late lunch together, and talking about me. I put down the phone and reached for O'Hanlon, but before I'd hacked my way through the first overgrown paragraph someone got my attention by clearing his throat. It was my friend with the long face and the silver beard.

"I couldn't help overhearing," he said.

"Neither could I."

"Was that gentleman serious?"

"He's a collector," I said. "They're like that."

"Not all of them, surely."

"He's like the rest of them," I said, "only more so."

"This writer," he said. "Gulliver Fairborn. It sounds as though he wants to . . . to possess the man. To stuff him and mount him on the wall."

I nodded. "Properly preserved," I said, "and perfectly displayed. It's a passion or a mania, or maybe both, but whatever it is he's got it. And you can see how it starts. He read a book and he liked it. Well, I read it myself."

"So did I."

"And I suppose I could say it changed my life."

"Some books have changed my life," he said, grooming his beard with his fingertips. "But then it was time to move on and lead my new life, not fill up the old one with memorabilia. I certainly didn't come away from any of them with the urge to have a jar full of the author's fingernail clippings."

We drifted into a nice bookish conversation, of the sort I'd envisioned when I decided to buy the store. I told him my name, which he'd already overheard, and he gave me a card proclaiming him to be Henry Walden, from Peru, Indiana.

"But I don't live there anymore," he said. "I had a little factory, a family business with about twenty employees. We made modeling clay, and then a big toy company came along wanting to gobble us up." He sighed. "I liked being in the clay business," he said, "but they made us an offer my brother and sister couldn't refuse."

He was outvoted, so he gave in gracefully and took the money, but he didn't want to go on living in the midst of two siblings he'd ceased to like and twenty out-of-work claymakers who'd ceased to like him. He'd always liked New York, and now he was staying at a hotel while he looked for an apartment and figured out what to do with the rest of his life.

"I've even thought—promise me you won't laugh—of opening a bookstore."

"I'd be the last person to laugh," I said, "and I think it's a great idea. Just remember the surefire way to wind up with a small fortune in the antiquarian book business."

"What's that?"

"Start with a large fortune," I told him. "Meanwhile, do you want some hands-on experience? You can help me carry in the bargain table."

"You're closing?"

"I'm afraid I've got an appointment half a mile uptown, and I've enjoyed our chat so much I'm running late. So if you'd like to give me a hand—"

"I could shop-sit for you," he offered. "God knows I've got nothing else to do. You wouldn't want me to close up, but if you'll be back at the end of the day . . ."

I took ten seconds to decide to leave him in charge. I could tell he was honest, but people have thought that of me, so how could I be sure? In less time than it would have taken to close up, I told him what to do and how to do it. "Anything else," I said, "people with books to sell, people who want to argue about the price, tell 'em to wait for me. And if there's anything I haven't covered, ask Raffles."

"Meow," said Raffles.

ELEVEN

K essler's Maryland Rye Whiskey," Martin Gilmartin pro-
nounced, holding his glass to the light. "Sounds like something
a bellhop would bring you." He took a sip, considered it.
"Sweet, but not cloying. Still, I don't think it will win me away
from scotch."

"No."

"But it has a distinctive taste. Got some body to it. And some
authority, I'd say." He took another sip. "Very American drink,
isn't it? Though I don't know of anyone who drinks it, American or otherwise. Still, people must. The bottle wasn't covered
with dust."

I'd asked if the club had rye, not a blend but a straight rye
whiskey, and the waiter had brought the bottle of Kessler's to
the table. I'd studied it like an oenophile peering at a wine bottle, trying to make out if it was chateau-bottled. I said it looked
all right to me, and he took it away and brought back a couple of drinks, and we were doing our part and drinking them.

"I could imagine John Wayne ordering this," he said. "In a
film, that is to say. Shoving his way through the bat-wing
doors of a saloon. The room goes dead silent. He bellies up to

the bar. 'Rye whiskey,' he says, putting that take-it-or-leave-it tone of his in each syllable." He took another sip. "It grows on you," he said.

We were in the downstairs lounge at his club on Gramercy Park. We were both wearing blue blazers and striped ties, but Marty managed to look a good deal more elegant than I. He always does. He's tall and slender and silver-haired, with the kind of looks and bearing that belong in a Man of Distinction ad—or in a club like The Pretenders, where the portraits on the walls were mostly of great actors of the past, Drew and Barrymore and Booth. They all looked at once dashing and distinguished, and so did my host.

Marty's a businessman and an investor and not an actor at all, except insofar as he plays his part in the drama of life. But there are non-actors among The Pretenders—a pulse and a checkbook seem to be the principal qualifications for membership. Marty's listed on the club's rolls as a patron of the theater, which generally means no more than that the member so designated goes to a play once in a while. But Marty's connection is deeper than that. He's an occasional angel for off-Broadway productions, and he's made a habit over the years of one-on-one interactions with individual members of the acting profession.

Individual female members, that is to say.

"It said in today's *Daily News* that she's an actress," I said, and hefted my glass of rye. "I suppose I should have guessed as much."

"Isis, you mean."

"Isis Gauthier. She's a beauty, Marty. I'll say that for her."

"It's not what you think," he said, and then looked aghast at his own words. "I can't believe I said that. 'It's not what you think.' Of course it is, it's very much what you think, so let me amend my statement. It's not *just* what you think."

"All right."

He raised his glass, found it empty, and motioned for the

waiter. When both our glasses had been refilled, he took a sip and heaved a sigh. He said, "I don't suppose you've ever met my friend John Considine."

"I don't believe I have."

"And why would you? John's a bond trader. Sails, plays a lot of golf."

"Is he a member here?"

"No, though I've offered to put him up. In a manner of speaking, he's a patron of the theater."

"In a manner of speaking."

"Quite. John's a happily married man, a father and grand-father, but sailing a boat and hitting a golf ball can only go so far. Over the years, John has had a series of friendships with some charming and talented young women."

"Actresses."

"For the most part. A little over a year ago, John and his wife attended a Psoriasis Foundation benefit here in the city. It was well past midnight by the time they returned to their home in Sands Point, and in their absence they'd had visitors."

"Burglars."

"Yes. They'd come and gone by the time the Considines re-turned."

"That's just as well," I said, "for the good of all concerned. Some burglars are capable of violence when provoked, and so are some of the people they visit."

"John was on the wrestling team at Colgate," he said. "Of course, that was a while ago. Since then he's had his share of good dinners, not to mention an angioplasty. So it was as well that he and his uninvited guests never met, especially since their visit struck him as less a violation than an opportunity."

I made the leap. "Insurance."

"You're very quick, but then so was John. He saw at a glance that he'd been . . . burgled? Or burglarized?"

"Either," I said. "Or eye-ther. Whichever."

He considered the matter. "Burgled," he said decisively. "A

robber robs, a mugger mugs, and, I suppose, a forger forges on. So a burglar burgles, and these burglars left a mess—chair cushions tossed around, furniture overturned. Bernie, you look appalled."

"Believe me, I am."

"So was Cynthia."

"Mrs. Considine."

He nodded. "John took her outside and made her wait in the car while he assessed the damage and alerted the authorities."

"Dangerous. Suppose they were still in the house?"

"Either he was blind to the risk or he was prepared to run it. He dashed upstairs to the master bedroom, where the evidence of a crime was unmistakable. Night tables upended, drawers dumped out on the floor."

"Barbarians."

"John did not linger. He phoned 911, then hurried downstairs to his wife. 'They left the safe wide open,' he told her. 'They cleaned it out. They got everything.' "

"But they hadn't?"

"It was a wall safe," he said, "concealed behind a print hanging in the bedroom. The print was worth a few dollars itself, but the burglars didn't recognize it, or didn't care. If they'd known to take it they'd have found the safe, and who knows? They might have been able to open it."

"If they didn't know enough to find it," I said, "they wouldn't have been able to open it. Unless your friend taped the combination to the back of the picture frame, like a fellow I paid a call on some years back."

"You're not serious."

"I guess he found it a useful aid to memory," I said, "and I guess he figured nobody would notice. And he was right, damn him. I didn't spot it until I was replacing the picture on my way out. I'd managed to get into the safe on sheer talent, but I'd have been in and out a lot faster if I'd seen what he left for me." I shook my head at the memory. "Never mind. John Considine cleaned out his own safe."

"He had some cash there," he said, "which wasn't covered by insurance, and which the IRS certainly didn't need to know about. He found another place to stash it. He also had some papers in the safe—the deed to the house, some bonds and stock certificates, a couple of promissory notes and mortgages he held. He added these to the litter on the floor, so that it would look as though the burglars had deemed them not worth the taking."

"They took the cash," I said, "and let the credit go."

"That's how he made it look. They took the jewelry, too. They had in fact walked off with Cynthia's jewel box, plus everything in the top dresser drawer, but she kept her best ten or twelve pieces in the safe. Those were the ones important enough to be listed specifically on John's homeowner policy. His pockets were bulging with them even as he was telling her he feared they were gone forever."

"Some would call him resourceful," I mused, "while others would label him a cad."

"The diem presented itself," he said, "and John carped it. In a sense, though, it slipped through his fingers. The police came and investigated, told him it looked like the work of a ring of burglars who'd been operating in the area, and held out little hope that the stolen articles would be recovered. John put in a claim for the full value of everything that had been stolen, excepting the unreported cash, of course, but including the several pieces of jewelry he'd stolen himself. The company paid. They're all terrible weasels, but in this instance they had no choice. There was no question that John owned the pieces, and that his policy covered them, nor was there any doubt in anyone's mind that a burglary had occurred. The claim was approved and the check issued."

"I thought you said something slipped through his fingers."

"And indeed it did." He picked up his glass. "This rye grows on one, doesn't it? Do you suppose we have time for another?"

"Time's not a problem. But I might need to drive or operate machinery."

"You'll want a clear head," he said, and put his glass down. "Back to John Considine. The company paid, and no sooner did John deposit the check than Cynthia went on a shopping spree. She had to replace everything that had been taken, and who could fault her for improving a bit on the original? By the time she was done, she'd spent every penny of the insurance company's payment, and some thousands of dollars more."

"So John was out of pocket on the deal," I said. "Still, in terms of net worth, he was ahead of the game, wasn't he? He was out a few thousand in cash, but he still had all the jewels."

"And what could he do with them?"

"Oh."

"Precisely. It would have been a different matter if he'd made his wife a party to the fraud. But such a course might have had unfortunate consequences of its own. John kept his own counsel. And he rented a safety deposit box and stashed the jewels in it."

"And there they remain."

"Not quite all of them."

"Oh?"

"At the time of the burglary, John had a special friendship with a young woman named . . . well, it hardly matters, as she's no longer a part of his life. He was quite taken with her at the time, and he gave her a bracelet, which had formerly reposed in his safe. It wasn't that distinctive in design, and it was worth a few thousand at the most. A substantial gift, but not wildly inappropriate. When they bade each other good-bye some months later, she did not offer to return the bracelet, nor did he feel he had the right to ask for it."

"And she's not a part of the story now."

"No."

"But another woman is."

He nodded. "Shortly after their breakup," he said, "or it may even have been shortly *before* that event, John met another young woman."

"An actress."

"Yes, as a matter of fact."

"I don't suppose she was living at the Hotel Paddington."

"She was," he said, "and that meant having to go through the lobby whenever he visited her, which John didn't much care for. On the other hand, the place has a certain artistic tradition, and an air of romance. And John was smitten with this girl."

"So much so that he gave her . . ."

"He says it was a loan."

"A loan?"

"According to him, he made that quite clear to her. She'd been cast in an off-Broadway show, a revival of *The Play's the Thing*, and the necklace they'd given her to wear was what you'd expect, something from the dime store. She thought it looked garish and tacky, and not at all what the role called for. She was an African-American actress playing a traditionally white role, and the last thing she wanted was to wear something tawdry. And John, in the grip of early passion, told her he had just the thing."

"A ruby necklace."

"With earrings to match," he said. "His instincts were good, at least for the short term. Because she absolutely loved the necklace. And why not? Burmese rubies set in twenty-two-karat gold are not that difficult to like. She thought it was the perfect thing for her character to wear, and she was as fond of it offstage as on. During the run of the play, she wore it onstage all by itself. Afterward, when she met him for a drink, she'd add the earrings."

"And he'd told her it was just a loan."

"So he says. Her recollection is somewhat different."

"The play's not still running, is it?"

"Its run ended some months ago."

"But I don't suppose she returned the jewels."

"No, and John was reluctant to press her. Why introduce a note of discord just when things were going so well between them?"

"If things were going that well," I said, "he could have let her keep them. Unless they were very valuable."

"The set of three pieces—necklace and earrings—was listed on John's insurance policy at sixty-five thousand dollars. That's what he'd paid for it, that's what he insured it for, and that's what they paid him."

"No wonder he wanted it back."

"Exactly."

"But he didn't press the point."

"No, he didn't. And then Cynthia began talking about the jewels."

"All the ones she'd lost? Or these pieces specifically?"

"The ruby necklace and earrings. She'd bought other jewelry, but she hadn't literally replaced what she'd lost. The rubies were her favorites. John had bought them for her on the occasion of a great financial triumph, so there was some sentimental value as well, for both of them. Now he began to regret ever having separated them from her, but he couldn't just find them, could he? So he invented a private detective."

" 'Invented?' Don't you mean . . ."

"Made him up," he said, "out of the whole cloth. 'I've consulted a chap,' he told her. 'A shady fellow, no better than he should be, but he's got contacts throughout the criminal world.' It would be this detective's task to buy back the necklace and earrings."

"I bet Mrs. Considine was impressed."

"Overwhelmed, according to John, and her reaction made him realize how important she was to him, and what a rotter he'd been, and shortsighted in the bargain. 'Actresses come and go,' he said, 'but a wife is forever.' He went to the Paddington and asked for the jewels back."

"And didn't get them."

" 'They're mine,' Isis said. 'You gave them to me.' It was a time for diplomacy, not strong emotion, but the latter gets in the way of the former. John said something regrettable about her acting ability, and she responded with some equally unfortunate remarks about his prowess as a lover. By the time the dust had settled, their affair was over. And she still had the necklace and earrings." He sighed. "It was then that he called me. I met him here and gave him lunch upstairs, and he told me everything I've just told you."

"He was recruiting you," I guessed, "to be the private detective."

"Do you think I'm the type, Bernie? A shady character? You're my sole contact in the criminal demimonde, and John doesn't even know about you. No, he just wanted a confidant, someone who knew the participants. Edna and I are friendly with him and Cynthia, you see, and at the same time I'd seen Isis onstage. I must say John's heat-of-the-moment comment was unwarranted. She's a perfectly adequate actress, and she lights up the theater."

"When was your lunch with John?"

"Friday."

"And his blowup with Isis was—"

"A few days before. I told John I'd see what I could do. He couldn't talk to her, they'd parted on bad terms, but perhaps a third party could get somewhere on his behalf. He thought I might offer her a decent sum for the rubies. He suggested five thousand dollars, which would be less than a tenth of their value, but a not insignificant sum. Coming from him, such an offer would be an unpardonable insult, essentially setting a price on her favors after the fact. Coming from a dispassionate friend, however, it might be another matter."

"So you came to the hotel, and—"

He shook his head. "I called her on Monday," he said, "and made a date for lunch on Wednesday. I met her at Le Chien Bizarre on East Thirty-ninth. You met her, so you must have noticed those blue eyes."

"They'd have been hard to miss."

"If she were a blonde from Sweden," he said, "I don't suppose those eyes of hers would be anything special. Context is everything, isn't it?" He pursed his lips, whistled soundlessly. "We had salads and omelets and shared a very decent bottle of wine."

"And went back to the Paddington."

"We were coming in," he said, "even as you were going out."

"I guess she'd agreed to return the jewels."

"Not exactly. We were going to continue our discussion."

"In her room," I said. "How long were you there?"

"A couple of hours."

"Discussing the situation."

"Quite," Marty said, looking like the cat who has done something naughty to the canary.

"I guess there was a lot to discuss."

"More than you might think. I had to take her side against John, and she was positively furious with him."

"Because he'd insulted her?"

"He'd done more than that. He'd taken the rubies."

"It's good we didn't have that third round of drinks," I said, "because I think the last round hit me harder than I realized. If John already had the rubies, why did he send you after them?"

"He didn't have them. But neither did she. She'd planned on wearing them to lunch, and when she looked for them they were gone."

I lifted an eyebrow.

"You don't believe her?"

Not for a minute. If her jewels were gone when Marty saw her at lunchtime, how did they magically reappear in her undies drawer that evening? But all I said was it seemed remarkably convenient.

"I had much the same thought," he allowed. "Yet her words had the ring of truth."

The necklace of falsehood and the ring of truth. "You said she was a good actress."

"I had that thought as well. All in all, I was inclined to give her the benefit of the doubt." He looked off into the middle distance. "She's attractive and personable. We enjoyed our lunch, we enjoyed a good bottle of Pommard, and we enjoyed each other's company. Did it occur to me that she might be lying about the disappearance of the jewels? Of course it did. Maybe they were in a dresser drawer, or tucked in one of the boots her teddy bear was wearing. I couldn't be certain, and at the moment I didn't care overly much."

"And why should you? They weren't your rubies."

"But John's my friend, and he'd entrusted me with a mission. Going to bed with his girlfriend didn't lessen my obligation to him. So I took care to let Isis know that, should the gems reappear as magically as they'd vanished, I could see that she wound up ten thousand dollars to the good."

"Didn't you say five thousand?"

"That was John's original idea, but he'd agreed I could go as high as ten if I had to. I barely mentioned the lower number, and then went right to the top. Why bargain with a woman you've just been to bed with, especially when it's somebody else's money?" He sighed. "The sum didn't bowl her over. I sensed she'd had the pieces appraised, or at least had some notion of their value. Her position never changed—she couldn't take the money because she didn't have the rubies. They'd been stolen, and she hadn't reported the theft because she'd taken it for granted it was John's doing."

"And she didn't have title, so what good would it do her to report the loss?"

"Exactly," he said. "When I saw you, Bernie, I didn't think about you in connection with John and Isis and the rubies, because I didn't as yet know they'd been stolen. Then afterward I remembered passing you in the lobby."

"But they were gone when she was dressing for lunch, and you'd already had lunch when you ran into me."

"Who's to say when you arrived, or how many visits you might have paid to the hotel? But it might not have been you. It could have been anyone John commissioned to go after the necklace and earrings. So I called him, and he was astonished at her effrontery. He flatly denied having anything to do with the jewelry's disappearance, and took it for granted she was lying, and was amazed she'd turned out to be such a devious bitch. The intensity of his reaction was convincing, and helped dispel any guilt I might have had about sharing a tender moment with the girl. I hadn't been poaching on my friend's preserve, because their relationship had clearly run its course."

"So you believed them both. Somebody took the rubies, but it wasn't him."

"That's correct. And then I thought of you once more, and I was going to call you today. But something made me call Isis last night, and she told me about the excitement at the Paddington. How she'd confronted a suspicious character in the hallway, and how he turned out to be a burglar and a murderer."

"A burglar perhaps, but—"

"You don't have to tell me, Bernie. I know the woman's death wasn't your doing."

"Everybody seems to know I'm not capable of murder," I said, "and all the same I keep getting arrested for it. You did me a big favor, bailing me out."

"I'm only sorry you had to spend the night in a cell. But, if you're inclined to return the favor . . ."

"How?"

"The rubies."

"Ah, the rubies," I said. "Who'll you give them to, have you decided? Your old buddy or your new girlfriend?"

"That's a question," he acknowledged. "And merely one of many. What sent you after the rubies? Was it sheer coincidence? Or did John know a shady private detective after all?"

"I don't know any private detectives," I said, "shady or otherwise. And I'd never heard of John Considine, and I guess I missed that Molnár revival, because I'd never heard of Isis Gauthier, either. I didn't go to the Paddington for the rubies. I went for Gulliver Fairborn's letters."

"And the woman who was murdered—"

"Was his agent, and she had the letters, and yes, I went looking for them. Somebody else found them first, and killed her, and the next thing I knew I was wearing handcuffs and hearing all about my constitutional rights."

"You didn't know about the rubies."

"No."

He looked at me, looked away, looked down at his hands. "I'm going to have another drink," he said, and raised a hand for the waiter. "Perrier for you this time?"

"No, rye's fine."

"I thought you wanted to keep a clear head."

"It's too late for that, and I'm beginning to think clear heads are overrated. I had a clear head last night, and what did it get me?"

The drinks came and we went to work on them. Then he said, "This is difficult, but there's no getting around it. You've just said you knew nothing about the rubies, and the last thing I want to do is call you a liar, and yet . . ."

"And yet you think I'm lying."

"Bernie, how on earth did you know the jewels were rubies?"

"You said they were."

"No."

"Of course you did, Marty. Burmese rubies set in twenty-two-karat gold. Remember?"

He shook his head. "First I mentioned the necklace she'd worn in the play, and I said John offered her a replacement. 'A ruby necklace,' you said, and only then did I describe the necklace and earrings. But how did you know they were rubies?"

"I could say something about the whole world of psychic phenomena, of which we understand so little."

"I suppose you could."

"But I won't," I said, and drank some more of my rye, hoping it would do more than Milt or malt to make me feel blameless. "I was lying, but at the same time I was telling the truth."

"Oh?"

"I never heard of Considine, or Isis, or the rubies. I went looking for some letters and found a dead body. All I wanted to do was get out of there."

"And?"

"And on my way out I took a shortcut through another room, and guess what I found in the underwear drawer?"

"You didn't."

"I did. I wasn't looking for rubies, not specifically. I'd have preferred cash, to tell you the truth, but what I found was rubies, and to my not entirely untrained eye they looked pretty good. So I took them."

"Because, after all, that's what you do."

"It seems to be. But she looked for the rubies that morning and couldn't find them, isn't that what she told you?"

"Yes."

"I hadn't even been to the hotel at that point. I didn't check in until a few minutes before I saw you. Anyway, she must have been telling you a story, don't you think? Unless she looked in the wrong drawer and honestly thought they'd been stolen."

He thought that one over. "I don't know," he said. "That sounds a little far-fetched, doesn't it? Wouldn't she go through all the drawers and make sure?"

"Probably, but—"

"She could have been lying," he said, "though it's hard to know why. Still, the possibility had occurred to me."

"You mentioned as much. You said maybe the rubies were stuffed in Paddington's boots."

"Paddington's—oh, the bear. Yes, I did say that, didn't I?"

"I didn't even notice a bear in her room. It certainly wasn't on top of the dresser."

"She kept it on the bed. It, uh, got moved to the little chair."

"I must have looked at the bed," I said, "but if there was a bear on it I never noticed. I don't remember a bear on the little chair, either." I frowned. "Come to think of it, I don't remember a little chair. Just a big Morris-type armchair."

"Well, *I* don't recall an armchair, but I can't say I was paying much attention to the furnishings. I remember the little side chair because she moved the bear to it, but I should be hard put to describe it to you. The only decorative note that sticks in my mind is that godawful painting."

"What painting was that?"

"Elvis on black velvet. I guess my horror showed. 'It's a black thing,' she told me. 'You wouldn't understand.' I'm sure she was being ironic, but—"

"Elvis on black velvet."

"You've seen them, haven't you? In the same sort of shops that sell pictures of dogs playing poker. I always wondered who would buy something like that, and now I know."

"I don't know how I missed it. I was in a hurry to get out of there, but it's not like me to be that oblivious to my surroundings. And it's a dangerous trait in a burglar. But I'd just seen a corpse and escaped from a murder scene while the cops were knocking on the door, and maybe that threw me off. I was too grateful to be off the fire escape to pay attention to where I was."

"But not too grateful to keep you from picking up some jewelry."

"Never mind that," I said. "I just realized something. I ran into Isis in the hallway outside Anthea Landau's room."

"So?"

"So what the hell was she doing there?"

"Didn't you say she was waiting for the elevator?"

"So she said, and eventually it came and she got on it, though not a moment too soon. But forget the elevator. What was she doing on the sixth floor?"

"What do you mean?"

"I may not remember Elvis on black velvet," I said, "but I remember that fire escape. I went out Landau's bedroom window and climbed down three flights of rickety iron steps until I found a room with nobody home. That was on the third floor, and that's where Isis lived, and—"

"No."

"No?"

"I distinctly remember," he said, "that her room was on the sixth floor. So she had every right to be waiting for an elevator in the sixth-floor hallway. But if her room was on Six, and if the room you broke into was three floors below . . ."

We looked at each other.

TWELVE

The cat uses the toilet," Henry Walden said. "But of course you would know that. You're probably the one who taught him."

"The only thing I ever taught him is to play shortstop," I said, and crumpled a sheet of paper into a ball, flinging it to Raffles's left. If he was at shortstop, then the ball was headed straight for second base. He pounced on it, robbing me of a base hit.

"Like that," I said, "but I don't know how much teaching was involved. He's responded like that from the very beginning. And I've gotten nowhere at teaching him to throw to first, and let's not even talk about turning the double play."

"He went right over to the bathroom door," Walden said, "which I'd closed, not realizing that you left it open for him. He scratched at the door, and I got the idea and opened it, and he went right in and hopped up onto the seat, and used it just as if it were a litter box."

"Did he flush?"

"Why, no."

"He never does," I said. "I'd have to say there's a limit to what you can teach him. He won't throw to first base and he won't flush the toilet after himself. Other than that—" I crumpled paper, hurled it "—he's not so bad."

I went on throwing balls of paper to catdom's Derek Jeter. I'd initiated the routine to hone Raffles's mousing skills, but as it turned out his mere presence was enough to keep my shop a rodent-free environment. He didn't actually have to do anything. Still, it wouldn't do to let him lose his edge, and for my own part I was pleased to discover that throwing balls of paper for him to chase was something I could still do after three stout glasses of Kessler's Maryland Rye.

There'd been some traffic in the shop, Henry told me, and he'd sold some books, collecting the marked price for each and remembering to charge the sales tax. He'd made out a slip for each sale, something I don't always remember to do, and had the carbon copies clipped together and tucked away in a corner of the cash register.

A woman had come in with a shopping bag full of books, hoping to sell them, and Henry had persuaded her to leave the books so that I could appraise them at leisure. I took a quick gander at them and saw Mark Schorer's biography of Sinclair Lewis, a first of James T. Farrell's *Gas-House McGinty*, and a batch of boxed Heritage Press editions, never hard to find but always easy to sell.

"Yes, I can use these," I told him. "I think the Farrell's genuinely rare. I know I've never seen a copy. The only thing harder to find is someone who collects the man, but if I get stuck with it I can always read it."

"They looked like good books," he said. "I didn't have the authority to make her an offer, but I didn't want her to sell them to somebody else, either."

I told him he'd done perfectly, and you'd have thought I scratched him behind the ear. He had a short list of phone messages, too, and I went over them. Carolyn had called to cancel our standing date for drinks. Something had come up. A man named Harkness, from Sotheby's, had called and left a number. And a woman had called several times and had declined to give her name, or leave any message at all.

I said, "The same woman each time? And she didn't say her name was Alice?"

"She never gave a name."

"Hmmm. Did she sound as though her name *might* have been Alice?"

That confused him, and I could understand why. I had the feeling I wouldn't have asked the question if I hadn't had that third drink at The Pretenders. Three stiff drinks on an empty stomach—empty unless you count the pastrami sandwiches, and I figured they'd used up all their absorbency neutralizing the cream soda.

It was past closing time. Henry gave me a hand with the table, and I closed the window gates and changed Raffles's water and did my other evening chores. Raffles had seen it before, but Henry stood around and watched, utterly absorbed, as if I was passing on the tricks of the bookselling trade with my every move.

I wanted to give him a few dollars, but he flat out refused to take money from me. It was a pleasant way to pass a couple of hours, he said, and who knew but that it might be good experience? He had to spend the rest of his life somewhere, and he could do worse than spend it in a bookshop.

"The best way to learn a business," he said, "is to work for somebody who's already in it. That's how you learned, isn't it? By helping out in somebody else's store?"

"No, I just plunged in," I said. I started walking, and he fell into step beside me. "I used to buy books from Mr. Litzauer, and he was talking about how he'd move to Florida in a heartbeat if he could just get a halfway decent price for his store, and I asked him what a halfway decent price amounted to in dollars and cents. He fumfered around a little, but then he came up with a figure and I said I'd buy the place."

"Just like that?"

"I'd come into a few dollars, and I figured why not? Otherwise I'd only piss it away on food and shelter. So I just jumped in with both feet. I didn't know zip about the business, and if I had I might have had the sense to stay out of it."

"But you love it," he said.

"Do I? I guess I do." And we walked along, talking books and bookselling, and before I knew it my feet showed they had a mind of their own, and a lousy one at that. They took me right to the Bum Rap.

I figured the least I could do was buy the guy a drink. We went in, and I sat where I usually sit, and he sat in Carolyn's chair, and when Maxine came over I asked Henry what he'd have. He asked me what I was having. I said I'd been drinking rye lately and figured I ought to stick with it, and he said that sounded good.

I didn't need that drink, but if I'd had it and left I'd have been all right. But then, wouldn't you know, Henry insisted on buying a round, and how was I supposed to refuse without offending him? There's no logical justification for the third round, I'll admit, but after the second round logic went out the window, if it had even strolled through the door in the first place.

It might have helped if I'd eaten something, but eating at the Bum Rap has never helped anybody but the makers of Alka-Seltzer. At one point Henry wanted to order a burrito, but I talked him out of it, and the next thing I remember was playing the jukebox. It's always a bad sign when I decide to play the jukebox. I always pick the same records—Bunny Berigan's "I Can't Get Started" and Patsy Cline's "Faded Love," and there's nothing wrong with either of those two, but it's still a bad sign when I play them, because it means I'm drunk.

Some places get all huffy when their customers get drunk, as if they'd sold you the booze never for a moment suspecting you intended to drink it. But no, you actually went and swallowed the terrible stuff, and then you had the poor taste to let it affect you. Well, shame on you, buster, and kindly take your business somewhere else.

But they're not like that at the Bum Rap. It's acceptable to be drunk there, as long as you don't disturb the other drunks. And I didn't disturb them. There was a point when I led them in song, and that might have disturbed someone with a fine ear for music, but all of us Bum Rappers seemed to be having a good enough time.

I don't have any clear memory of getting out of there, but all at once we were on the street, me and my new best friend. I rushed to the curb and hailed everything that came along—trucks, vans, off-duty cabs, and a bus. None of them stopped, curiously enough, but a cab did, finally, and I made Henry take it.

"I'll get the next one," I said. "Nothing to it." And off he went, and I caught myself just as I was about to hail a blue-and-white police cruiser.

I kept my arm down, but even so it seemed to me that the two cops were looking at me as they sailed on by. "Bernie," I said to myself, talking out loud and trying not to slur my words, "Bernie, old boy, you're drunk as a lord, tight as a tick, high as a kite. You've got to get home before you get in trouble. Wait for a yellow car with a light on top. That's the kind to wave at. It's the only kind to wave at."

I may have erred on the side of caution, because a cab or two got by me before I could get my hand up. But eventually I must have snagged one, because the next thing I knew I was riding in it. And I was tired, too, so much so that I could barely keep my eyes open.

I must have closed them. They were closed when I became aware of the cabdriver, to whom I had evidently bonded. "My frien', my frien'," he was saying, with a certain degree of urgency, and one of those accents that can cope with no more than one consonant at the end of a word. "My frien', we are here. You wan' to sleep, you mus' go to your room."

I didn't see why he couldn't leave me alone. But I sighed and opened my eyes. I leaned forward and squinted at the meter. It was hard to make out and I decided I was reading it wrong, because what I thought I saw was $3.60, and it generally costs me ten bucks plus a tip to get home, which is one reason the subway generally gets my business.

But this would have been a bad night for the subway.

I got out, leaned against the cab, got out my wallet, and found a ten and two singles. "Your meter's wrong," I said. "You ought to see about getting it fixed."

He took the money, looked at the bills, then looked at me. I asked him if something was wrong. Wasn't that enough money? Did he want more?

"Is plenny money," he said. "You go in your house, okay?"

"Okay," I said, and looked around. "Where is it? Where are we?"

"Where you say."

"Where I say?"

"Where you say to take you. We here, my frien'. You go to your bed, okay?"

"Okay," I said, and let go of the cab for a moment, and when I reached for it again it was gone. I got my balance, no easy task, and I turned around for a good look at my house, which I have to say didn't look like my house at all.

Well, that might explain the low fare. The cabby, upset at having a fare sleeping in his cab, had just dropped me any old place—and I, willing to believe we'd gone all the way to the Upper West Side, had insisted on paying him accordingly.

But where the hell were we?

I straightened up and focused on the building in front of me, and either it was swaying or I was, and logic suggested the instability was mine. There was something written on the canopy, but how was I going to read it?

Definitely not my building, no matter what the driver said. And yet it did look familiar.

Was I intent on visiting a friend? This certainly wasn't Carolyn's place on Arbor Court, although the meter would have been about right. Some other girlfriend? I didn't know where Alice Cottrell lived, we'd only been to my place, but maybe I'd given the driver some ex-girlfriend's address, out of force of habit. Well, force of nonhabit, since I didn't have any old girlfriends I was in the habit of dropping in on. Force of rye whiskey, call it.

I walked up to the entrance, and it still looked familiar. I opened the door and went in, and the entranceway looked familiar, too. I looked past some chairs and couches to a fireplace, and I looked up over the fireplace, and I saw a little furry chap in a royal blue hat and a bright red jacket and boots the very color of the cab that had brought me here.

Oh.

I straightened up, and I walked a perfectly straight line over to the desk, where a round-shouldered man with the air of a defrocked accountant was reading one of Patrick O'Brian's sea stories of the Napoleonic Wars.

"Jeffrey Peters," I said. "Room 415. I'd like my key, please."

THIRTEEN

I woke up eight hours later, well rested, glad to be alive, with a clear head and a feeling that all was right with the world, and if you believe that I know a bunch of really nice guys who'd love to play poker with you.

Because that's not how it happened at all. A pair of sensations woke me, one centered an inch or so behind my forehead, the other in the pit of my stomach. My head, throbbing, alerted me that to move was to risk death, while my stomach advised me that it was about to reject what I'd been unwise enough to put into it.

I stayed right where I was, eyes clenched shut, trying to will the day away. I wasn't sure where I was, but it didn't feel like my own bed. And I couldn't dismiss the awful sensation that I wasn't alone in it.

I forced my eyes open, and another pair of eyes looked back at me from only inches away. Little shoe-button eyes, and of course it was Paddington, and that brought it all back, or at least as much as I was destined to remember, the last moment of which I've already told you about—marching carefully across the lobby and demanding my room key. I couldn't recall what had happened after that, but it wasn't hard to recon-struct, for here I was in my room.

I got up and showered and shaved. My head didn't literally split in two, nor did I get sick to my stomach. The little kit with my shaving gear, which I'd tucked into my suitcase, held as-pirin as well, and a good thing. I put on clean socks and un-derwear—in case of a traffic accident, or a police frisk—and the shirt and slacks and jacket I'd been wearing the day before.

The shirt and pants were on hangers, I was pleased to note, and the jacket was hung over the back of the chair. That, it seemed to me, was a Very Good Sign. If I'd had it together suf-ficiently to hang up my clothes, then I couldn't have been too bad, could I?

Ah, the little lies we try to tell ourselves. Memory, the thief of self-esteem, assured me I'd been in a bad way indeed. Just because I was neat didn't mean I'd been sober.

Just for openers, telling the cabby to take me to the Paddington had not been the act of a sober man, or even a halfway sane drunk. I had to get back to the hotel, had to fig-ure out a way to reclaim my tools and gloves before they turned up in an evidence locker, had to get my hands on Cyn-thia Considine's rubies before somebody else did.

But how? The last I'd seen of the Hotel Paddington, and it of me, I'd been wearing handcuffs and a hangdog expression. If I had to return to the scene of the crime, a bit of indirection seemed called for. Illicit entry via the basement, say. A little ca-pering across the rooftops. I couldn't just walk right in as if I owned the place.

But wasn't that essentially what I had done? I'd walked in, if not like the owner, at least like a tenant in good standing. And why not? I'd paid my rent in advance, and no one had checked me out or given me my money back. If it had been Carl Pillsbury behind the desk, or if the redoubtable Isis Gau-thier had been curled up on a sofa in the lobby, I wouldn't have had such an easy time of it. But what did the nearsighted night clerk know of Peter Jeffries, or Jeffrey Peters, or whoever I'd claimed to be? Easygoing lad that he was, he'd just slapped my key on the counter without even checking the register.

Maybe my mind, freed by rye whiskey from the rigid parameters of conventional thinking, had worked all of that out for me, all in the few seconds it took me to provide the cabdriver with an address. I considered the possibility, and then reluctantly shook my head. (A bad idea, aspirin or no aspirin. The last thing my head needed was a good shaking.)

No, I hadn't thought my way into the Paddington. I'd blundered, and come up lucky.

I picked up Paddington, and he looked none the worse for wear. Either the cops had returned him after his x-ray ordeal, which seemed unlikely, or the hotel had replaced him, which also struck me as odd. Never mind. He was here and so was I, and he could stay here but I had work to do.

I picked up my watch, and when I saw what time it was I held the thing to my ear to see if it was still ticking. It wasn't, of course; it was digital, and had never ticked in its life. But the little seconds were passing visibly, so it was still working, and what it told me was that it was 3:37 in the morning.

I'd somehow assumed it was later than that. I'd taken it for granted that, having found a quiet place to pass out, I'd have had the good sense to remain unconscious until a civil hour. Now, knowing it was still the middle of the night, I immediately felt exhausted.

The bed beckoned. I glared at it and stalked out the door.

The sign on the stairway entrance reminded me I couldn't get back in. The warning was meant for lesser mortals, but suppose my tools were not where I'd left them? Oh, I could walk down to the lobby, but I remembered how much fun that had been the last time I did it. I patted my pockets and found a wooden toothpick, then pushed the snaplock back with my thumb and jammed the toothpick in next to it, wedging it in place. Now the door would close without locking, and anyone entering from the fourth-floor hall would notice nothing out of the ordinary.

The stairwell still smelled of smoke. That was fine, just so long as no one had started a fire.

And nobody had, as far as I could tell, at least not a serious fire, because the firehose mounted on the stairwell wall at the fifth-floor landing looked undisturbed. I unscrewed the heavy brass nozzle—what a fine blunt instrument it would make— and shook out my handy-dandy ring of picks and probes and my little flashlight, the whole array double-wrapped in a pair of plastic-film gloves. Then, from the canvas hose itself, I drew out the little jewelry case that still contained a ruby necklace and earrings. I slipped various articles into various pockets and finally screwed the nozzle back on the hose.

I walked back down to Four, and I had the door open and was retrieving my toothpick when I changed my mind and let the door swing shut. If knowledge was power, I realized, I was a ninety-seven-pound weakling, and I didn't even have to send in the coupon to Charles Atlas and get the secrets of Dynamic Tension going for me.

I sat down on the top step and started ticking off the things I didn't know. I didn't write out a list, but if I had it might have looked something like this:

THINGS I NEED TO KNOW AND DON'T

1. Who killed Anthea Landau?
2. Where did the knife come from, and what happened to it?
3. Why hadn't I heard from Alice Cottrell?
4. Speaking of Alice, why couldn't I reach her?
5. How did the jewels get into that room on the third floor?
6. Where were the Gulliver Fairborn letters?
7. How was Isis Gauthier connected to Anthea Landau?
8. How was I going to get out of this mess?

I walked down one more flight of stairs, and it's an indication of the efficiency of my mind that I searched my pockets for another toothpick to jam the lock, so I'd be able to return to the stairwell. Light dawned when I reached for the knob and there wasn't one. I got out my tools and opened the door.

When I emerged from that third-floor room, the proud possessor if not the lawful owner of a ruby necklace and earrings, I of course hadn't bothered to note the room number. Why bother? I had other things on my mind, and it didn't seem like something I would ever need to know. The room was just something I'd passed through, and I wouldn't need to pass through it again. I'd already taken what was worth taking. Why go back?

Still, it wasn't terribly difficult to narrow it down. I'd been in Anthea Landau's bedroom when I ducked out onto the fire escape. The room I'd wound up in was three floors below, and if it wasn't directly beneath Landau's it wasn't that far from it. Landau's room number was 602, so the place to start was 302, and if that didn't pan out I could try the rooms on either side of it.

I got my bearings and found Room 302, conveniently if unimaginatively tucked between Rooms 301 and 303. No light showed beneath any of their doors, but it was getting on for four in the morning, so the same could be said for most of the doors in the hotel, and indeed most of the bedroom doors in the whole city. New York may be the city that never sleeps, but at that hour a good number of its citizens tend to close their eyes.

I'd have liked to join them. My headache was back, and I felt a great weariness. I couldn't quite catch my breath, and wasn't even sure it was worth catching. Once I caught it, what would I do with it?

I stared at all three doors and felt like one of the dimmer contestants on *Let's Make a Deal.* I had to pick one of those doors, and what was I going to trade for whatever was behind it? My freedom? My future?

I stepped up to 302, put my ear to it to no particular purpose, then took out my tools and picked the lock. It yielded without a fuss, and I slipped inside and drew the door shut.

I stood absolutely still, letting my eyes accustom themselves to the darkness. The curtains were drawn, but they were a less efficient lot than Anthea Landau's, and once my pupils had had time to dilate I could see just about enough to keep from bumping into the furniture.

But I could hear enough to keep me from moving.

What I heard was breathing, the deep slow breathing of a sleeper. It was curiously reassuring, signifying as it did that the room's occupant was alive. If I had to walk in on somebody, I'd just as soon the person was still oxygen-dependent.

Get out, I told myself. *Somebody's home, and they don't know you're here, and if you leave quickly and quietly they may never find out. So what are you waiting for?*

But if I left, I still wouldn't know if this was the right room. I'd just know somebody was in it, and what good did that do me?

I got out my pocket flash and positioned my thumb over the little button. I wouldn't need very much light, and I wouldn't need it for very long. As soon as I saw Elvis on black velvet, I'd know I was in the right place. As soon as I'd assured myself he wasn't there to be seen, I'd know I wasn't.

I aimed the flashlight at the wall, tapped the button, let go of it almost immediately, and repeated the procedure at intervals of a few feet, working my way around the room. There was, I managed to establish, no painting on black velvet on any of the room's four walls, not of Elvis, not of a big-eyed waif, not of a sad-faced clown.

Wrong room.

I reached for the doorknob, turned it ever so gently, opened it a crack and paused to listen for signs of life in the hallway, then got out of there and closed the door. I played a little mental game of eeny meeny miney mo, trying to guess which of the remaining doors concealed Elvis on black velvet. I wondered, too, what version of Elvis the painting showed—Elvis Young or Elvis Old? Elvis lean and hungry or Elvis puffed up with too many peanut butter and banana sandwiches? Elvis bright-eyed and bushy-tailed or Elvis with a pharmaceutical glaze? I hadn't seen the painting myself, and—

Of course I hadn't. I'd heard it described by Marty Gilmartin, and *he'd* seen it in Isis Gauthier's room up on Six. So why was I looking for it down here on Three?

I'll tell you, a mind is a terrible thing to have, especially when it doesn't work any better than mine did. I had a killer hangover, and that explained a lot, but I wondered if there might not be a little more to it than that. Could I still be drunk? Was that possible?

It didn't seem the least bit fair. One or the other, okay, fair enough, I'd earned it. But both at once? Wasn't it like lightning and thunder? They were both the result of the same phenomenon—in this case, strong drink and plenty of it—but the lightning got there first, and had disappeared by the time the thunder came rolling in.

It occurred to me that I ought to go back to bed and sleep this off, whatever it was. But opportunity had knocked, hadn't it? And wasn't it my job to open the door?

In this case, the door to 302. I'd already opened it, and now I opened it again. This time I didn't actually enter the room. I stood at the door, using my pocket flash to supplement the light that slanted through the opening I'd created, and looked around for something familiar.

I saw something unfamiliar, and that was just as good. When I'd come in from the fire escape, heading for the door to the hallway, the dresser had been on my right, the bed on my left. And the layout in this room was the mirror opposite. I went over it in my mind, like the guy in the tower of the Old

North Church—*Let's see now, did Mr. Revere say one if by land and two if by sea, or was it the other way around?*—and decided I had it right. This wasn't the room where I'd found the rubies.

I closed the door a second time. I thought of doing what Sleeping Beauty had neglected to do—i.e., fasten the chain lock to keep out people like me. That's not hard if you have the tools for it, and I did, but it's not the sort of task to undertake unnecessarily when you're either drunk or hungover, or possibly both.

Next I cracked 301, and the door moved only a couple of inches before the chain lock stopped it. I could have unlocked it—it's slightly easier on balance than relocking the thing, and there's more point to it—but I knew the room was occupied, so why barge in if I didn't have to?

I saw what I could through the narrow opening. The layout was as I remembered it, but this room had twin beds, and I realized now that the room I'd entered from the fire escape had a double. So this wasn't it.

That left Room 303, and it was the one lock that gave me a hard time. Don't ask me why. It was the same basic mechanism as all the others, and it should have been every bit as easy to pick. But it wasn't, lending further credence to my drunk-and-hungover-both-at-once hypothesis.

I'd have been embarrassed if anyone had seen me fumbling with the damned lock, and the chances of being embarrassed in just that fashion increased with every minute I spent standing there in the hallway. There'd been no one coming or going—it was, after all, the middle of the goddam night—but it seemed to me I was pushing my luck.

The lock was old, and some of its pins and tumblers were worn, and sometimes the result is a lock that just about falls open if you give it a hard look. In this case, though, my picks kept slipping around inside, and at one point I gave up and tried my room key. There was a chance it would work, albeit a slim one, but long shots do come in every once in a while, and wouldn't it be nice if this was one of those times?

Dream on. . . .

I put the key back in my pocket, got back to business, and had better luck this time around. I cracked the door and let my flashlight do the walking, and there was a double bed right where it was supposed to be, and no one was in it. I slipped in, drew the door shut, and collapsed into a chair.

I used my flash again, less hurriedly this time, and was able to say with certainty that this was the room I'd been in the other night. I hadn't been paying attention, and thus couldn't consciously remember the room and its furnishings, but it turned out I was able to recognize them when I saw them. The litter on top of the highboy dresser was familiar, too. I opened a couple of drawers, and I was in the right place. The second drawer held feminine undergarments, but this time there was no jewelry stashed there.

I could put the rubies back where I'd found them. If the room's occupant hadn't yet noticed their absence, I'd have concealed my actions entirely. If she'd realized they were gone, she'd find them and wonder if she was losing her mind.

But was I losing mine? Why on earth would I want to put the jewels back? I wasn't sure who the rightful owner was, or if the rubies had one. Cynthia Considine? Her husband, John? Isis Gauthier? I didn't see that any of the three had anything approaching a moral equivalent of clear title. Ms. 303 had as good a claim as they did, and wasn't my own claim every bit as good as hers?

I decided it was, and the jewelry case stayed in my pocket.

But another question arose. What exactly was I doing here?

I had to sit down to think about that one. I'd never stopped to question the impulse to come to this room, and then I'd been so caught up in the process of finding the right room and picking my way past its lock that I hadn't had time to wonder what I'd do once I was inside.

And it was a logical place to be, wasn't it? Now that I'd located the room, now that I was in it, I could look around until I learned whose room it was. And then I'd very likely know who had taken Isis Gauthier's rubies, and then I'd know—

What?

I'd probably know the name of some morally bankrupt friend of Isis's who'd cast a greedy eye on the rubies and seized an opportunity for theft when it presented itself. There wasn't much I could do with that information, unless I wanted to convey it to Isis, in the hopes of getting back on a first-name basis with her.

Would it bring me any closer to Gulliver Fairborn's letters? Would it help me learn who killed Anthea Landau? I'd had eight questions on the little list I hadn't written down, and the only one it might answer was *How did the jewels get into that room on the third floor?*

Still, I couldn't get away from the idea that everything was tied together. Otherwise coincidence played too large a role. And, if everything was indeed intertwined, then any bit of data I picked up might lead to something else.

I put on my gloves—I'd already left no end of prints in this room, but that didn't give me a reason to leave still more—and I got busy. There was a lamp on the little desk—brass, with a green glass shade, and now that I saw it I remembered it from my first visit. I switched it on and went around the room, looking at things, trying to find something that would identify the occupant.

It would have been easier if I'd happened to be a cop. I'm sure some of the clothing had labels or laundry marks that could have been traced back to the purchaser. For that matter, all a cop would have had to do was flash his badge at the desk clerk and demand the name of the person registered in Room 303. That wasn't foolproof, it might lead only to an alias in the Peter Jeffries mode, but it was yet another option that cops have and burglars don't. (When you look at all their advantages, it's amazing we ever get away with anything.)

I was in the closet, examining the clothes as if in the hope that her mother might have sewn in name tapes before sending her to camp, and pondering laundry marks and labels as if they were going to tell me something. I popped the catches on a small suitcase, the kind with wheels and a pull-up handle. A few years ago nobody but stewardesses had them, and now it's the only kind you see. This one was empty, and I closed it up and turned off the closet light, and I was on my way out of there when something flickered in my memory. I'd just seen something. Now what the hell was it?

A luggage tag.

Well, of course. People tie tags on their suitcases, with their names and addresses and phone numbers, so that the airlines, having lost their luggage for them, can, once in a blue moon, find it again. (It's also handy if someone steals your bag. If he likes the general quality of your possessions, he knows right where to come to get more. And, if you tucked a set of keys in your bag, all the better.)

I spun around, leaned over to peer at the luggage tag, and of course the light was too dim to make it out. I straightened up and reached to switch on the closet light, and as soon as it came on I switched it off again.

Because I heard a key in the lock.

Oh, God. Now what?

Stay in the closet? No, I couldn't, the desk lamp was on. I got to it in a hurry and switched it off, while the key went on jiggling in the lock. The worn pins and tumblers evidently presented the same sort of problem even if you had a key, and what had been a nuisance a few minutes ago was a godsend now. Back to the closet? No, the bathroom was closer—and in less time than it took to have the thought I was in it with the door closed.

And just in time, because I could hear the door open, and a moment later I could hear it close. I didn't hear the light switch, but when she switched the light on in the room some of it showed under the bathroom door.

Good I'd stayed out of the closet. I've been in closets a couple of times in the past when householders turned up unexpectedly, and I always managed to escape detection, but I didn't like my chances this time around. It was a cool night, and she'd almost certainly have been wearing a jacket or a coat, and the first thing she'd do was take it off, and thus the first place she'd go was the closet.

And where did I think was the *second* place she would go?

The bathroom, of course, and what was I going to do when she burst in and found me there? I couldn't pretend I was a plumber sent to fix a dripping faucet. I wasn't dressed for it and I hadn't brought the right tools for the job.

Should I lock the door?

Hell, she'd hear it if I did. Unless I covered the sound by coughing or flushing the toilet, and then she'd hear *that*. And even if she didn't, she'd find out that the bathroom door was locked when she tried to open it. And she'd call downstairs, and they'd send somebody up, and the next thing you knew I'd be having my rights read to me. They're important rights, but there's a limit to how often I want to hear about them.

There was a window, the glass frosted so that I couldn't tell if it led to the fire escape. It didn't look as though it had been opened since the last time it had been painted, and there was no guarantee I could open it, and no chance at all I could do so without making a lot of noise. It was a tiny window, too, and no cinch to climb through, and—

The doorknob turned. The door opened.

FOURTEEN

But by then I was standing in the bathtub, cowering behind the shower curtain, feeling every bit as secure about the whole enterprise as Janet Leigh in *Psycho*.

She turned on the light as she entered. This didn't surprise me, but it didn't make me happy, either. The shower curtain was somewhere between opaque and translucent. I could see shapes through it, but only if I worked at it. The more light there was, the more clearly I could see.

If the shower curtain had been designed by the inventor of the one-way mirror, I might have welcomed the extra illumination. But every quid has a pro quo, and the better I could see, the more easily I could be seen in return.

Even with the light on I couldn't tell much about my visitor. Based on the ordinariness of her silhouette, I could estimate that she was not too tall and not too short, and neither a wraith nor a blimp. But I could have guessed as much without having seen her at all, and I'd have been right ninety percent of the time. Anyway, I had more to go on than the blurred shape visible through the plastic curtain. I'd seen the clothes in her closet.

Well, I knew one thing more now. I knew she was proper, even prim. Fastidious, at the very least.

Because the first thing she did after turning on the light was close the door.

I don't know. Maybe everybody does this, or maybe it's a girl thing. But when I'm alone in my apartment, I'll tell you right now that I don't close the bathroom door when I have to take a whiz. I'm sure there are people who do—I was in a room with one of them now—even as I am sure there are people who run water in the sink while they are thus occupied, so that they won't be able to hear what they're doing.

She didn't do that, and I could hear her loud and clear. This might have been provocative, even exciting, if I'd been a little kinkier than God made me, but under the circumstances all it was was disturbing. Not because I was offended, but because I was envious. The gentle tinkling sound made me aware that I, too, had a bladder, and a hitherto unnoticed need to empty it.

I'm not going to dwell on this, but it's something to profit from if you've been contemplating a life of crime. It's not all glamour and big profits. You're going to spend a fair amount of time wishing you had the chance to pee.

My guest had the chance, and she was taking it. Then she stood up and flushed, and then she washed her hands, and who could have expected less of someone who'd bothered closing the door?

Then she opened the door and walked through it, and then my blood froze, because, casually and conversationally, she said, "Your turn."

Not that I wouldn't welcome a turn, as I've already explained. If I hadn't quite reached the shifting-one's-weight-from-one-foot-to-the-other stage, I could already see it looming on the horizon. But when had she spotted me, and how had she masked her discovery so well, only to tip it off so offhandedly? *"Your turn"*—and while I was taking my turn she'd be on the phone, telling the number-cruncher downstairs to call 911.

And she left the door open.

I should point out that all of this happened quickly, and that I didn't have a whole lot of time to think about it. Otherwise I'd have figured it out, as you very likely have, but before my drunk/hungover (choose one) mind could run through its gears, a taller silhouette passed through the door, pausing to draw it shut. Then he strode manfully over to the commode, bent over to raise the seat, straightened up, and went at it.

I'd draw the curtain here, but for the fact that I was behind it. He did what he'd come there to do, flushed, washed his hands, dried them on a towel, and switched off the light on his way out the door. He didn't close the door this time.

So I got to hear them making love.

Some years ago, when I was a teenage kid embarking on a career in burglary, the whole enterprise (I blush to admit) bore a distinct undercurrent of sexual energy. You can blame it on my youth; it seems to me there was a sexual aspect to everything back then.

I suppose a Freudian might have contended that I started breaking into houses in the first place in hopes of sneaking a peek at the primal scene—i.e., my own parents, doing the dirty deed. God knows what lurks in the unconscious, but I have to tell you that was the last thing in the world I wanted to see, and if I'd wanted to spy on my folks I wouldn't have gone looking for them in other people's houses. I'd have stayed home.

But that's not to say I wouldn't have welcomed a glimpse of somebody else doing something I wasn't supposed to see. I didn't go looking for it, and in fact took great pains to make sure other people's houses were empty before I came calling. All the same, I was frequently stirred by what I found. An unmade bed would send my mind reeling, just at the thought of what might have taken place in it mere hours before I arrived on the scene. A bra, a pair of panties—I didn't steal them, I didn't stand around sniffing them and pawing the ground, but I was damn well aware of them.

Once, then, I'd have found it thrilling to be so close to a coupling couple, intensely aware of them even as they were wholly unaware of me. Maybe, if I'd managed to get in touch with my Inner Adolescent, I could have summoned up some excitement even now, but I'm not so sure. I think those days are gone, and good riddance.

Because, as much as I enjoy the sport as a participant, I've long since outgrown any interest in it as a spectator. I've seen a few XXX-rated movies over the years, and I don't think I'm a prude about it, but I'd just as soon get through life without ever seeing another.

So I stood there and listened to their lovemaking, wishing I or they or all of us were elsewhere, engaged in some other pursuit. Watching TV, say, or playing pinochle, or sharing a pizza. I didn't have to close my eyes—they were in the other room, and I was behind a curtain—but I'd have liked to put my fingers in my ears, to shut out sounds I didn't much want to listen to.

And I did that at one point, only to take them out a moment later. Because, see, I needed whatever information my ears might bring me. I didn't know a damn thing about them beyond the fact that one was male and the other female. So far I hadn't heard a word out of him, and the only words she'd said were "Your turn" as she left the bathroom, and that hadn't been enough to let me know if it was a voice I recognized.

Maybe they'd talk. Maybe they'd say something that would serve to tell me who they were, or answer some of the questions on my unwritten list. So I listened, and all they did was make the sounds people make when they're thus engaged. Some grunting, some groaning, some mumbling, some moaning, and the occasional sharp intake of breath and small sigh of appreciation.

And then, at the very end, it got discernibly exciting for her.

It may have been every bit as thrilling for him as well, but he was man enough to keep it to himself. She got verbal, and pretty noisy, and I tried to tune it out, and then a phrase caught my attention and I listened more intently than ever, and yes I thought yes it was yes!

I knew who she was.

I don't know how the dictionary defines "anticlimactic." I suppose I could look it up, but so could you, if you care. I don't, because I know what it is. It's standing in a bathtub, desperate for a pee, after two people in the next room have finished making love.

Now what?

I couldn't hear a thing, and just what did that mean? Probably just that they were lying there in companionable silence, either gathering their strength for another round of the same or drifting off to sleep. Either way, I was stuck.

I stayed where I was, and I found myself thinking about Redmond O'Hanlon and the candiru. Suppose I was swimming in the Amazon, feeling the same urgency I felt now, and knowing that to pee was to send an engraved invitation to every candiru in the neighborhood. How long could I hold out?

Well, you get the idea. I don't know how far I might have gone with that line of thought, or what action it might eventually have prompted, but sounds from the other room intruded. They were moving about, I realized, and having a conversation, though in voices too low-pitched for me to make out.

Footsteps approached, and the bathroom light came on. Oh, Christ, were they going to shower? It wasn't exactly unheard-of after a romp of this sort, but—

It was the woman, and I was pleased to discover that she was less fastidious than I'd thought earlier. She wet a towel in the sink and dabbed herself with it, then blotted herself dry with another. She left, and it was his turn, and wouldn't you know the son of a bitch peed again? And flushed, and washed his hands, and switched off the light and left.

Then there were more sounds of movement, and then the light went out. Not the one in the bathroom, that was already out, but the one in the bedroom. And next I heard an unimaginably sweet sound, that of a door closing and a key turning in a lock.

I waited a moment—to make sure that was really what I'd heard, to give them a chance to come back for whatever they'd forgotten. I'd have waited longer, to give them a chance to walk clear to the elevator and back, but I have to say I'd already waited long enough.

I drew the shower curtain, climbed out of the tub. I didn't have to raise the toilet seat. He'd left it up, loutish inconsiderate male that he was.

Not me. I am, after all, a sensitive New Age guy. When I was done, I put the seat down.

I'll tell you, all I wanted to do was get out of there. But I did remember to check the closet. The suitcase was still in place. I don't even know that either of them ever bothered going into the closet. It seemed to me they were too busy scuttling in and out of the bathroom.

I took a good look at the tag on the suitcase, and the name on it was Karen Kassenmeier, with an address in Henrietta, Oklahoma. I thought about copying it down, but why bother? I recognized the sounds she'd been making toward the end. I'd heard them before, and the woman who'd made them certainly hadn't introduced herself as Karen Kassenmeier.

And who was he, and why did he get to make those particular sounds come out of her mouth? I probably should have nudged the shower curtain aside just long enough to get a quick look at him. But I'd have just seen the back of him while he was using first the toilet and then the sink. I probably wouldn't have recognized him.

They'd made the bed, I noticed. But they hadn't changed the sheets, so there was a good chance he'd left some DNA behind.

And it could damn well stay where it was as far as I was concerned.

Odd that they'd stop to make the bed. . . .

I went back for another look, and my legendary powers of observation determined that they hadn't made the bed, having never unmade it in the first place. The chenille bedspread bore unmistakable (not to say unmentionable) evidence of the very sort of activity I had so recently overheard. They were what you'd expect, along with one thing I wouldn't have expected—a blackish mark, roughly the size and shape of the palm of one's hand, directly above one of the pillows.

I wondered what it was. I didn't much want to touch it, but I took a long look at it. Could it have seeped through from beneath? If so, I didn't much want to see the source of the seepage. But I made myself lift up a corner of the spread for a peek at the pillow beneath it, and what I saw was an ordinary white pillowcase, with no blackish mark on it, and indeed nothing out of the ordinary about it.

And was that what I wanted to be staring at when she—or both of them—came back?

No, emphatically not. I wanted to be in my own room, staring at the undersides of my eyelids. And, in not much time at all, there I was and that's what I was doing. It was getting on for five o'clock, and I'd draw less attention leaving the hotel at a decent hour than slinking off before dawn. And why chase all the way uptown to my apartment only to hurry back a couple of hours later to open my shop? My rent was paid. I might as well get some use out of the room.

It says right on the aspirin bottle not to take the stuff more often than every four hours, but the person who wrote that didn't have any way of knowing how I was going to feel right now. I'd gulped a couple more first thing upon returning to the room, and now I lay on the bed in the dark and waited for them to kick in.

Paddington Bear lay beside me. I'd taken off all of my

clothes. He'd kept his on, including his boots. I tried to keep my mind on Paddington, but it would have none of it.

It kept insisting on returning to Room 303, and what I'd encountered there. Well, no, there hadn't been an actual encounter, and thank God for that, but I'd glimpsed her through a plastic shower curtain and heard her through an open door.

The glimpse didn't tell me much more than that she sat down to pee. The unmistakable cries of passion, cries that had previously resounded within the walls of my own apartment, they told me a good deal more.

The luggage tag swore she was Karen Kassenmeier. But I knew better.

She was Alice Cottrell.

FIFTEEN

Remarkably enough, I was open for business a few minutes after ten. Raffles met me at the door and rubbed up against my ankles, assuring me he was on the brink of starvation. It was a convincing performance, but it didn't stop me from calling Carolyn at the Poodle Factory.

"I didn't feed him," she said. "I just opened up myself a few minutes ago. It was a long night."

"For me, too."

"I know," she said, "because I tried to reach you and I couldn't. I called late, too. Where were you, anyway?"

Someone was at the door. "I'll tell you during lunch. What kind of food should I get?"

"I don't know," she said. "Nothing too far out, okay? I couldn't face breakfast this morning, so that'll give you an idea. Lean towards bland."

I don't know what kind of a night Raffles had had, but he had no trouble facing breakfast. My first customer was joined by a second, and while they poked around in different corners of the shop I went through the bag of books Henry Walden had persuaded a woman to leave for my appraisal. They'd looked good at first glance the previous afternoon, and they looked even better after a thorough examination. No great rarities, no *Tamerlane and Other Poems*, but good salable books in decent shape, the sort that look good on my shelves and move quickly off of them.

I made notes and jotted down numbers and worked out how high I could safely go for the books, and I'd just come up with a figure when Henry Walden stepped over my threshold, looking as though he'd spent the previous night meditating at a Zen temple instead of knocking them back at the Bum Rap. He was wearing a different sport jacket and a clean shirt, and his eyes were bright and his skin clear. His silver beard and mustache were, as always, perfectly groomed, and his tan beret was cocked at a rakish angle.

"Good morning," he said. "That was enjoyable last evening."

"I enjoyed it myself," I said. "As much as I remember of it, anyway. The drinks hit me pretty hard."

"Really? You didn't show it."

That was nice to hear, but I didn't want to put too much stock in it. People say it all the time. *"Oh, really? Both the dog and your mother-in-law? That's funny, because you didn't seem drunk at all."* Yeah, right.

We chatted a bit, and then he found some books to look at while I made a couple of phone calls. I reached Marty Gilmartin at his office and told him the books he was looking for—I didn't want to say rubies—were in a safe place. I didn't add that the safe place was halfway to the bottom of a sack of dry cat food in my back room.

"But don't say anything," I said. "To either of them."

"John or Isis," he said. "Not until we know what we're going to do with the, uh, books."

I rang off and tried Alice Cottrell's number, or at least the number she had given me, which now seemed no more credible than anything else she'd told me. There was no answer, and I can't say I was surprised.

* * *

The woman who'd left the bag of books still hadn't turned up at noon. I hung the cardboard clock face in the window, indicating I'd be back at one, and asked Henry if he felt up to giving me a hand with the table. I wound up leaving the table out on the sidewalk and retrieving my clock sign.

"I've got a shop-sitter," I told Carolyn. "A customer with time on his hands. I can't afford to pay him anything, but he doesn't seem to want to be paid. He likes hanging around, and he says he's learning the business."

"I had that guy Keith," she said. "Remember him? He wanted to be my apprentice. He was happy to do all the shit work if I'd just teach him the dog-grooming game. It would have been a good deal, but I couldn't stand having him around. He got on my nerves."

"I don't think Henry'll get on my nerves," I said. "He didn't this morning, and they're pretty raw."

"Your nerves?"

I nodded. "Rough night."

"You and me both."

"I thought you were with Erica."

"I was."

"I thought you stayed with Lavoris and soda when you were with her."

"I thought so, too," she said. "What's for lunch, Bern? I couldn't face breakfast, so I'm pretty hungry."

"Me too," I said. "I don't know what's for lunch."

"You bought it and you don't know what it is?"

"I went to the Uzbek place."

"Two Guys from Tashkent?"

"Right, and you know what that's like. The menu's on the blackboard, but who knows what any of the words mean? I just pointed at things and handed them money, and one guy gave me food and the other guy gave me change."

"That makes two guys, all right." She opened a container,

sniffed. "Somehow," she said, "I don't think this is going to be bland."

"Oh, hell," I said. "I forgot."

She took a forkful and her eyes widened. "A long way from bland," she announced.

"Leave it. I'll get you something else."

"No, stay where you are. Maybe that's the wrong move entirely, eating bland food when you feel like this. Maybe spicy food is what you really need."

"Well, this is spicy. I think it would take rust off old pipes."

"My pipes are getting older even as we speak. This is tasty, isn't it? I bet it fixes me right up."

"I hope so."

"And if it makes me any worse, I'll go home. And that wouldn't be the worst thing in the world, either. What do you figure this is, Bern?"

"No idea."

"Maybe we're happier not knowing. That's probably a lot of crap, bland food for an upset stomach. Like bland food for an ulcer."

"You haven't got an ulcer."

"I will," she said, "if we keep eating Uzbek food. How come you had a rocky morning?"

"I had drinks with Marty," I said, "and then I had drinks with Henry."

"Henry the shop-sitter."

"Right. Marty and I had Kessler's, and Henry and I had Old Overcoat."

"Old Overholt."

"Whatever. They both liked rye just fine, and they both handled it okay, too. But I wound up with a snootful."

I told her how the night had ended, only to begin again at half past three in the morning and end a second time when I got back to bed an hour or so later.

"Gee," she said. "I thought I had a wild evening."

"What happened?"

"Erica had a business triumph to celebrate," she said. "So she took me to the Lorelei Room."

"Sixty floors up? Posher than posh? Views beyond description? That Lorelei Room?"

"That's the one. I was wearing this outfit she made me buy, and I felt really weird, but she kept telling me I looked beautiful, and halfway through my second Rob Roy I started to believe her."

"Where did the Rob Roys come from?"

"The waiter brought them. Oh, why Rob Roys and not Campari? Because it was a celebration. That made it a special occasion, so it was okay for us to get a little tiddly."

"Tiddly."

"And the views were amazing. You could see Jersey, you could see Queens. Though what's such a big deal about being able to see a couple of places you wouldn't dream of going to?" She shrugged. "Anyway, it was swank, Bern. It makes a pretty dramatic change from washing rottweilers."

"All part of being in New York."

"Rottweilers, the Lorelei Room, and Two Guys from Tashkent." She helped herself to one of the little fried dumplings, popped it into her mouth, chewed, and reached for her iced tea. "People outside of New York," she said, "will live a lifetime without getting to taste Uzbek food. They don't know what they're missing."

"Poor bastards."

"Whereas we, on the other hand, don't know what we're eating. Bern, where was I?"

"Sixty stories high, not counting the Rob Roys."

"And that's what we were doing, too. Not counting the Rob Roys. But this is the part I gotta tell you. A couple of guys came over and hit on us."

"Oh?"

" 'Oh?' Is that all you can say?"

"What else do you want me to say? You're a couple of attractive women, and it's not that hard to believe that a couple of guys might put the moves on you."

"Bern, guys don't hit on me."

"Not ever?"

"Once every couple of years," she said, "some drunk wanders into the Cubby Hole or Henrietta Hudson's and doesn't realize he's in a dyke bar, and if I'm standing in front of him and he's drunk enough he'll come on to me. But outside of that, no, guys leave me alone. Because it's fairly obvious that I'm gay."

"Well, you weren't in the Cubby Hole last night."

"No, and I wasn't wearing slacks and a blazer, either, and my hair's longer than I've worn it since I was a kid in pigtails, and I had lipstick on, Bernie, and eye shadow, for Christ's sake."

"No kidding. Eye shadow?"

"And things I don't know the names of. Erica made me up. We were at her apartment, and you'd have thought we were teenagers at a slumber party, doing each other's makeup. Except she did her own, because I wouldn't have known what to do."

"Eye shadow," I said. "So they hit on you and you told them to get lost, and—"

"No."

"No?"

"I started to, and Erica gave me a kick. Then she looked up at them with eyes big as saucers and said sure, we'd love it if they would buy us a drink. And they sat down at our table, and we quick drank our Rob Roys to make room for the round they were buying us."

"That's really weird," I said. "What did she have in mind?"

"That's what I wondered. I thought maybe the booze had hit her. You know how there are these people who never drink very much, and you wonder why not?"

"And then one night they have a few, and you find out."

"Right. I thought maybe that was her story, in which case I was going to have to find a way to get her out of there. But then she went to the ladies' room and motioned for me to come along." She frowned. "Guys don't do that, do they? Make a social event out of going to the bathroom?"

"Not the kind of guys I tend to hang out with."

"I have to go along with the guys on this one, Bern. I don't seem to develop a craving for company when I have to go to the jane. I just go and come back. But Erica didn't even have to go. She just wanted a chance to talk in a male-free environment."

"And?"

"And that was okay with me, because I had a question for her. Like what are we doing with these two clowns? And she told me to play along."

"Play along?"

"It'll be fun, she said. We can just sort of lead them on and jolly them along and then give them the slip."

"You were wearing a slip?"

"Very funny, Bern. I tried to talk her out of it but she was taking charge and topping the whole scene. 'We're celebrating,' she reminded me, and they could pay for the celebration, and that would really be something to celebrate."

"So you went back to the two visiting firemen—"

"Meteorologists, Bern. They were two meteorologists from the Midwest, in town for the big meteorologists' convention."

"I didn't know there was one."

"Neither did we, and I'll spare you the weather jokes, which is more than they did for us. They bought us some more drinks and then they bought us dinner."

"At the Lorelei Room? It must have cost them . . ."

"In round numbers, a fortune. But what did they care? It was going on the old expense account, and it was bread on the water, because what girl would fail to show her appreciation to the guy who'd just spent a couple hundred dollars feeding her?"

"I've always operated at a lower financial level," I said, "but a surprising number of women have failed to do just that."

"Even when they've heard your Mel Tormé record?"

"Even then. You must have wondered how you were going to get rid of them."

"I was too busy worrying about how I was gonna get through the next five minutes. I just sat there feeling dopey, and I guess that was all I had to do. Meanwhile, Erica was flirting like crazy."

"With a couple of weathermen."

"You didn't need them," she said, "to know which way the wind was blowing. Actually, they were pretty decent fellows."

"I bet their wives didn't understand them."

"I don't know why not. God knows I did. What's to understand? They were horny and wanted to get laid. I felt the same way, but with a difference."

"And all the while Erica was flirting her head off."

"Her head was the least of it. She kept leaning forward to give Ed a peek down her dress, and I'm positive he had a hand on her leg. Phil put his hand on my leg, and I wanted to stick a fork in it."

"What did you do?"

"I had some more wine. I just poured it in there on top of the Rob Roys, and with coffee I had a pony of B&B."

"I guess that's more feminine than straight brandy."

"I'd have preferred the brandy," she said, "and instead of a pony I'd have had a whole horse. Because I had this horrible sense that we were going to go back to their hotel with them, or take them to Erica's place, or something."

"And—?"

"And that too," she said, "because it wouldn't be the first time a woman swore she was gay and turned out to be bisexual. Before the guys hit on us, I was actually starting to worry about you."

"That I'd turn out to be bisexual after I swore up and down I was a lesbian?"

"Erica was full of questions about you," she said. "Everything from how did we get to be friends to where you live and what you have for breakfast. It was enough to make me wonder, and then the guys turned up, and . . ."

"And you thought you'd wind up going home with them."

"Right, and then we'd wake up the next morning, and Erica'd say, 'Ohmigod, we sure were drunk last night, and I don't remember a thing,' and I'd have to pretend I didn't remember, either, but I'd remember. I decided the hell with that, and I'd figure out some way to keep it from happening, but I didn't have to. They paid the check, and we rode down on the elevator with them, and the next thing I knew Erica and I were in a cab and Phil and Ed were on the street, watching us go out of their lives."

"Welcome to New York," I said.

"We went to my place for a change," she said, "and she was really excited by the whole thing. 'Pretend I'm a man,' she said. 'Fine,' I said. 'You're a man. How about them Yankees, huh?' But she made me play along, and it was really weird."

"I can imagine."

"And then it was her turn. 'Now pretend *you're* the man,' she said, and that was weird, too. I don't even like talking about this stuff, Bern."

"Me neither. I've never been much on locker-room conversations."

"Or powder-room conversations, either. But I didn't have any more conversations with Erica, because I fell asleep right away. I woke up early, but she was already dressed and gone, so all I woke up with was a hangover."

"Where do you think it's going?"

"The hangover? I think it's going away, thanks to Two Guys

from Tashkent. Oh, you mean me and Erica? I don't know. I guess time will tell. How about you and Alice?"

"I think it's already gone."

"And how about Gulliver Fairborn's letters, and those rubies you found? And the murder of Anthea Landau? And everything else that's been going on?"

"I don't know," I said. "Once I realized that was Alice squealing with passion, I thought what a coincidence it was that she was in this room. But it wasn't a coincidence at all, not if it was her room. And I thought about it some more, and I saw the real coincidence."

"What was that?"

"The jewelry. John Considine stole it from himself and gave it to Isis."

"On loan."

"According to him, but either way she had it. And then it wound up in Alice Cottrell's room. Now that's a coincidence."

"It wound up in your pocket," she said, "and that's not a coincidence. It's theft, and maybe that's how it got in Alice's room."

"She's a jewel thief?"

"Why not?"

"And, because she's an accomplished thief herself, she has to rope me in to swipe some letters so she can return them to Gulliver Fairborn?"

"Maybe she's not a jewel thief, Bern."

"Then what is she? And how did she wind up with the jewels? And, and . . ."

"And what, Bern?"

"I don't know," I said, "but it's getting complicated."

SIXTEEN

In the time I was gone, Henry had made a couple of sales and settled with the woman who'd left the bag of books. He paid her in cash from the register and got her to write out a receipt, and he even saved me money; he'd offered her twenty-five dollars less than I'd been prepared to go, and she'd taken it without argument.

Mr. Harkness from Sotheby's had called again. I didn't feel like calling him back, nor could I see the point in trying Alice Cottrell's number, because I'd figured out that it wasn't her number after all. So what I did instead was stand there talking books with Henry, who leaned on my counter with his chin in his hand and talked about the impression Thomas Wolfe had made on him at an admittedly impressionable age. "I thought *Look Homeward, Angel* was just wonderful," he said, "and then a few years ago I tried rereading it, and I couldn't get anywhere with it."

"Well, you can't go home again," I said.

"Maybe that's it, although there are some books I can read over and over. But I think you have to be young when you read Wolfe."

"It's the same with Dr. Seuss."

"I don't know," he said. "I like *The Cat in the Hat* better than ever. And the one about the kid with all those hats."

"Bartholomew Cubbins," I said. "Maybe you just like books about hats. I've got a copy of *The Green Hat* around here somewhere. By Michael Arlen. I've had it for years, and if you read it you can tell me if it's any good. What about *Nobody's Baby*? If you'd read it when you were seventeen you'd be saying it changed your life, but I don't suppose you did."

"I was well past seventeen when it was published."

"But you read it?"

"When it came out, and I've looked at it a few times since then."

"But I don't suppose it changed your life, did it?"

"I suppose everything does," he said thoughtfully. "Even the morning paper, even the quiz on the back of the Special K box. One's a different person for having read it, whatever it happens to be."

That got us into a nice philosophical conversation. I'd bought the bookshop in the hope of conversations like this one, and I gave myself over to it wholeheartedly. I stopped in mid-sentence and turned at the sound of the door opening, and there was a woman who looked familiar. I couldn't place her until she said, "Hi! What are you doing here?"

It was Isis Gauthier, and I didn't recognize her until she spoke because she looked very different. She wasn't dressed like Paddington Bear this time around, but looked just fine in jeans and a pink Brooks Brothers shirt. Her cornrows had transformed themselves into straight shoulder-length hair with red highlights, which, clever fellow that I am, I realized had to be a wig.

"I come here all the time," I said. "It's my store. What are *you* doing here?"

"Not you," she said. She was looking at Henry, who straightened up, his hand dropping to his side. "Oh, sorry. I thought you were somebody else." Now she turned to me. "I *know* it's your store," she said. "And I know what you do when you're not running it, too. And I think we ought to have a talk." Then she turned and looked at Henry again.

"Time I got some lunch," Henry said diplomatically.

She was silent until the door closed behind him. Then she said she'd spoken to Marty, who told her he'd spoken to me. "He says you didn't kill Miss Landau," she said, "but that's the same thing that policeman said. You went there to steal something but you couldn't find it."

"I hate the way that sounds," I said. "As if I'm a crook, and incompetent in the bargain."

I gave her my best disarming smile, but I couldn't see that it had any effect. "You're a burglar," she said, "and you came to my hotel to steal something. And somebody got into my room and stole my rubies. Now it doesn't seem like much of a leap to think you had something to do with it."

"I see your point, but—"

"Marty says you didn't," she went on. "But here's the thing, see. When I first told him my rubies were missing, I could tell he wasn't buying it. He thought it was a way for me to keep them without flat out refusing to give them back. 'Oh, Ah'd be happy to give dem back so poor Miz Considine don't be pinin' away for dem, but Ah cain't, on account of somebody done stole dem.'"

"'Glory be, Miz Scarlett, what do Ah know about birfin' babies?'"

She gave me a look. "But now he believes me," she said. "He had a conversation with you, and now he believes me. What does that tell you, Mr. Rhodenbarr?"

"I guess he came to his senses."

"What it tells me," she said, "is that he knew I hadn't faked the theft of the rubies, because you admitted taking them. You must have made an earlier visit to the hotel, before the night I ran into you in the hallway."

"And then I returned to the scene of the crime?"

"You found out the Paddington's security wasn't that great, and you wanted to see what some of the other rooms might hold. But what I want to know is how you came to my room in the first place. Did John Considine send you?"

"I've never met the man. And if I'd already stolen the rubies on his behalf, why would he send Marty to talk you out of them?"

"Maybe he didn't know you were successful. Maybe you decided not to tell him, because you thought you could do better selling the rubies to somebody else than settling for whatever he promised you for them."

"That's a lot of maybes for one sentence."

"It's two sentences, with one maybe in each."

"Is that all? Well, it still seems like a lot."

"Too hypothetical for you?"

"Call me hypothetical," I said.

"Is that a song cue?" She braced one hand on her hip and cocked her head. To the tune of "Call Me Irresponsible" she crooned, "*Call me hypothetical. Toss in . . .* toss in what?"

"Alphabetical," I suggested.

She made a face. "*Toss in theoretical.*"

"Better."

"*Don't leave alphabetical out.*"

"I like it," I said, "and I'm glad I was able to make a modest contribution. I think we've got a hit on our hands."

"I think you changed the subject," she said sternly, but she didn't look as stern as she sounded. A smile was trying to play with her lips. It wasn't getting a whole lot of encouragement, but it was hanging in there.

"You think I have your rubies," I said. Note the possessive pronoun; it was my way of letting her know I was on her side. "Suppose you're right."

"I knew it!"

"Whoa," I said. "Let's keep it hypothetical, okay? I didn't

say you're right, I said suppose you're right. As a matter of fact, I never stole anything from you."

"And that's the truth, right?"

"Gospel."

"And I'm just supposed to take your word for it? The word of a burglar?"

I said, "The jewels disappeared from your room, right? Well, I've never set foot inside your room. I don't even know what room you're in."

"Then how do you know you've never been in it?"

"Because you're on the sixth floor, and the only sixth-floor room I've been in was Anthea Landau's."

"Poor Anthea," she said. "She was nasty to most of the other tenants, but she was always perfectly nice to me. 'If you ever write a book,' she told me, 'you just bring it straight to me, dear.' " She fixed her gaze on me. "You just admitted it!"

"Admitted what?"

"That you were in her room."

"It's not much of an admission," I said. "It's not as though we were in court. Anyway, they found a fingerprint of mine in there. The point is I wasn't in your room, and I never saw your Elvis on black velvet."

"Then how do you . . . oh. Marty must have told you."

"He was impressed. Can we get back to my hypothesis? Suppose, just for the sake of argument, that I have your rubies."

"Argument's the word for it. All right, I'll play your little game. You don't have the rubies, but suppose you did."

"What would it take to make you happy?"

"To make me happy? Give me the damn rubies back and I'll be happy as a lark."

"Is that what it would take? The rubies themselves?"

"What are you getting at?"

"I'm just trying to find out what the main attraction is here," I said. "Is it a handful of pretty red stones, or is it what they're worth?"

"Keep talking."

"Would you settle for what the rubies are worth?"

Her eyes flashed. They were still blue, I noted, but a little less startling. I must have been getting used to them.

"John Considine tried that on," she said. "He told Marty to offer me five thousand dollars. Five thousand dollars!"

"A veritable pittance."

"I'd say it's about as veritable as pittances get. An appraiser told me they're worth eighty thousand dollars."

"That's more than they were insured for, but it's probably not far off. Look, forget five thousand dollars."

"I forgot it the moment I heard it."

"And forget eighty thousand too, while you're at it. Suppose you could get twenty thousand."

"Twenty thousand dollars."

"In nice quiet cash."

"It's less than they're worth."

"Assuming they're genuine, and assuming—"

"An expert appraiser said they were. Genuine Burmese rubies, he said."

"It's interesting about rubies," I said. "The best ones come from Burma and Sri Lanka. They're the major exporters of quality stones."

"I know."

"And who do you suppose are the biggest importers of synthetic rubies?"

She looked at me. "You're going to tell me Burma and Sri Lanka, aren't you? What's the point?"

"Figure it out."

"I saw a shop on the highway with a sign. 'We Buy Junk and Sell Antiques.' Is that what the folks in Burma and Sri Lanka are doing?"

"If they are," I said, "and if they can get away with it because it's virtually impossible to tell synthetic rubies from the real thing, then rubies might not be an ideal long-term investment."

She frowned. "I wasn't thinking about selling them," she said. "If I did, I'd get more than twenty thousand. I wore them onstage, you know."

"In *The Play's the Thing.*"

"You saw me? No, of course not. Marty told you."

"I heard you were sensational."

"You're just making that up, but I still like the way it sounds." She came up with a real smile this time. "I loved those rubies," she said. "I felt wonderful wearing them. Especially because John gave them to me. But when I stopped feeling that way about John, I still felt the same way about the rubies."

"And now?"

"Twenty thousand dollars is a lot of money. I'd miss the rubies. As a matter of fact I miss them already. Still, I could get a lot more use out of the money. But you're not offering it to me, are you?"

"We're just being hypothetical, remember?"

"Is that what we're doing?" She arched an eyebrow. "I'd like my rubies back, Mr. Rhodenbarr."

"Bernie."

"I'd like my rubies, Bernie. Or my twenty thousand dollars. But you don't have the jewels or the money, and we're just being hypocritical."

"I think you mean hypothetical."

"Not necessarily," she said, and headed out the door.

The store was quieter for the absence of Isis, and a drabber place altogether. She brightened things up even when she wasn't wearing all the colors of the rainbow. I was all alone. Henry hadn't come back, and I didn't know if he was going to.

I picked up the phone and tried Alice's number, or what I'd been given to think was Alice's number, and it went unanswered, as seemed to be its habit. I hung up and took a moment to Think Things Through, and I realized something.

I could wash my hands of the whole mess.

I'd gotten involved to impress a girlfriend and do a favor for a writer whose book had—oh, all right—changed my life. *Nobody's Baby* may not have saved me from a life of crime, but my worldview was forever altered by it, and you couldn't say the same for the quiz on the back of the Special K box. And so I'd tried to retrieve Fairborn's letters, but someone else had beaten me to it, and they were well beyond my reach by now. If you're going to look for a needle, at the very least you ought to know which haystack to look in. And I didn't. Anybody could have taken them, and they could be anywhere by now.

So Fairborn wouldn't get his letters back, but he wouldn't blame me, because he didn't know I existed. He might or might not blame Alice Cottrell, and she could blame me if she wanted, but she'd effectively disappeared from my life, reappearing only to share her squeals of excitement with some faceless stranger. I couldn't convince myself I owed her a thing.

I'd managed to walk in on a murder scene and get arrested for it, but I wasn't languishing in a cell, and sooner or later the charges would be dropped. Even if they never found out who killed Anthea Landau, they didn't have a case against me.

What did that leave? The rubies? Well, fine. I hadn't checked lately, but I was pretty sure they were still covered with cat food and safe as houses. Whether or not John Considine was willing to pay twenty grand to get them back, and whether or not Isis decided to take the money, was not really my problem. It was Marty's, as soon as I passed the jewelry on to him, and he could figure it out.

And where did that leave me? Well, for the moment it left me with a bag of books I'd just purchased, and they weren't doing me any good where they were. I took them out and stacked them on my counter and set about pricing them, then placing them where they belonged on my shelves. *Gas-House McGinty* was hard to price; I checked a couple of price guides to no avail, wound up leaving it unpriced for the time being.

Idly I opened the book to the first page of text and started reading, and I was halfway down page three when a familiar voice jarred me out of Farrell's narrative. "Well, well, well," Ray Kirschmann boomed, and I straightened up and closed the book with a snap.

"Hey, Bern," he said. "You look like you just got caught red-handed, an' all you're doin' is readin' a book. You got a bad conscience or somethin'?"

"It's a valuable book," I said. "I shouldn't be reading it. Anyway, you startled me, Ray."

"Man's got a store, he's gotta expect somebody might walk into it every once in a while. It's one of the risks of retail. Even if it's a fake store an' all he really is is a burglar."

"Ray . . ."

"Those letters turn up yet, Bern?"

"No," I said, "and they're not going to. I was looking for them, I admit it, but somebody got there first."

"An' stabbed Landau."

"Evidently."

He frowned. "Seems to me," he said, "you said the other day that you had the letters."

"No," I said, "*you* said I had them, and I said they were in a safe place."

"Safe from who?"

"Safe from me," I said, "and I have to say I don't care where they are, or who took them."

"Bern, what happened to our deal?"

"Nothing happened to it, but not even Steven can make something out of nothing. There's nothing for us to split, Ray."

"So you're out of it."

"Right."

He started to say something, but the phone rang and I reached to answer it. It was Hilliard Moffett, the world's foremost collector of Gulliver Fairborn, just calling to remind me of the intensity of his interest.

I stopped him in midsentence. "I don't have the letters," I said, "and I never will. And I'm a little busy right now."

I hung up. Ray said, "What we were sayin', you washed your hands of the whole business."

"Absolutely."

"So you ain't been back to that hotel, the padded bears."

"The Paddington," I said, "and no, I haven't. How could I? I don't think they'd let me in."

"When did anybody ever have to let you in, Bern?"

The phone rang again. I made a face and picked it up, and it was Lester Eddington, the Fairborn scholar, to say that he perhaps ought to stress how important it was that he receive copies of the Fairborn-Landau correspondence, and that on consideration he realized he could pay quite a bit more than the cost of making copies. Several thousand dollars, in fact, and—

It helps when you know your lines, and I didn't have any trouble remembering mine. "I don't have the letters," I said, "and I never will. And I'm a little busy right now."

I hung up. "You keep tellin' people that," Ray said, "an' pretty soon you're gonna believe it yourself. Tell me somethin', Bern. What did you do last night?"

"What did I do?"

"Uh-huh. You hang out with Carolyn?"

"No, she had a date."

"So what did you do?"

"I had a few drinks at the Bum Rap," I said.

"All by your lonesome? You know what they say about drinkin' all by yourself."

"I suppose it's better than being all by yourself and not drinking," I said, "but I had company."

"An' then?"

"And then I went home."

"To your place on West End an' Seventy-first."

"That's where I live," I said. "That's my home, so when I decide to go home, that's where I go to."

"You coulda gone home with whoever you were drinkin' with," he said. "To her home, is what I mean."

"It was a guy."

"Well," he said, "I never thought you were that way, Bern, but what's it to me who you go home with?"

"I went home alone," I said, "to my own home, and all by myself, and—"

And the phone rang. I picked it up and barked into the receiver, and there was a pause, and a Mr. Victor Harkness of Sotheby's said he'd been trying to reach me, and he guessed I hadn't had an opportunity to call him back.

"This is unofficial," he said, "so let's just call it an exploratory inquiry. Miss Anthea Landau had made arrangements for us to handle the sale of the Fairborn letters. She'd brought in some representative letters, so we'd had a look at them, but she wouldn't leave them with us. But we gave her an advance, and she signed our standard agreement, and it's binding on her heirs and assigns."

"I doubt that would include me," I said. "I can't imagine why she would mention me in her will. I never met the woman."

There was a long pause, and then Mr. Harkness tried again. "My point, Mr. Rhodenbarr, is that we have a vested interest in the material. It will be the highlight of our January sale of books and documents. Its value to us thus exceeds somewhat the commissions we'd expect to collect on the sale, which would in themselves be substantial."

"That's interesting, but—"

"Consequently," he said, "we could pay a finder's fee. In cash. No questions asked."

"And you can do that?"

"The letters remain the legal property of Miss Landau," he said, "no matter in whose hands they may be at the moment. And our arrangement with her remains in force. Should we succeed in recovering the letters, we'd be under no obligation to account for the manner in which they came into our possession."

I took a deep breath. "I don't have the letters," I said, "and I never will. And I'm a little busy right now."

I hung up. "You're repeatin' yourself," Ray said. "I'll tell you, Bern, you sound like a broken record."

"Records are made to be broken."

"Uh-huh. So you went straight home last night, huh?"

Where was he going with this? "I went to the Bum Rap," I said. "I already told you that."

"Having drinks with some fag friend of yours."

"His name's Henry," I said, "and he's not gay, or at least I don't think he is. What difference does it make?"

"It don't make none to me. I didn't go home with him."

"And neither did I."

"No, you went home alone. What time?"

"I don't know. Eight or nine o'clock, I guess. Something like that."

"An' you went right home."

"I stopped at the deli and bought a quart of milk. Why?"

"Prolly to put in your coffee. Oh, why am I askin'? Just makin' conversation, Bern. So you went home an' you were there alone all night, is that right?"

"That's right."

"An' this mornin' . . ."

"I got up and came to the store."

"An' opened up, an' fed your cat, an' did the things you always do."

"Right."

"An' you just walked out your door, right? You didn't notice a thing?"

Oh, God. I had to ask, even though I didn't want to hear the answer. "Didn't notice what, Ray?"

"The dead girl," he said, "lyin' smack in the middle of your living-room floor. There was hardly room enough to walk around her, so I guess you musta stepped right over her. Funny you didn't even notice."

SEVENTEEN

A dead woman," I said.

"Girl, woman. Suit yourself, Bern. It don't matter what you call her on account of she ain't likely to answer. Poor dame's dead as a hangnail."

"In my apartment."

"Unless you moved out an' somebody else moved in. You still livin' in the same place, Bern?"

"Uh," I said.

"I guess it ain't a bad place to live," he said, "or you wouldn't be livin' there, an' it must be a good place to die, too, 'cause that's what she used it for. Not that she didn't have help."

"She was murdered?"

"I'd say so. People'll shoot themselves now an' then, and sometimes they'll stab themselves, but it's rare for somebody to do both."

"She was . . ."

"Shot an' stabbed, right. Shot in the shoulder an' stabbed in the heart, or close enough to it to be just as good. The ME says death was pretty much instantaneous."

"At least she didn't suffer," I said, "whoever she was. Was it the knife wound that killed her?"

"For the gunshot to kill her," he said, "it woulda had to be blood poisoning, because she had the wound all bandaged up. The doc wouldn't go out on a limb, but what he said was it was a minimum of twenty-four hours old. She got shot, she got patched up, and she went over to your place and got herself stabbed to death."

"When did this happen, Ray?"

"Sometime last night, from the looks of things. While you were home sleepin', Bern."

"Who found the body?"

"Couple of uniforms."

"They were just passing through my apartment and happened to notice her there?"

"Respondin' to a call."

"When was this?"

"Around eleven this mornin'. Some neighbor told your doorman there was suspicious sounds comin' from your apartment in the middle of the night."

"So he waited until morning? And then he told the doorman?"

"She. You know a Mrs. Hesch?"

"Down the hall from me. A nice lady."

"Well, she heard something in the middle of the night, but don't ask her when. Because I already asked an' I got everything but a straight answer. She went back to sleep an' woke up wonderin', so she knocked on your door an' you didn't answer, an' then she called you on the phone an' you still didn't answer, so she told your doorman."

"And he called it in?"

"He tried you on the intercom, and then he went upstairs and banged on the door, but you didn't answer, and neither did she."

"She?"

"The dead girl. So he went an' phoned it in."

"And a couple of uniforms came and forced my lock," I said. "Damn it, anyway."

"Relax, Bern."

"If you knew how many times I've had to replace that lock . . ."

"You don't have to replace it this time, because nobody forced it. The doorman had a key."

"He did?"

"The one you left with him."

"I figured it must have disappeared. If he had a key, why didn't he open up right away?"

"Maybe he was afraid of what he might find. Maybe he did open the door an' saw her from the doorway an' got the hell out an' let the uniforms find her for themselves. What the hell difference does it make? She was dead on the floor this mornin', an' she'd been dead for a while."

"How long?"

"For the time bein' I'm just guessin', but say six or eight hours. She probably got herself killed sometime in the middle of the night."

"When did you come into the picture, Ray?"

"Right away. Me an' you are linked in the department's computers, Bern. There's a flag with my name on it that pops up anytime your name comes up. It didn't take long for somebody to call me."

I looked at my watch. "It took you a while to get here, though."

"Yeah, it did. I figured, why hurry? I might as well wait an' hear what the ME had to say. An' I wanted to find out who she was, just in case you never managed to catch her name."

I already had a pretty good idea, but I had to ask. "Who was she, Ray?"

"The name Karen Kassenmeier ring any kind of a bell?"

She'd been alive at four-thirty in the morning, I thought. Gloriously alive, making triumphant noises on the spread-covered bed in Room 303 at the Hotel Paddington. Then the guy had hustled her out of there and took her north and west to my apartment, where he stabbed her and left her for dead.

"Bern?"

Unless she went up to my place on her own and met somebody else there. I had no way of knowing if the man she'd been with in Room 303 had killed her, or if it had been somebody else. And it didn't make too much difference, since I didn't know who he was. But why my place?

"Uh, Bern . . ."

Maybe because she knew where it was. Maybe she realized she was in danger, and thought I could save her.

"Hey, Bernie? Where'd you go?"

"I'm right here," I said. "I was thinking, that's all. Her name's not Karen Kassenmeier."

"Sure it is."

"No, it's not. As a matter of fact—"

The phone rang.

"Answer that," Ray said. "An' the hell that ain't her name. It's good solid police work turned it up, includin' takin' prints off her cold dead fingers an' runnin' 'em by Washington. Karen Ruth Kassenmeier from—"

"Oklahoma," I said. "Henrietta, Oklahoma."

"If it ain't her, how come you know where she's from? An' whyntcha answer the phone, because it's givin' me a headache."

"They all want the same thing," I said. "You want me to answer it? Fine, I'll answer it, and I'll tell this one the same thing I told the other two. And then I'll tell you the real name of the woman who's been calling herself Karen Kassenmeier."

I grabbed the phone.

"I don't have the letters," I snapped, "and I never will. And I'm a little busy right now."

"Bernie? Is that you?"

"Uh," I said.

"I guess I picked a bad time," she said. "I'll try you a little later."

"Wait," I said, but the line went dead. I looked at the receiver for a moment, but that never really accomplishes anything, and eventually I gave up and put it back in its cradle.

"Well," he said, "let's hear it."

"Huh?"

"The name," he said. "The real name of the dead dame on your floor."

"She's not still on my floor, is she? Don't tell me they haven't moved her."

"Quit stallin', huh? Who is she?"

"Karen Kassenmeier," I said.

"That's what I said. You were gettin' ready to say somethin' else."

"No, not me."

"Of course you were. I know what I said, an' I know what you said, an' what I'd like to know is what you almost said an' why you decided not to say it."

"Whatever it was," I said, "that phone call just drove it straight out of my mind. That's what you get for making me answer it."

"Bern—"

"Whatever it was," I said, "I'm sure it wasn't important. And if I ever remember it I'll be sure to let you know."

Her name's Alice Cottrell—that's what I'd been ready to tell him, and if the phone call hadn't emptied my mind, it had certainly changed it.

Because that was Alice Cottrell on the phone.

"Here you go," Ray said. "Take a look."

"I hate this."

"No kiddin', Bern. You liked it, I'd have to start worryin' about you. Nobody likes to look at dead bodies. Why do you think we bury 'em?"

"So we won't have to look at them?"

"Reason enough," he said. "Well? What do you think?"

I turned away. "I've never seen her before," I said. "Can we go now?"

"I didn't go home last night," I said.

"Jeez, that comes as a shock to me, Bern."

"I had a reason for saying I did."

"Of course you did, an' the reason's you're a liar. A guy lifts things for a livin', you don't hardly expect every word outta his mouth's gonna be the truth. Half the questions I ask you, main reason I ask is to see what kind of a story you come up with."

"You don't expect the truth from me?"

"If I did," he said, "it'd mean I ain't learned a thing over the years, because you been tellin' me lies since the day we met. An' why should I hold it against you? We done each other a lot of good over the years, Bern."

"That's true."

"Put a lot of dollars in our pockets. An' I wound up makin' a couple of righteous collars along the way, too."

"Sometimes it was me you collared, Ray."

"But nothin' ever stuck, did it? You always came out okay."

"So far."

"You ever meet this Kassenmeier, Bernie?"

"No," I said. "I thought I did. For a minute I thought she was someone else."

"She looked familiar?"

I shook my head. "Earlier. Before I saw her, I thought the woman in my apartment might have been, uh, another woman."

"And who would that be, Bern? Never mind, don't strain yourself makin' up a story. You changed your mind on that before you got anywhere near the morgue. If I was guessin', I'd say that was her on the phone."

He pulled up next to a hydrant—where would cops park

without them?—and we walked around the corner to my store. Henry was ringing a sale as we entered. He'd returned from lunch around the time Ray started badgering me to take a look at the late Karen Kassenmeier, and I'd left him to mind the store.

I hadn't introduced them before, so I did now. "This is Ray Kirschmann," I said. "He's a police officer. And this is Henry Walden. He used to own a clay factory."

"I didn't know clay was somethin' you made in a factory," Ray said. "I thought you just dug it up, like dirt."

You did, Henry told him, but then you had to process it, which involved removing the impurities and adding compounds to keep it from drying out. Then you dyed it and packaged it and shipped it to the stores.

"An' then people give it to their kids," Ray said, "an' the little bastards track it into the carpet, which you never get it out of. You workin' for Bernie, Henry?"

"He lets me hang out here," Henry said, "and I lend a hand when I can. It's more interesting than making clay."

"If you like books," Ray said. Henry said he liked them a lot, and that he liked the kind of people you met in bookstores. You met all kinds, Ray agreed. Henry asked if I needed him for anything more, and I said no, that I'd be closing fairly soon. Henry said he'd most likely see me tomorrow, and stopped on his way out to give Raffles a pat.

"Nice enough fellow," Ray said, when the door closed behind him. "Was he here the other day when I came by?"

"It's hard to remember who was and who wasn't. He's been hanging around a lot."

"Henry Clay. Wasn't there somebody famous named Henry Clay?"

"He was the man who said he'd rather be right than be President."

"There you go."

"But his name's not Henry Clay, Ray. It's Henry Walden."

"Same difference. What it did, it rang a bell. An' so did his face, but then it didn't. Like he was familiar at first glance, but at second glance you realized you were seeing him for the first time."

"At second glance, you were seeing him for the first time."

"You know what I mean. If you saw that beard you'd remember it, wouldn't you? Extinguished an' all. Bern, speakin' of familiar. Namely the dame we just saw. I know she wasn't who you thought she was, but are you sure she didn't look the least bit familiar?"

"She looked dead."

"Yeah. Well, there's not a whole lot of doubt on that score."

"She looked as though she'd been dead forever, Ray. As though she'd been born dead, and bad things happened to her ever since."

" 'Cordin' to what we got on her, she's forty-six years old. The worst thing ever happened to her was gettin' stabbed to death last night, but up until then she got arrested a whole batch of times an' went away more than once."

"For what?"

"Theft. She was a thief."

"A thief in my apartment."

"Yeah, that's a first. She musta been lookin' to steal somethin'."

"I suppose so."

"You don't seem concerned. Why's that?"

"Well, she didn't get away with anything, did she, Ray?"

"No, but whoever killed her might have walked off with what she came to take."

"I don't know what she came to take," I said, "and I didn't have anything worth taking."

"How about your life, Bern?"

"Huh?"

"She had a gun in her purse."

"A gun," I said.

"Little bitty one. Hadn't been cleaned since the last time it was fired."

"Maybe she shot the person who stabbed her."

"An' then put the gun back in her purse?" He made a face. "What it mighta been," he said, "is the gun she got shot with a couple of days ago."

"The shoulder wound."

"Uh-huh. It's the right size. Twenty-five-caliber, perfect if you want to stop a charging cockroach."

"If somebody shot her in the shoulder," I said, "how does the gun wind up in her purse?"

"Maybe the guy who shot her a while ago is the same guy who stabbed her last night. She falls down dead an' he gets rid of the gun by stickin' it in her purse."

"That makes a lot of sense."

"It makes no sense at all," he said, "but what does?"

"Maybe she shot herself originally," I suggested.

"Now that makes sense, Bern. Woman wants to kill herself, she shoots herself in the shoulder."

"She shot herself accidentally."

"It's her gun an' she has an accident with it."

"Why not?"

He thought it over. "Whole lot of arrests on her sheet," he said. "I didn't see where she was ever charged with possession of a firearm."

"People change."

"So I keep hearin', but I ain't seen much evidence of it. She got charged twice with assault. Charges dropped both times. Didn't use a gun, though."

"She used a knife," I said.

"How'd you know that, Bern?"

"The way you paused. I could sense the punch line looming in the distance. She did use a knife?"

"Yeah, she stabbed a couple of guys."

"But I bet she didn't have a knife in her purse."

"Nope."

"Or found on the premises."

"Well, you got a drawer full of knives in your kitchen. But no, they didn't find the murder weapon at the crime scene. The thinkin' is the killer took it away with him."

"Was it the same knife?"

He smiled approvingly. "Very good," he said. "You'd make an okay cop, if you weren't a crook instead."

"Who says a person can't be both? Was it the same knife used to kill Anthea Landau?"

"If we had the knife," he said, "it'd be easier to say one way or the other. All they can tell so far is it's possible. What do you say, Bern? Any ideas where we might find the knife? Any thoughts on who mighta stuck it in Kassenmeier?"

"No."

"You know somethin' about Kassenmeier, Bern. You say you never saw her, an' you say you didn't know nothin' about her, but I saw the look on your face when I mentioned her name the first time. You didn't look like you were hearin' it for the first time."

"I never heard it before," I said, "but I'd seen it."

"Seen it where?"

I thought about it. Was there any reason to hold out on him? There had to be, but I couldn't think what it was.

"She was staying at the Paddington."

"How would you know that? That's where you were last night, isn't it?" He didn't wait for an answer. "Lemme use your phone," he said, and he was reaching for it when it rang. "Shit," he said, and picked it up himself. "Bernie's Bookstore," he said. "Who's this, Carolyn? Sorry, my mistake. Hold on."

He handed me the phone. Alice Cottrell said, "Bernie? Is that you?" I said it was. "Who was that just now?" A police officer, I said.

"Oh, then you can't talk," she said. "That's all right. Look, I wanted to let you know that everything's taken care of. I got what we were looking for."

"How'd you manage that?"

"It's too complicated to explain. But I called Gully in Oregon, and he couldn't be happier. I ran the whole batch through a shredder and fed the shreds to the incinerator. I'm at the airport myself. They're about to call my flight to Charlottesville."

"Uh . . ."

"Bye, Bernie."

The phone clicked in my ear. I held it out to Ray.

"Your turn," I said.

"Nothing," he said. "No Kassenmeier. Not at the Paddington."

While he was on the phone, I'd brought in my bargain table and begun the process of closing up. I could have waited for him to give me a hand, but I'd still be waiting. Cops, I've learned, tend to avoid heavy lifting.

"Maybe she checked out," I suggested.

"We know she checked out," he said, "because you generally do when somebody sticks a knife in your heart. But she didn't check out of the hotel because she never checked in in the first place. What makes you so sure she was there?"

"I was in her room."

"Last night?"

"And once before."

"But you never met her."

"No."

"An' you didn't know who she was."

"No."

"Then how'd you know it was her room?"

"Her suitcase was in the closet."

"An' all you gotta do is look at a suitcase an' you can tell whose it is?"

"I can if there's a tag on it with her name and address. But maybe she used another name when she registered."

"And had her own name on her luggage tag?" He frowned.

"She had ID in her purse in three different names. I tried 'em all on that fruit at the hotel just now."

"Which fruit would that be?"

"The lounge lizard with the Shinola hair. Carl Pittsburgh."

"Pillsbury."

"Whatever. He never heard of her, no matter what name she used."

"Then she used a fourth name. And she couldn't have checked out of the hotel, because the room was still occupied around four in the morning. She may have been at my place by then, but she must have planned on returning to the Paddington. Her suitcase was still in the closet and her clothes were still in the dresser drawers."

"Maybe I oughta go have a look," he said. "You wouldn't happen to remember the room number, would you?"

I picked up the phone and tried a number. No one answered, and I can't say I was surprised.

"Sure, I remember the number," I told Ray. "Want to trade?"

EIGHTEEN

It was getting on for nine that night by the time I got over to the Bum Rap. I didn't really expect to find anybody there—except, of course, for those people you always find there, and never find anywhere else. But Henry was there, his tan beret perched on his long egg-shaped head, his sensitive fingers stroking his silver beard. He had a drink in front of him, and wore an expression of perfect repose that suggested it wasn't his first.

"Your friend was here," he said. "Carolyn. A charming woman."

"Was she drinking Campari?"

"Is that what it was? She called it Lavoris. She ordered one for herself and a double scotch for you."

"And drank my scotch and left the Lavoris."

"You mean she's done that before? She had a second scotch, insisting that one was for you as well, and when the waitress brought it she told her to take back the Lavoris. 'I'm not drinking anything tonight,' she told her. 'Not even the mouthwash.' Then she bought me another drink and told me if I drank too much I should have something from the Uzbek restaurant. What do they have at the Uzbek restaurant?"

"Uzbek food," I said.

"Well, she seems to think highly of it. She finished her second drink—well, *your* second drink—and threw some money on the table and marched out of here. She said she had to meet somebody and straighten her out. Here's the waitress. What would you like to drink?"

"I suppose I should stick with scotch," I said, "since that's what I've had so far, even if I haven't had any of it for myself. Is that what you're drinking?"

"Actually," he said, "this is rye."

"Oh?"

"You got me to try it last night, and I ordered it today more or less automatically."

"And you liked it just as well today?"

"It grows on you."

"You think it might turn out to be your regular tipple?"

"It might at that."

I ordered rye for both of us, and raised mine when it came. "To books that change a person's life," I said, "for better or for worse. Why a clay factory, Henry?"

"Come again?"

"How'd the business get started in the first place? Do they dig a lot of clay around Peru, Indiana?"

"They used to," he said. "That's how the business got started. Then, after it had been established for many years, the clay deposits were exhausted."

"I know how they feel."

"So we bought the raw clay down south," he said, "and shipped it to Peru, where we did the processing and packaging."

"And shipped it all over America."

"All over the world. Wherever there are little children, and carpets for them to track it into."

I worked on my drink. We both fell silent for a long moment, and someone put a quarter in the jukebox and played a Patsy

Cline record. It wasn't "Faded Love," but it was still terrific. Neither of us said a word until Patsy was done.

Then I said, "Cole Porter was born in Peru, Indiana."

"He was for a fact."

"And there's no clay there."

"Not anymore. The deposits—"

"Are about as exhausted as they can get, because they were never there in the first place. There used to be considerable alluvial clay deposits quite a ways east of Peru, however, near a town called Huntington."

He thought this over. "You know quite a bit about clay," he said, "for someone who's not in the business himself."

"I went to a bookstore. Not my own, but the Barnes & Noble on Astor Place. I wanted to check the *Mobil Travel Guide*, and the only travel books I carry are the kind that warn you about the toothpick fish."

"What does a toothpick fish do?"

"It embeds itself in the olive fish," I said, "and the two of them float around inside a martini fish. Forget the toothpick fish, all right?"

"All right."

"There's a clay factory in Huntington," I said, "and according to the *Mobil Guide* they offer free tours of it. Anybody who wants can just show up at the front door and they'll give him a tour of the factory."

"There could be a clay factory in Huntington, too," he said. "Why not? It's less than fifty miles from Peru to Huntington."

"It looked farther than that on the map."

"Well, it's not. They're both on the same river, the Wabash. Couldn't there be clay deposits near both towns?"

"There could."

"And couldn't there just as easily be a clay factory in Peru as in Huntington?"

"I don't see why there couldn't," I said, "but the fact is there isn't. There's Cole Porter's birthplace, and there's the circus museum, and there's the locomotive monument commemorating the city's railroad history. But there's no clay factory."

"Maybe not," he said, "but there could be."

"Have you been to Peru, Henry?"

He nodded. "Pretty nice town. The locomotive monument's pretty impressive."

"How about Huntington?"

"It's nice, too. I took the clay factory tour."

"I figured you might have. Is some big conglomerate buying up the clay factory?"

"Jesus, I hope not."

"You just made that part up."

"Sure."

"And you moved the factory from Huntington to Peru . . ."

"Well, it sounds better," he said. "Huntington's so damned generic. As a name for a town, I mean. Peru, now, that has some zing to it."

"Zing," I said.

"Peru's a country. The Incas, the Andes, Machu Picchu. Exotic-sounding, and then you go from that to Indiana. Peru, Indiana. Plus there's the fact Cole Porter was born there, which not everybody knows, but still, it's a little extra flavoring. If a man's going to have a clay factory, why not float it forty or fifty miles down the Wabash to Peru?"

"Because it sounds better."

"Well, yes."

"I guess *Nobody's Baby* changed your life more than most people's."

"I guess it did."

"Gulliver Fairborn," I said.

"Ridiculous name."

"Distinctive, though. More so than Henry Walden. Ray called you Henry Clay, but he tends to get names wrong."

"Not an uncommon failing."

"I wonder if that was in your mind when you picked the

name. The story about the clay factory unconsciously led you to choose the name Henry. Or it could as easily have been the other way around."

"So many things could."

"Henry Walden. Henry for Henry David Thoreau? And that would lead straight to Walden Pond."

"Where, as far as I know, there are no alluvial clay deposits." He picked up his drink and contemplated it. "The goddam scholars pull that crap all the time," he said. "Pick apart every sentence a man writes, looking for hidden meanings. If they ever wrote anything themselves they'd know it doesn't work that way. It's hard enough to get any kind of meaning into the work, never mind a hidden one. What tipped you off? It couldn't have been the location of the clay factory."

I shook my head. "You looked familiar."

"To you?"

"Yes, but just vaguely, and I didn't think about it much. But you looked familiar to other people, too. In fact one of them thought she recognized you and said hello to you."

"That stunning black girl."

"Isis Gauthier. You were standing with your chin in your hand, and she greeted you, and you dropped your hand and turned and she apologized for her mistake. Because once she saw your beard she knew you weren't the man she thought you were."

"And that set you thinking?"

"No, it takes more than that to set me thinking. But Ray had the same reaction. He thought he recognized you, and then he decided he didn't. And that got me wondering why you'd looked familiar to me, and it was because I saw you the first time I walked into the lobby of the Paddington. You were sitting there reading a copy of *GQ*. It was you, except you didn't have the beard or the beret. You were wearing sunglasses, weren't you? And it seems to me you had a lot more hair."

"Henry Walden," he said. "Master of disguise."

"I guess it's no great trick to disguise a man nobody's ever seen in the first place, a camera-shy fellow who's elevated anonymity to the level of an art form. The beard-and-beret combination was perfect, because it made you a type, the distinguished older man taking the trouble to look artsy-bohemian. And the perfectly trimmed silver beard's so eye-catching that it's what registers the strongest when anybody looks at you. I saw the beard and I knew I'd never seen it before on anybody else, and that meant I hadn't seen you before. But I had."

"I suppose I wanted you to know," he said. "Otherwise I wouldn't have spent so goddam much time hanging around the bookshop."

"You even bought books."

"You didn't make much money off me."

"Not on the books you bought from me," I said. "I'm talking about the books you bought from Pericles Book Shop and sold to me. The books you said some woman brought in. I was shelving them, and something made me look on page 151 of one of them. That's where Stavros Vlachos pencils in his code cost. He'd marked that book, and you know what? He'd marked all of them."

"I didn't know about that."

"That's why he does it there, instead of on the flyleaf like everybody else. I called him, and he remembered the sale and described the man who'd picked out the books and paid in cash. He told me what you paid, too, and you took a major loss on the deal, didn't you?"

He smiled. "You told me how to make a small fortune in the book business, remember?" He shrugged. "I was lurking in your shop under false pretenses, and I guess I felt I owed you something."

"How'd you get there the first time? You must have followed her."

"Her," he said heavily. "I saw her at the hotel. I took a room there, that's how come I got to sit around the lobby reading a magazine. I blew into town wearing a wig and sunglasses and checked in under a phony name. Not Gulliver Fairborn, and not Henry Walden, either. And I was just settling in when that wretched child showed up."

"That's funny," I said. "She speaks well of you."

"Oh?"

"She told me how you wrote to her in Virginia, upset at the prospect of your letters to Landau being auctioned off. She was on a mission to retrieve those letters and return them to you. According to her, she's accomplished it."

"What do you mean?"

"Half of it, anyway. I had a phone call from her while I was with Ray. She got the letters. Then she called you in Oregon—"

"Oregon?"

"You get around, don't you? She called you, and I guess all you wanted now was assurance the letters were destroyed, because she fed them to a paper shredder and burned what it spat out. I wonder where she got it."

"Got what?"

"The paper shredder. Did she bring it with her from Charlottesville? Do you suppose they have them at Kinko's? And how much do they charge to use them?"

He sighed. "It would be nice," he said, "to run Tiny Alice through a shredder. Or a wood chipper, say. If she got her hands on those letters, then they haven't been destroyed. And God knows they're not going to be returned to me."

"She's going to sell them?"

"I don't know what she's going to do with them. Did she tell you about our liaison? The love affair of the century, starring Alice Cottrell as Lolita?"

"Briefly."

"I'll bet. What did she say?"

I gave him an abridged version and he shook his head throughout. He kept shaking his head, and when I'd finished he took a sip of rye and let out a long sigh. "I did write to her," he said. "There was something in that *New Yorker* piece of hers that struck a chord. And I received letter after letter in response. Her own situation was impossible, she wrote. She had to get away. Her father was molesting her almost daily and her mother was beating her with a wire coat hanger, that sort of thing. Eventually she wore me down. I told her she could come for a brief visit."

"And?"

"And the next thing I knew she had arrived, and she was harder to get rid of than a summer cold."

"I understand she stayed for three years."

"More like six months."

"Oh."

"She had her own bed, but she'd wait until I fell asleep and then crawl into mine."

"She said she was a virgin."

"Maybe she was. I certainly did nothing to change her status, much as she tried to get me interested. She had more tricks than a White House intern, but so what? She was a scrawny little runt of a kid, and I'm not wired that way." He shook his head. "She's probably hoping there's a letter or two where I confide in my agent about the exciting young woman who's just come into my life."

"What was in the letters, Henry?"

He smiled. " 'Henry.' I guess you might as well go on calling me that. What was in the letters? I don't even remember. Anthea was my agent, and it was a close author-agent relationship."

"And you wanted the letters back."

"I wanted them to disappear, to cease to exist."

"Why?"

"Because I don't want people pawing over them and finding little glimpses of me in them. It's the same reason I live my life the way I do."

"Yet people find you in everything you write."

"They find the part I'm willing to show," he said. He looked off into the distance. "It's fiction," he said, "and I get to make it the way I want it to be, with a clay factory relocated from Huntington to Peru, say, if that's where I want it to be. I don't care who reads my fiction, or what they think they find there."

"I see."

"Do you?" His eyes probed mine. "Say you're having a conversation with somebody. You don't mind if he can hear the sentences you're speaking, do you?"

"If I minded, I wouldn't say them in the first place."

"Exactly. But suppose, while he was listening to you, he was also reading your mind. Picking up the unvoiced thoughts buzzing around in your brain. How would you like that?"

"I get it."

"The fiction I write is my conversation with the world. My private life is private, an unspoken conversation with myself, and I don't want any mind-readers eavesdropping on it."

"So it doesn't matter who gets the letters," I said. "A collector or a scholar or a university library, or even Alice Cottrell. It's the same invasion of privacy wherever the letters wind up."

"Exactly."

"Isis Gauthier," I said.

"Don't know a thing about her, except that she's stunning and well-spoken."

"Karen Kassenmeier."

"Who's she?"

"A dead thief," I said. "How about the hotel clerks? The failed actor who dyes his hair, his name's Carl, and the myopic accountant-type, whose name I never got."

"I believe it's Owen. And there's at least one more clerk, a woman named Paula, with a big nose and a chin like Dick Tracy."

We were still at the Bum Rap and my companion was still

supporting the rye whiskey distillers of America, but I'd switched to Perrier.

"I didn't really get to know any of the clerks," he said. "Or anybody else at the hotel. I went there with some fantasy of talking Anthea into returning the letters, but I couldn't even work out how to approach her. I couldn't offer her the kind of money the letters would bring at auction, and I couldn't threaten her, either. What could I do, sue her? Charge her with unethical conduct?"

"Stab her," I suggested, "and take the letters by force."

"Not my style. As a matter of fact, action of any sort's not my style. And getting to the hotel was about as much action as I managed. Then I sat around the lobby, wearing a wig and sunglasses, and drinking enough rye whiskey to face the world each day."

"I understand it can do more than Milt or malt."

" 'To let us know it's not our fault,' " he finished. "Where on earth did you come up with that? Did I blurt it out the other night?"

"Alice quoted you."

"Christ," he said. "And she remembered after all these years?"

"You wrote it in the book you autographed for her."

He snorted. "I never gave her a book. She already had one, she quoted it back at me endlessly, and I certainly never signed or inscribed a book for her. But the line itself is one I used to say rather often." He took a breath. "Back to the Paddington. I sat around and I sipped, and that's about all I did."

"And you came to my store."

"Yes. Alice turned up, and I recognized her even if she didn't see through my disguise. And I followed her down here, and I found myself fascinated by your involvement in the process. You were a dealer in antiquarian books, but you also seemed to be something else. A burglar, as it turned out."

"Well," I said.

"And then other people kept coming to the shop, each of them with his own interest in the letters. So *I* kept coming, fascinated, wondering what would happen. You agreed to steal the letters, didn't you? For Alice?"

"For you," I said. "So that they could be returned to you."

"That was her story. And did she say I would pay you?"

"She said you didn't have much money."

"God, that's the truth, and the Hotel Paddington's getting most of it. So what were you going to get out of it?"

"Nothing," I said.

"Nothing? You were going to do it out of the goodness of your heart?"

"Well, see," I said, "I figured I owed you something. You wrote *Nobody's Baby*, and that book changed my life."

"Henry," I said. "Henry, I may have an idea."

"About the letters? About getting hold of them?"

"I have some ideas about that, but this is something else. I thought—"

"About Anthea's murder? And this other murder, the one that happened at your apartment?"

"More ideas," I allowed, "but what I thought—"

"About the rubies you mentioned? I still don't understand how the rubies fit into the whole thing."

"Neither do I, exactly, though I have an idea or two. But this is a little different. It's more about you being broke, and about a person being entitled to a decent return on his efforts. And I guess what it's mostly about is the whole notion of what does and doesn't constitute invasion of privacy."

"Oh."

"So let me run it by you," I said, "and you tell me what you think. . . ."

NINETEEN

Ray Kirschmann scratched his head. "I dunno," he said. "Them's the famous letters people are gettin' killed right an' left over? They don't look like much to me. He a fag?"

"I don't think so."

"You sure? 'Cause what kind of regular guy writes all his letters on purple paper? If that ain't fag stationery I don't know what is." He picked up a sheet. "Half the time he don't even fill more than half the page, you notice that? And the typing's terrible. Crossouts all over the place. A police officer turns in a report lookin' like this, believe me, he's gonna hear about it."

"Well," I said.

"An' look at this, will you? He can't spell for shit, an' what he says don't make sense. 'In high dudgeon, Gully.'"

"What's wrong with that, Ray?"

"He spelled 'dungeon' wrong. It don't have a *d* in it, at least it didn't last time I looked, an' he left the *n* out. And dungeons ain't high in the first place, Bern. They're down in the basement."

"I guess you're not impressed."

"I'm impressed that somebody's gonna pay decent money

for this crap," he said. "That impresses me a whole lot. An' I'll be impressed six ways from Sunday if you wind up sortin' out these two murders an' I get to close the case. I don't see how you're gonna do it."

"Maybe I'm not."

"Maybe you're not," he agreed, "but you got some record for pullin' rabbits outta hats. Just comin' up with these is pretty good rabbit-pullin'. You gave me a phone number, I checked the reverse directory an' gave you the address, an' the next thing you know you got a stack of purple letters in your hand. I bet you just rang the doorbell an' asked for them, didn't you?"

"I said I was working my way through college. When you say that, people do what they can to help out."

"Yeah, you oughta be sellin' magazine subscriptions. But you keep pullin' those rabbits, so I gotta give you the benefit of the doubt, whether it's reasonable or not. An' when it's over," he said, flicking the stack of purple paper, "when it's over, me an' you can cut the cake, an' that's right down the middle."

"Even Steven."

"Same as always. So I'll put the rest of it together for you, Bern. If you come up with a murderer, that's gravy. If you don't, then all we wind up with is money. An' what's so bad about that?"

"Here you go," Carolyn said. "All done. What do you think?"

"Looks good to me," I said, "and I can't thank you enough."

"No," she said, "as a matter of fact, you can't. Not nearly enough. Although it was almost fun, in a sort of harebrained way. 'The quick brown fox jumps over the lazy dog.' What's the point of that sentence, anyway? Besides the fact that it's got all twenty-six letters."

"I think that's it."

"It's also something of a slur on dogs, and I certainly never heard of it happening in real life. Foxes generally get the hell away from dogs as fast as they can. They don't waste time on gymnastics. Unless the fox was rabid."

" 'The rabid brown fox jumped over the lazy dog.' "

"I think I did it that way once, as a matter of fact. And there's another twenty-six-letter one, something about packing my bag with six liquor jugs, but that was a subject I wanted to avoid altogether. Anyway, Bern, I hope you're happy."

"Pleased," I said. "I won't be happy until this is over."

It was the day after my heart-to-heart with that little old clay-maker with the silver beard, and I was in the bookstore, although I hadn't bought or sold any books to speak of. I kept busy by training my cat, throwing crumpled-up balls of purple paper. I'm not sure cats can distinguish colors, or if they care. He pounced on them as eagerly as he ever had on white ones.

He'd gone far to his right for one when the phone rang. I picked it up and said, "Barnegat Books," and a voice I recognized said, "Bernie."

"Oh, hi, Alice. How was the trip to Charlottesville?"

"Uneventful," she said, and I could believe it. "Bernie, I just got some very disturbing news."

"Oh?"

"The file of correspondence," she said. "It was incomplete."

"There was a letter missing?"

"Half the file was missing, if my information is correct. I thought I had the whole thing, and I only had half of it."

"The half you shredded and burned."

"Yes, that's right. The other half . . . God, this is crazy."

"I'll say."

"I beg your pardon?"

"Nothing. You know, I wondered about the letters. I didn't have a chance to tell you yesterday, but . . ."

"But what?"

"Well, it just so happens I found a whole batch of letters. Typed, and on purple paper."

"You found them?"

"Uh-huh. See, there was a disturbance in my apartment the other night."

"I think I read something about that."

"In the Charlottesville paper? I'm surprised they covered it."

"Bernie—"

"A woman was killed," I went on, and crumpled a sheet of purple paper. "When I heard about it, the first thing I thought was that it was you."

"Me?"

"But then you called, and you can imagine how relieved I was to hear your voice. I'm relieved right now, as far as that goes."

"Bernie . . ."

"And I can hear you clear as a bell," I said. "It's a great connection. You'd think you were right here in the city."

"Bernie, these letters you found . . ."

"When I got back to my apartment—"

"You found them at your apartment?"

"No, if they'd been there the cops would have hauled them off, along with the dead woman and her purse and whatever else she had with her. But they missed one thing, a scrap of paper with my address written on it in a feminine handwriting."

"Your address."

"Uh-huh. And underneath it there was another address, and it was of an apartment on East Seventy-seventh Street."

"I see."

"Well, I didn't. But I went there, and, long story short . . ."

"You found the letters."

"Right. I wasn't looking for them, because you'd already told me how you'd managed to get hold of them and they were destroyed. So I figured these must be fakes, or maybe they were copies, but whatever they were they probably ought to be destroyed, too."

There was a pause. She was waiting for me to say more, and

I let her wait. Finally she said, her voice higher than before, "And you . . . destroyed them?"

"Not yet."

"Thank God."

"But I will as soon as I close up the store and . . . Did you just say 'Thank God'?"

"Bernie, don't destroy the letters."

"No?"

"I'd better see them."

"Why, Alice?"

"To authenticate them. To make sure they're the whole lot. I just think I should, that's all."

"I suppose I could bring them to Charlottesville," I said. "But it's a little hard for me to get away right now. But maybe sometime after the first of the month—"

"Don't come to Charlottesville."

"No? I suppose I could FedEx the letters, but—"

"I'll come back to New York."

"I'd hate for you to make a special trip."

"Bernie, I'm in New York right now."

Duhhh. "I thought it was an awfully clear connection," I said. "Well, that's perfect, Alice. You can come to the party."

There was a pause. Then, "What party?"

"My party," I said. "Seven-thirty this evening at the Hotel Paddington. You know where the Paddington is, don't you?"

"Bernie . . ."

"What am I thinking? Of course you do. Come to Room 611."

"Room 611?"

"Not Room 602, where Anthea Landau lived and died, and not Room 415 or 303 either. I don't suppose they'll stop you at the desk, but if they do, just tell them you're coming to Mr. Rhodenbarr's party."

Another pause, longer than before. Then she said, "Who's coming to this party, Bernie?"

"Ah," I said. "Well, we'll have to see, won't we?"

*   *   *

"So this is Paddington," Carolyn Kaiser said. "Nice-looking bear, Bern."

I bounced him on my knee. "He's a good fellow," I agreed.

"And this is *the* Paddington. I like the place, but your room's not much, is it?"

"The mice are hunchbacked," I said.

"The one upstairs is a lot nicer. Bigger, and it's a good thing, because it's crowded as it is. You couldn't fit all those people in here."

"They've started arriving?"

"They've arrived," she said. "I don't know what happened to fashionably late. They started showing up a little before seven, but Ray held everybody in the lobby until ten minutes after. Now they're all in 611, trying not to stare back at the King."

"Elvis on black velvet," I said. "It makes a strong statement."

"The eyes follow you around the room, Bern. Did you notice that?"

"That's great art for you."

"They even follow you," she said, "after you leave the room. I could feel them on me when I was out in the hallway, and coming down here on the elevator."

"Can you feel them now?"

"Nope."

"Well," I said, "let's go up and make sure they're still open."

TWENTY

Isis Gauthier's room was a lot nicer than mine. It was larger, of course, and better furnished, and the window afforded a nice view of Madison Square. Elvis gazed down from above the mantel, and the fireplace beneath that mantel, unlike mine, had escaped being bricked up. It was in fact a working fireplace, and it was working now. You couldn't really see the fire, it was out of sight behind an almost opaque fire screen, but you could smell woodsmoke in the air, even as you could hear the occasional crackle.

The room would have been warm enough without the fire. It had been cool earlier when I laid the fire, but it was warm now, and I don't know that it was the fire on the hearth that made the difference. Jam enough people into a room and they're going to be warm, especially if some of them are a little hot under the collar to begin with.

We had a full house, all right. Isis Gauthier was there, looking much as she had on our first meeting, her hair in cornrows and her clothes a Paddingtonian riot of primary colors. Marty Gilmartin was nearby, more quietly dressed in muted tweed. Alice Cottrell wore a business suit and looked businesslike, and so did a man I'd never seen before, a very tall and very thin fellow with a narrow nose. I recognized everybody else in the room, so I worked it out that he had to be Victor Harkness from Sotheby's, and I'd say he looked the part.

Gulliver Fairborn wasn't there, with or without his silver beard and tan beret, with or without his wig and sunglasses. But the World's Foremost Authority on the author and his works was present in the person of Lester Eddington. He had his shirt buttoned right for a change, but he still looked gawky and geeky, and no doubt would until *Glamour* magazine gave him a makeover.

Hilliard Moffett, the World's Foremost Collector, was present as well, his bulk stuffed into gray flannel trousers and a houndstooth jacket, both of which he'd outgrown. He sat forward in his chair, looking more like a bulldog than ever. *I have my checkbook*, he looked to be thinking, *so what are we waiting for?*

There were only so many places to sit, and a couple of people were standing. Carl Pillsbury, star of stage, screen, and hotel lobby, was leaning against a wall, and managing to look as though he leaned against walls all the time. His white silk shirt was spotless and his dark slacks were sharply creased, but his black shoes were due for a shine. I guess he'd used up all the shoe polish on his hair.

Ray Kirschmann was standing, too, in—big surprise—an ill-fitting blue suit, and there was another cop posted next to the door. I hadn't met him before and never did get his name, but it wasn't hard to tell he was a cop, given that he was in uniform. And Carolyn Kaiser was there, of course, along with her friend Erica Darby. They both looked so feminine it was hard to believe nobody had rushed to give them a seat.

I went over and took center stage, which put me right in front of the oriental screen, which in turn was in front of the fireplace. I could hear the fire, which gives you an idea how quiet the room was. You'd have thought these people would have plenty to say to each other, but nobody was saying a word. They were all looking at me and waiting for me to say something.

I wasn't sure how to begin. So I began the way I always do, given half a chance.

"I suppose you're wondering why I summoned you all here," I said. "It's hard to know where to begin, and I'm not sure that the answer is to begin at the beginning. In the beginning, a man named Gulliver Fairborn wrote a book called *Nobody's Baby*. If you feel it changed your life, well, you're not alone. A lot of people feel that way, including most of the ones in this room.

"It certainly changed Fairborn's life, for better and for worse. It enabled him to make a living doing the only thing he really cared about—writing. But it made it difficult if not impossible for him to lead the anonymous life he longed for. He stayed out of the limelight, he shunned correspondence and interviews, he never allowed himself to be photographed, and he lived under assumed names. Even so, his privacy got violated from time to time.

"And a major violation was looming on the horizon. A woman named Anthea Landau, a longtime resident here at the Paddington, had been Fairborn's first literary agent. Now she made arrangements to offer the letters he'd written her for sale to the highest bidder. Anything with Fairborn's signature on it is rare, and actual letters from him are right up there with hen's teeth."

"I have a couple of his letters," Hilliard Moffett said, "including one to a real estate agent in Hickory, North Carolina, inquiring about houses for rent. As far as literary correspondence is concerned, I don't think he's written anything of the sort in years. When he delivers a manuscript to his current agent, he just sends it by express mail with a false return address and no note enclosed." He sighed. "He's not an easy man to collect."

"So the letters to Landau would be valuable," I said. "Even priceless."

"Nothing's priceless," said Harkness from Sotheby's. He sounded as if he was quoting the firm's motto, and who am I to say he wasn't? "Except in the sense that the price could only be determined by discovering what the material would bring at public auction. I saw a sampling of the letters, and felt confident they would bring a substantial sum, certainly in the high five figures, and possibly well into six figures."

"The letters haven't been sold yet," I said, "so we don't know what they'll bring. But we do know that they were valuable enough and desirable enough to bring some interesting people all the way to New York. Some of them are here now, in this room. There's Hilliard Moffett, for instance, who already told you he has a couple of Gulliver Fairborn's letters. He wanted the others."

"I collect the man," he said.

"And Lester Eddington, who knows a lot about Fairborn."

"He's my life's work," Eddington told us. "Moffett, I'd be interested in seeing that letter to the North Carolina realtor. I know he spent two years in the Smoky Mountains, and it would be useful to pin it down."

"The letter's not for sale," Moffett snapped, and Eddington told him a copy would suit him just fine, or even a transcription. Moffett grunted in reply.

"And then there was Karen Kassenmeier," I said.

I looked around, and every face I saw looked puzzled, except for Ray, who knew the name, and the other cop, who didn't seem to be paying attention.

"Karen Kassenmeier was a thief," I said. "She wasn't a perfect thief, because she got caught a couple of times and went to prison for it, but she was pretty good at what she did, and she didn't shoplift at the dime store. She stole high-ticket items, and the word was that she stole them to order."

"And she came to New York, Bern?"

"From Kansas City," I said, "according to the tag on her suitcase. But the airlines didn't list a passenger named Kassenmeier on any of their Kansas City-to-New York flights in the past two weeks."

"So she came earlier," Moffett said, his jowls wagging.

"Or she used a false name," Isis Gauthier suggested. "Criminals use aliases all the time, don't they? Why, I met a man just the other day who called himself Peter Jeffries, or Jeffrey Peters. I can't remember which, and neither could he."

"It's not that easy to use an alias on an airplane," I said. "You have to show photo ID when you board, and you pretty much have to pay with a credit card or draw more attention from security than anyone would want, especially a thief. And if she used an alias, she wouldn't have gone on using a luggage tag with her own name on it."

"She might," Erica said. "Criminals are stupid. Everybody knows that. Otherwise they wouldn't get caught."

"Sometimes they have bad luck," I said, a little defensively. "Anyway, we know she used her own name because there's a record of the flight she took. Three days before Anthea Landau was killed, Karen R. Kassenmeier was on a United flight from Seattle to JFK."

"They got her name on the whatchacallit, the passenger manifest," Ray said. "An' there's prolly a record of her flyin' from Kansas City to Seattle, which'll turn up if we look for it. What did she go an' steal in Seattle, Bern? The dome off the stadium?"

"I don't think she stole anything, although she may have. My sense of Karen is that temptation was one of the things she found hard to resist. But she went to Seattle to meet with somebody who wanted those letters very badly. Somebody who lived in Seattle, say, or who drove in from someplace an hour or so away. Bellingham, for instance."

Hilliard Moffett thrust out his jaw. "That's ridiculous," he said. "Pure conjecture. Bellingham's a considerable distance from Seattle, a stone's throw from the Canadian border. And you say this woman is a thief, and comes from Kansas City. How would I know her?"

"You're a collector," I said. "When Landau was killed and I was arrested, you came straight to my shop. You as much as told me you'd buy the letters, even if they were stolen, even if I'd killed to get them. I didn't have the sense that you'd never made that kind of offer before."

"You've no proof for any of this."

"I don't suppose it would be hard to find," I said. "Kassen-meier probably stayed at a hotel in Seattle, and it wouldn't be hard to find out which one. If she made any telephone calls, there'll be a record. If she met a pudgy fellow with Brillo hair and a face like a bulldog—"

"I beg your pardon!"

"Make that a heavyset gentleman," I said smoothly, "with curly hair and an assertive jawline. If she met a fine-looking fellow like that, in the hotel lobby or at the coffee shop or in a bar in the neighborhood, somebody's sure to remember. But why fight it? Nobody's asking you to cop to conspiracy. You just let her know how important the letters were to you, and where they might be found."

"There's nothing illegal about that."

"Certainly not. And maybe you advanced her some money for expenses."

He thought about it. "That sounds as though it might be illegal," he said, "so I'm sure I did nothing of the sort. And if anybody did give her expense money, I'm sure it must have been cash, so there'd be no record of it."

"So she came to New York," I went on, "and she took a room here in the Paddington. But here's a curious thing. After she turned up dead, the police checked to see if she was registered here. And she wasn't."

"What's so curious about that?" Lester Eddington wondered. "It may be difficult to use a false name on an airplane, but how hard is it at a hotel?"

"Not that hard," Isis said. "Bernie did it, even if he did have a little trouble keeping it straight."

I brightened. We were back to first names!

"It's a nuisance," I said. "Unless you have a fake credit card to match your fake name, you have to pay cash and leave deposits. She still might have done that, just to keep her name away from the scene of the crime she was planning, but we know she didn't."

"How do we know that?"

"We know what room she occupied," I said. "Ray?"

"Actin' on information received," that worthy announced, "I made a check of the hotel records concernin' recent registrations in the room in question. The room was on the hotel's books as unoccupied for the entire past week."

"Wait a minute," Isis said. "If there was no record, how did you happen to know what room she was in?"

"Information received," Ray said.

"Received from whom?"

"From me," I said.

"And how did you happen to stumble on the information?"

"I happened to be in that room, and—"

"You happened to be in it."

"Twice," I said. "The first time I didn't know whose room it was, and I didn't really care. I was on my way from the fire escape to the hall, and all I wanted was to get out of the building altogether, because I'd just come from Anthea Landau's apartment."

"That's the dame who got killed," the uniformed cop said. "You were in her apartment?"

"That's right, and—"

"Am I missing something?" He turned to Ray. "Why isn't he in a cell?"

"He's out on bail," Ray said.

"He's out on bail and he's putting on a show for us?" Ray gave him a look, and he shrugged. "Hey," he said, "I just asked. I didn't mean nothing by it."

The room went quiet, and I let it stay that way for a moment. Then I said, "There was something I noticed in that room on my first pass through it. As a matter of fact, I found something in that room on my first visit, and, uh, I took it along with me."

"Ray," the uniformed cop said, "did you happen to read this guy his rights? Because he just admitted to a Class D felony." Ray gave him another look, and he opened his mouth and closed it.

"It was a piece of jewelry," I said, and glanced at Isis, who registered this information and nodded thoughtfully. "I subsequently found out that it had been the property of one of the hotel's permanent residents, and that she didn't live in the room I'd taken it from. Someone had evidently stolen it from her and put it in the room where I found it."

"That's interesting," Hilliard Moffett said, "if a bit hard to follow. But what does it have to do with two murders and the disappearance of the Fairborn-Landau correspondence?"

"I'll get to that."

"Well, I wish you'd speed it up," he said, a little testily. "And could someone open a window? Between the body heat and the fireplace, it's getting awfully warm in here."

I looked at Isis, and she turned to Marty, and he walked over to the window and opened it.

"What I did," I said, "was put two and two together, which is to say I put 602 and 303 together. The room numbers," I explained, when I saw some puzzled faces. "Landau was in 602, and someone entered her room and killed her, and made off with the letters from Fairborn. And 303 was the room where Karen Kassenmeier was living, and where I found the stolen jewelry. Of course I didn't know the jewelry was stolen when I, uh, picked it up, and I didn't know it was Kassenmeier's room until I went back to it a second time."

"You went back to it . . ."

"To find out whose room it was. I figured there had to be a

connection between the theft and homicide on the sixth floor and the missing jewels that turned up three floors below. Anyway, I went there and found a suitcase in the closet with Karen Kassenmeier's luggage tag on it. I might have found more, but I heard somebody at the door."

"Kassenmeier?"

"That's what I assumed," I said. "I didn't know her name yet, I hadn't had time to read the luggage tag, but I assumed the person at the door was the room's current occupant. It was the middle of the night, so it didn't figure to be a friend paying a call."

"It could have been another burglar," Isis suggested. "Like you."

"Not like me," I said, "because this burglar had a key. What I did was hide."

"In the closet?"

I looked at Alice, whose question it was, and who seemed surprised at having raised it. "Not the closet," I said. "And a good thing, because I have a feeling they looked in the closet."

" 'They'?"

I nodded at Isis. "There were two of them," I said. "A man and a woman. I was in the bathroom, behind the shower curtain, and I didn't get a look at either of them. I stayed where I was, and they used the bedroom and left."

"They used the bedroom?" Erica said. "How?"

"Well, not to sleep."

"They had sex in it," Carolyn said. "Right, Bern?"

"They did," I said, "and then they left."

"Kassenmeier and some guy," Ray Kirschmann said, and glanced at Carolyn. "Or maybe it wasn't a guy."

"It was," I said.

"What did you do, hear his voice?"

I shook my head. "He left the toilet seat up," I said.

"The pig," Isis said.

"I never really heard his voice," I went on, "except in an undertone, and I certainly didn't recognize it. But I recognized *her* voice, and it wasn't Kassenmeier's."

"How could you tell? You said you never met Kassenmeier."

"I never did," I said, "so if I recognized this voice—"

"Then you knew who the person was," Marty said. "The woman."

"Yes. She was the person who got me interested in Anthea Landau and her file folder full of letters. And now she turned up in a room where I'd found some stolen jewelry, and then she left and I checked the luggage tag and read the name Karen Kassenmeier. So my first thought was that this was her room, and that she and Kassenmeier were the same person, even if I had met her under another name. One of the names was an alias, and they were both the same person."

"Maybe you were right," Alice Cottrell said levelly. "How can you be sure they weren't the same person?"

Because Karen Kassenmeier's dead, I thought, *and you're sitting here trying to look innocent.* But what I said was, "I saw Karen Kassenmeier at the morgue, and she wasn't anyone I'd seen before. But even before then, I had the feeling the woman I overheard wasn't the same person whose room it was."

Ray said, "Why's that, Bern?"

"The bed was made." That put a puzzled look on every face in the room, so I explained. "The two visitors made love in Room 303, and then they left, and when I saw the bed it had been made up."

The man from Sotheby's, Victor Harkness, cleared his throat. "All that would seem to establish," he said, "is that they're neat."

"I couldn't see how they'd had time to make the bed," I said, "and it was very professionally made, as if the chambermaid had done it. In fact it looked the same as it had looked before they got there, and there was a reason for it. They'd never un-made the bed in the first place."

"You mean they . . ."

"Had sex on top of the bedspread," Isis Gauthier finished for him, and made a face. "That's even worse than leaving the toilet seat up."

"I suppose they were in a hurry," I said, "and they probably wanted to avoid leaving evidence of their visit to the room, evidence Karen Kassenmeier might notice when she returned to it. But they did leave some evidence, and it enabled me to determine who the man was."

"DNA," the uniformed cop said. "But how would you get samples for comparison, and when did you have time to run tests, and—"

"Not DNA," I said, "and that wasn't the kind of evidence that was left behind. Maybe they practiced safe sex."

"I hope so," Isis said. "Everybody ought to."

"Who was the man?" Carolyn asked. "And what was the evidence that pointed to him?"

"It was a black mark."

"On his record?" Victor Harkness suggested. "A blot on his copybook?"

"Don't forget his escutcheon," I said. "But this was a black mark on the bedspread. At the top, over the pillow. Right where his head would be." While they thought about it, I added, "Remember what I said earlier, about hearing a key in the lock? That was one of the reasons I assumed it was the room's occupant coming home. But it wasn't, yet it was somebody with a key. Of the two people in that room, I knew the woman, and I couldn't think of any reason she would have a key to another person's hotel room. But maybe the man had access to a key. A key to Room 303, say, or a master key, a key that would open any room in the hotel."

"A key to the door," Carolyn said, "and a black mark on the bedspread."

"A picture begins to emerge," I said. "A picture of a hotel employee. Someone who could put Karen Kassenmeier in a room without officially registering her. Someone who would thus know what room she was in, and would be able to get in and out with no trouble. Someone whose hair is as black as the telltale mark on the bedspread, and not because that's the way Mother Nature made it. Carl, you've been at the Paddington for years. Is there anyone you know of who fits that description?"

TWENTY-ONE

Everyone looked at Carl Pillsbury, and I have to hand it to him—he was as cool and as bold as a brass cucumber. He frowned in thought, took his chin between his thumb and forefinger, pursed his lips, and emitted a soundless whistle. "Someone who works for the Paddington and dyes his hair," he said. "Now a couple of years ago we had a fellow who wore a toupee, but that's not the same thing, is it? But I can't think of anyone who uses hair coloring."

"Then somebody musta turned you upside down," Ray said, "an' stuck your head in the inkwell, 'cause that mop of yours looks about as natural as Astroturf."

"Me?" he said, his eyes widening. "You actually think I color my hair?"

"Everybody knows you do, Carl," Isis said.

"Everybody?"

"Everybody in the tristate area."

"It's obvious?"

"I'm afraid so."

"I have a pretty good idea what happened," I said, "although there are a few gaps here and there. I know you're from the Midwest originally, and so was Karen Kassenmeier. The two of you aren't that far apart in age. I think you knew each other way back when, or else you met here in New York."

"That's ridiculous."

"I suppose it's possible she approached you cold when she got here," I said, "but that's hard to believe. She must have known you."

"That would explain something," Hilliard Moffett said. "I certainly never suggested anything criminal when I met that woman in Seattle—"

"Whether you did or not," Ray assured him, "we got bigger fish to fry. An' whatever you did you did in Seattle, an' this here's New York, an' I don't see no Seattle cops in this room. So just say whatever you got to say."

"All right," Moffett said, and stuck out his jaw. "She had an interesting reaction when I mentioned the name of the hotel. Until then she'd seemed noncommittal, lukewarm to the whole notion, but then she brightened. 'The Paddington,' she said. 'I wonder if he's still there.' I asked her what she meant, and she just shook her head and pressed me for more details."

"That proves nothing," Carl said. "She once knew someone who once worked or lived at the hotel. So what?"

"You'd be surprised what good police work can turn up," Ray said. "Once we take a good long look at both your backgrounds, don't you think we're gonna find somethin' puts you an' her in the same place at the same time? You could cop to it right now an' save everybody some trouble."

"Even if I knew her once," he said, "it still proves nothing."

"Here's what I think happened," I said. "She showed up at the hotel and told you she wanted to check in under a false name. You had an even better idea: she wouldn't register at all, and you'd stick her in a room. That would save her upwards of a hundred and fifty dollars a night."

"What makes you think I would do anything like that?"

"It's not exactly unheard-of in the business," I said. "It's a good way for a desk clerk to make a few dollars for himself. Like a bartender forgetting to charge for drinks, with the understanding that the customer will show his appreciation with an oversize tip. But Karen Kassenmeier was offering you more than the chance to knock down a few dollars on an off-the-books rental, wasn't she? She could afford to, because you could provide more than a place to stay. You could get her into Anthea Landau's room."

"Why would she need me for that? You already said the woman was a professional thief."

"She was a pro at liftin' things," Ray said, "but there's nothin' on her sheet shows she ever opened a door she didn't have the key to."

"You could get her in," I said. "That had to be worth something to her. You could find a spare key to Landau's room, or lend her your passkey. And you could tip her off as to when Landau was out of the hotel, so that she could get in and out without encountering the woman."

"We had a case like that a couple of years back," Ray said. "Big midtown hotel, an' we started gettin' reports of things missin' from the rooms. No signs of forced entry, and it was almost always cash that was taken, an' another thing—the victims were almost always Japanese businessmen."

"At some midtown hotels," Erica said, "that's just about all you find."

"This one got a lot of 'em," Ray said, "but it was still pretty clear they were gettin' targeted. An' we looked into it, an' we found it was worse than we figured, because a lot of the Japs was gettin' knocked off an' not botherin' to report it. We knew it had to be somebody on the inside, an' we narrowed it down to this one clerk, but we couldn't make a case."

"What happened?"

"You tell me. There was this one Jap we talked to. He got knocked off, an' he knew some other people who got knocked off, an' I guess maybe we let on which clerk we suspected." He looked off into the distance, recalling the moment. "Funny guy," he said. "Woulda made a hell of a poker player, 'cause he didn't show nothin' in his face. An' when he stretched out his arms you could see he had tattoos on his wrists, an' there was more tattooin' that showed when he loosened his tie an' unbuttoned his collar. An' one more thing that was pretty funny. I mean, he was the kind of guy that if he was an American you'd figure him to have a pinkie ring. But there was no way in hell he could manage that."

Somebody obligingly asked why.

"No place to put it," Ray said. "Both his pinkies were gone. Funny, huh?"

"Yakuza," I said. "Japanese gangsters. What happened to the clerk?"

"Well, must be he took the money an' ran," Ray said, "because he disappeared, an' nobody ever saw him again." He shrugged. "But just to be on the safe side, I stayed outta sushi bars for the next month or so."

Carl had the look of someone who'd eaten a little too much Uzbek food. I guess he didn't like stories where the hotel clerk disappeared.

"Maybe you'd worked a deal with her before," I said to Carl. "For one reason or another she knew you weren't an altar boy, and she made her pitch and you liked the sound of it. As a matter of fact, you had an idea of your own."

"I don't know what you're talking about."

"People say that all the time," I said, "and it's hardly ever true. You know exactly what I'm talking about. You told her about a woman living right here at the Paddington, a fellow member of the theatrical profession, who was wearing an extremely valuable necklace with matching earrings."

Isis's jaw dropped, and she wheeled on Carl. "You son of a bitch," she said. "I thought we were friends."

"Don't believe him, Isis."

"Tell me why I should believe you instead, Carl."

"For God's sake, he's a self-proclaimed burglar."

"Actually," Carolyn put in, "I think 'admitted' would be a better word for Bernie than 'self-proclaimed.' It's not as though he goes around making proclamations. If anything, he's a little ashamed of being a burglar."

"Then why doesn't he stop burgling?" Isis wanted to know.

"Just between us, I think it's an addiction."

"Has the man tried therapy? Or some sort of twelve-step program?"

"Nothing seems to work."

"But I live in hope," I said. "Carl, you and Isis were both actors. You were still jockeying a desk in a hotel lobby and she was getting work and wearing rubies. Maybe that gave you a resentment, or maybe you just saw some easy money. You gave your friend Karen a key and a room number and told her what to look for. And I guess she was a pro, all right, because she got out with the jewelry and otherwise left the place the way she'd found it."

"I didn't know anyone had been in there," Isis said. "I always thought burglars made a mess."

"Only the low-level ones," I said.

"All I knew was that the necklace and earrings were gone. I looked for them and they were gone. I thought I'd misplaced them, and then I started thinking the, uh, friend who gave them to me had taken them back. And finally I found out that you were a burglar, and I decided you must have taken them."

"Well, I did," I said, "but Kassenmeier took them first. She stuffed them in the back of her underwear drawer." I shook my head. "The cobbler's children go barefoot, all right. A pro like Kassenmeier goes and hides the rubies in the first place a burglar would look. I guess she was in a hurry to get back to work on the job that brought her here in the first place, the Fairborn-Landau letters."

I drew a breath. "Now here's where the timing gets a little tricky," I said. "The day of Landau's murder was the same day I first came to the Paddington. I checked in around lunchtime, collected my bear, and went to my room."

"You took a bear?" Isis said. "You came here to commit burglary and you wanted a bear in your room?"

"I don't see what one thing has to do with the other," I told her. "It's a cute bear. Point is, while I was checking in I picked up an envelope from the floor. It was there to be picked up because I had just that minute dropped it. It had Anthea Landau's name on it, and it was my way of finding out which room she was in. All I had to do was watch where Carl put it."

"I didn't put it anywhere," Carl said. "I left it on the desk."

"For the moment," I said. "But by the time I'd put my things away and went back downstairs, you'd tucked it in Landau's pigeonhole."

"How could you tell?" Lester Eddington asked. "There must have been a dozen envelopes in as many pigeonholes."

"This one was purple."

His eyes lit up at the news, as did Hilliard Moffett's. "Like every letter Gulliver Fairborn ever wrote," Moffett said.

"I wanted something distinctive," I said, "so I'd be able to spot it. And I had purple on the brain because I knew it was Fairborn's favorite color for correspondence. So I bought some purple paper and envelopes at a stationery store." I drew a folded sheet from my breast pocket, waved it around. "Like this," I said, and put it back. "I put a blank sheet in an envelope and left it at the desk, and it was in Anthea Landau's pigeonhole when I left my key on the way out. And when I picked up my key that evening, it was gone."

"She picked up her mail."

"That's what I assumed. But Anthea Landau had become increasingly reclusive in recent years. She rarely left the hotel, and didn't often leave her suite of rooms."

"I had to go to her room to examine the letters she was going to consign to us," Victor Harkness put in. " 'You'll have to come to the hotel,' she said, arranging to meet me in the lobby. When I called from the lobby she said, 'You'll have to come upstairs.' "

"So I hardly think she would come downstairs for her mail," I said. "I think she would have it brought up to her."

Everyone looked at Carl. "So?" he demanded. "What does that have to do with anything? When I was on my break I took her mail up and slid it under her door. There are a few guests who get that service. Miss Landau was one of them."

"So you slid it under her door."

"That's right."

"Is it? What if I told you someone saw you knocking on her door?"

"I slid the mail under her door. If I knocked, it was just to let her know I'd brought her mail. I did that sometimes."

"And walked away without waiting for the door to be opened."

"Yes."

"What if I told you someone saw you wait until she opened the door?"

"Nobody saw me." He colored. "Look, who can tell one day from the next? Maybe she opened the door. She sometimes did, if she was standing right next to it when I knocked. What difference does it make?"

"I'm guessing now," I said, "but I think my guess is pretty close to the truth. I know you knocked and I'm sure she let you in, and then I think you did something to make sure she'd sleep soundly. Was she drinking a cup of tea? Did you put something in her tea?"

"That's ridiculous."

"It may not have been tea," I said, "and she may not have been drinking it right there in front of you, whatever it was. But one way or another you slipped her some kind of a mickey."

"If he did," Ray said, "there'll be traces somewhere. In the cup if she didn't wash it, an' in her if she drank it." Marty asked if they'd found anything. "No," Ray said, "on account of we didn't look. When a woman's been hit over the head an' stabbed to death, you don't generally order a toxicology scan to find out if she took poison. But I can order it now, an' if she did we'll know about it."

"It wasn't poison," Carl said. "My God, I wouldn't poison anybody."

"It was just something to help her sleep."

"She hadn't been sleeping well," he said, "and she never left those rooms, and I knew Karen was getting tired of waiting. She'd go in while Miss Landau was asleep, and if she wasn't sleeping soundly—well, I was afraid of what might happen."

"With good cause, as it turned out."

"Oh, God," Carl said. "I probably shouldn't say any more. I've said too much already."

"Well, you got the right to remain silent," Ray said smoothly, and ran the whole Miranda warning past him. "An' that goes for everybody in this room," he added. "All of you's got the right to remain silent, an' all the rest I just read. But you want my opinion, you'd be crazy to quit talkin' now."

"I would?"

"You broke some laws," he said, "an' no question you were an accessory, but if you help us clear the case an' tie the whole thing to Kasimir—"

"Kassenmeier," I said.

"Whatever. You do that, you're in good shape. And she's dead as a doorknob, so what's the harm in that?"

"She killed Miss Landau," Carl said. "I mean, you already know that, don't you?"

"Why don't you tell us what happened?"

"There's not much to tell. I gave the drug time to work, and then I called Miss Landau. She didn't answer her phone, so I assumed she was sleeping soundly. Then I called Karen in her room and told her to come down and pick up a key. She did, and went upstairs with it. The next thing I knew, Miss Landau was dead."

"What happened?"

"All I know is what Karen told me. She went in and Miss

Landau woke up and confronted her. Karen stabbed her and got away without being seen."

"Aren't you leaving something out?"

"I don't think so."

"When they found Kassenmeier in my apartment," I said, "she'd been shot in the shoulder, and it didn't happen on West End Avenue, either, because the wound had been cleaned and dressed and was already starting to heal. Landau shot her, didn't she?"

"Oh, that's right," he said. "I forgot that part."

"Well, a minor detail like that could slip a person's mind easily enough. She called you, didn't she? From Landau's apartment, saying she'd just taken a bullet in the shoulder. You told her to stay where she was, and you went upstairs and took her to your own room, the one you've had since you moved into the Paddington twenty-odd years ago. It was closer than the room you'd put Kassenmeier in, and you had first-aid supplies there, tape and gauze pads and antiseptic. You bandaged her up and left her there to rest. And you went back to Landau's apartment."

"Why would I do that?"

"To see if there was anything you could do for the woman. You wouldn't just leave her there, would you?"

"No, of course not," he agreed. "But there wasn't anything I could do for her, so I—"

"Sure there was."

"I beg your pardon?"

"It's funny about the gunshot," I said. "I smelled gunpowder when I was in Landau's place. I didn't recognize it at first, but then I did, and that's how I found out I was sharing space with a dead woman. I assumed she'd been shot, and I was puzzled when I learned later that she'd been hit over the head and stabbed. But of course it makes sense when you realize that Landau was the one who did the shooting. She surprised a burglar in her room and shot her."

I paused, feeling the way Carl did when he heard how the Japanese gangster had made a hotel clerk disappear. I don't like stories where somebody shoots a burglar.

"And Karen stabbed her," I went on. "That's interesting, when you stop to think about it. Somebody pulls a gun on you and takes a shot. It hits you in the shoulder. You want to make her stop shooting, so what do you do? You pull a knife and stab her."

"It sounds like self-defense," Ray said, "but it ain't, not when you're busy committin' a felony at the time. It's murder, no question about it."

"It's also unlikely. Someone's shooting you so you go for a knife?"

"Karen carried a knife," Carl said. "It had gotten her in trouble in the past."

"I know," I said, "but she never stabbed anybody while she was working. She saved it for her personal life. So she wouldn't have been creeping around Landau's apartment with a switchblade in her hand, would she? It'd be in her purse, which she probably set down the minute she walked into the room, if she even brought it with her in the first place, which seems doubtful. Even if the purse was on her person when Landau started popping caps, do you suppose she'd start rooting around in it, looking for her trusty knife?"

"What's the difference?" Isis wanted to know. "One way or another this Kassenmeier woman stabbed Anthea, didn't she?"

I shook my head. "Nope," I said. "Not a chance."

"But—"

"She hit her over the head," I said. "She picked up something with a little heft to it and swatted the old lady. It wouldn't take much of a blow to knock her out."

"And then she stabbed her," Carl said.

"Why?"

"To make sure, I suppose."

"To make sure she'd wind up facing homicide charges? All

she wanted to do was get out of there and get her shoulder fixed. Landau was out cold, and was no danger to Kassenmeier. All she needed to do was scoop up the Fairborn file and go home."

"Who else would have a reason to kill her?"

"Suppose she opened her eyes again after Kassenmeier got out of there. Maybe she picked up the phone and called the front desk. Or maybe she woke up after you'd already returned to the crime scene, Carl. To tidy up, or to pick up the Fairborn file if Kassenmeier hadn't already grabbed it. Or maybe just to see what else you could steal."

"That's ridiculous."

"If you went through Kassenmeier's purse and brought the knife along, that's premeditation. If Kassenmeier left the purse behind, and you went back for it, and then Landau woke up and you pulled the knife purely on impulse, well, you might have better luck with that story."

The best pause I ever heard was Jack Benny's, when a holdup man said, "Your money or your life." Carl was almost as eloquent, standing there with his mouth hanging open.

"Well," I said, "that's saying a mouthful. But there's no rush. You'll have plenty of time to work up a story."

"Wait," he said. "I shouldn't be saying anything, but I shouldn't have said anything from the beginning, should I? For God's sake, I've been on *Law & Order*. I know how you people work."

"That just about makes you law enforcement personnel," Ray said. "Which is why we're givin' you a chance to go on record."

Carl rolled his eyes. "Spare me," he said. "I know this is a trick, and I don't care. I'll tell you the truth, if only to get it clear in my own mind. It doesn't matter. Nobody's going to believe me."

"I have a feeling you're right about that," I said, "but let's hear it."

"It was the way you said," he told us. "Up to the time when I was on the desk and Karen called from Miss Landau's room.

She was hysterical, and all I could make out was that she'd been shot. I left the desk unattended and raced up there, and found her bleeding from a shoulder wound and Miss Landau unconscious on the floor. She was alive, though. One side of her face was bruised, I guess where Karen hit her with the Scotch tape."

"She hit her with Scotch tape?"

"Miss Landau kept it in a heavy brass desktop dispenser, and that's what Karen hit her with. She just picked it up and threw it, and it evidently hit Miss Landau and knocked her cold. It weighed a ton."

"I know the thing he's talkin' about," Ray confirmed. "We found it on the desk in the front room."

"That's where I put it," Carl said, "when I was tidying up. Maybe that's where Karen found it. Does it matter?"

"Not to me it don't," Ray said, "and not to Kasimir either, bein' as nothin' does at this point. Keep talkin'."

"I moved Miss Landau," he said. "I know you're not supposed to, but I couldn't just leave her lying on the floor like that. She was a little old lady, you know, and light as a feather. I picked her up and put her in the bed."

"Which is where she was when I got there," I said, "but there was a difference. She was dead."

"I know," he said. "She was dead when I went back. First I went to my room, with Karen, who was at least able to walk. I had first-aid supplies in my room, as you guessed, and I cleaned the wound and put on a sterile dressing. I had three weeks' work a few years ago on *General Hospital*, so I'm not entirely without experience in such matters. I don't know if any of you watch the show, but I was the lupus patient who wasn't expected to live. I surprised everybody."

"Not for the last time," I said. "I suppose you put her to bed, too."

"Of course. And then I rushed back down to the lobby, just to make sure prospective guests weren't rushing the desk. It was quiet, so I went right back to the sixth floor and into Miss Landau's apartment. I didn't even look at her right away, because I knew I'd have to call an ambulance and get her looked at, and before I did that I had to straighten up the place. I wiped off the Scotch tape dispenser and put it back on the desk, I closed the drawers Karen had left open, I found the gun where it had fallen and found Karen's purse where she'd put it down. And, incidentally, she did take it with her when she entered the apartment, so that she could stuff the letters in it before she left. It was a big purse, large enough to accommodate a thick nine-by-twelve envelope."

"Sounds like the one she had with her when she got killed," Ray said. "She didn't have no thick envelopes in there, but there was a handy little gun, and it coulda been the one she got shot with."

"I did everything I could think of," Carl said, "and then I went for a look at Miss Landau, and she was in the bed, right where I'd left her. And she was dead, stabbed in the heart with Karen's knife."

"How do you know it was Kassenmeier's knife?"

"Because it was the kind she carried, a folding stiletto with mother-of-pearl sides and a four-inch blade. And it was sticking out of her chest."

"I didn't see a knife," I said. "Of course the bedclothes might have covered it."

"There was no knife stickin' out of her when we got to the scene," Ray said.

"I took the knife away," Carl said. "I know you're not supposed to do that, but—"

"For Chrissake," the uniformed cop said, "you're not supposed to do *any* of the shit you did."

"I know."

"Like taking the knife's the least of it."

"I know."

"Well, go on," the cop said. "I didn't mean to interrupt. Go on. You took the knife."

"And washed the blood off it," he said, "although I know there would have been traces that would have showed up under forensic examination. I know that."

"Well, sure," Ray said. "You were on *Law & Order.*"

"But it still seemed a worthwhile precaution."

"After you took the knife—"

"I put it back in her purse."

"Along with the gun," I said.

"Well, yes."

"What else was in there?"

"In the purse?"

"Right. There wasn't a thick nine-by-twelve manila envelope by any chance, was there?" I shrugged. "I mean, it's obvious, isn't it? How else would you have been so sure it would fit?"

"I looked for the envelope," he said, "because she'd told me that she had had a chance to find the letters before Miss Landau confronted her. But I couldn't find them, and I thought whoever had used the knife had found the letters at the same time. But the purse was heavier than it should have been, and I looked again, and there was a zippered section tucked away behind a flap. And that's where the envelope full of letters was."

"So you didn't have to go through the files."

"No. I got in and out as quickly as I could."

"And what did you do with the letters?"

"I took the purse back to my room," he said, "where Karen was resting. I didn't know what to say because I didn't know what had happened. Who stabbed Miss Landau? I was sure she was alive the first time I saw her, and I know she was dead when I went back, and I swear to God it wasn't me who stabbed her." He stopped himself, frowned. "I," he said. "It wasn't I who stabbed her."

"Well, it wasn't me either," Ray told him. "So keep talkin'."

"You took the purse back to the room," I said.

"Yes."

"With the knife still in it."

"Yes."

"And the gun, of course. Landau's gun."

"Yes."

"And what about the letters?"

"What about them?"

"What did you do with them? Because you couldn't have given them to Kassenmeier or she'd have been out of there like a shot, mission accomplished. Where did you stash them, Carl?"

He sighed. "In the other room."

"Which room? Room 303?"

"Yes. Karen was in my room, and I thought . . . well, I don't know what I thought. I didn't really have time to think."

"And you stashed them there before you went back to your room."

"Well, on my way. It wasn't on my way, not literally, but . . ."

"I get the picture. I'll be a son of a bitch. You must have been tucking them away while Isis and I were getting on a first-name basis in the sixth-floor corridor. You got the letters out of Landau's room a few minutes before I let myself into it, and then you stashed them three floors below just before I came into that room off the fire escape. Why couldn't you have put that envelope in the underwear drawer? Look what a lot of trouble you'd have saved me."

"I . . ."

"Where did you put them, anyway?"

"On a shelf in the closet."

"And then you went back and told Karen where you'd put them."

"Uh . . ."

"You didn't, did you?"

"Not exactly."

"What did you tell her?"

"That Miss Landau was dead. I didn't mention the knife, though, so I guess she assumed she'd died from getting hit with the Scotch tape dispenser."

"Hell of a way to go," Carolyn said.

"So she thought she'd killed her."

"I suppose she did, but then when the story came out on the TV news, she knew Miss Landau had been stabbed."

"And then she must have thought *you* did it."

"I told her I didn't, that whoever got the letters must have found her knife at the same time, and used it on Miss Landau. I don't know if she believed me."

"So you didn't tell her where you'd hidden the letters."

"No. I thought she might find them when she went back to her room, but she didn't. What she did find was that her rubies were missing."

"My rubies," Isis said.

"Well, yes, but by this time Karen thought of them as her rubies, and they were gone. I didn't know what to think when she told me that. Was she lying, so that she wouldn't have to share the proceeds with me? And if not, what had happened to them?"

"In the meantime," I said, "I'd been arrested. And you knew I was a burglar."

"But what would you be doing in Room 303? I decided it must have been the same person who stabbed Miss Landau."

"Well, a person who'd stick a knife in a little old lady probably wouldn't draw the line at jewel theft," I said. "But let's focus on that person and forget the rubies for a minute. Who do you figure it was?"

"I have no idea."

"You know," I said, "that's hard for me to believe. I think you have a pretty good idea."

He lowered his eyes. "I've thought about it," he admitted.

"No kidding."

"And I honestly don't know."

"But you honestly do have an idea."

"No, I—"

"That person's the reason you didn't bring the letters back to your own room," I said. "It's the reason you didn't tell your old buddy Karen that the envelope she swiped was on a shelf in her own closet. You were working an angle of your own, weren't you?"

"I wasn't double-crossing Karen," he said. "I was planning on giving her the letters."

"When?"

"In another day or two. After I'd had a chance to—"

"To have copies made," I said.

"Yes."

"Because a certain person wanted copies," I said, "and made you an offer for them you really didn't want to refuse."

"I never even met this man," Lester Eddington asserted. "I need copies of all of Gulliver Fairborn's correspondence, but I'm in no position to offer very much money, and I certainly wouldn't be a party to a felony."

"Relax," I said. "It wasn't you."

"But who else would want copies? Moffett here is a collector. He wanted the originals, and anyway he was the one who brought in Karen Kassenmeier in the first place. Sotheby's already had the right to auction the letters."

"And I just wanted to give them back to the poor guy who wrote them," I said. "But there was somebody else, somebody who wanted to write a book of her own. That's why she recruited me, but she didn't want to leave anything to chance, and she redoubled her efforts after I tried for the letters and came up empty. Well, Carl? Is she the one you think killed Anthea Landau?"

Carl didn't say anything.

"Cat's got his tongue," I said, and turned to look long and hard at Alice Cottrell. "Well? Did you kill her?"

TWENTY-TWO

Bernie," she said, as if she'd just been stabbed in the heart herself, and by someone as dear to her as Brutus was to Caesar. "Bernie, I can't believe you think I'm capable of murder."

"You've been capable of enough other things," I said. "You got me into this mess in the first place, making up a story about wanting to retrieve the letters for Gulliver Fairborn out of kindness. That way you'd get the letters without laying out a cent."

"But that's the truth," she said. "That's why I wanted them."

"Because Fairborn wrote to you at your home in Charlottesville."

"I may have told a few fibs."

"Fibs?"

"White lies, then. I don't live in Charlottesville and Gully didn't write to me. But I knew how upset he must be, and I knew what a favor it would be to him if those letters could cease to exist. And I had passed your bookstore several times, and knew that its proprietor had a sideline career as a burglar—"

"What he is, he's a burglar," Ray put in, "with a sideline sellin' books."

"—so I thought I could persuade you to do something nice for a great writer."

"And a mediocre one, too."

"I beg your pardon?"

"I get *Publishers Weekly* at the shop," I said. "I don't usually have time to read it, and there's not much in there for a used-book dealer, but I finally got around to going through some back issues, and guess who's got a proposal making the rounds? I forget who your agent is, but it's not Anthea Landau. You're going to be writing a memoir, aren't you? All about your affair with Gulliver Fairborn."

"That's not all it's about," she said. "I've led an interesting life, and people will be interested in reading about me."

"But just in case they aren't, a little dirt on Fairborn wouldn't hurt. You gave me a sample of what you were going to be writing, telling me more than I really wanted to know about one of my literary heroes. As it turned out, it was more than you knew."

"I'm a fiction writer," she said. "I suppose it's natural for me to improve on the truth a little."

"You weren't going to return his letters, were you?"

"Eventually I might have. Or I might have destroyed them. Or I might have sold them to you, Mr. Moffett, or passed them on to you, Mr. Harkness. And I might have even run off an extra set of copies for you, Mr. Eddington. But what does it matter what I might have done? I didn't get the letters."

"You really wanted them, though. Even before I went into the Paddington, you got close to Carl and made him a similar offer. But instead of appealing to his better nature and making it sound like an act of charity, you put your body on the line."

"That's not a nice way to put it."

"You didn't have much to offer in the way of money," I said, "but you're sexy, and Carl was vulnerable. And you made it clear it wouldn't cost him anything to get the letters for you. You'd copy them and return the originals, and he could do as he pleased with them."

"Carl gets around," Carolyn said. "He's sleeping with Karen, and he still can't resist Alice."

"Karen and I were never lovers," Carl said.

"Just good friends," Isis said. "You got her to sleep in your own bed and you weren't even tempted?"

"I always figured Carl was a little light on his feet," Ray said. "But then why would he go for Alice here?"

Carl rolled his eyes. "If a man has manners," he said, "or a bearing that's in any way theatrical, people jump to the conclusion that he's gay. It so happens I'm not. But some of my best friends are, and Karen was one of them. Not a best friend, exactly, but a gay woman."

"So you weren't interested in her sexually."

"No."

"But you were interested in Alice."

"She's an attractive woman," he said, "and seductive, and very persuasive. She offered me two thousand dollars, which I'm still waiting for, incidentally—"

"Don't hold your breath," Alice said.

"—and she indicated that we'd celebrate success in a manner I'd find very gratifying. The morning after Miss Landau was killed, she called to find out what had happened. And I told her I had the letters."

I turned to Alice. "I wondered why I didn't hear from you," I said. "Everybody else called or dropped in, but you stayed away. If nothing else, I figured you'd want to know whether or not I had the letters. But you already knew."

"All that's true," she said. "But I didn't kill the Landau woman. I wasn't even there that night."

"You could have been," I said. "You could have sashayed right past the desk while Carl was running around breaking laws and betraying old friends."

"But why would I kill Anthea Landau?"

"She was an agent," I said. "Didn't you say she turned you down once? Maybe you were harboring a resentment."

"You can't believe that."

"Not for a moment," I said. "Because how would you have known to look for a knife in Karen Kassenmeier's purse? Besides, the person who killed Landau is almost certainly the same person who killed Kassenmeier. The killer probably used the same knife. And that pretty much lets you out, because Kassenmeier was up at my apartment getting stabbed to death at just about the same time that you were knocking off a quickie with Carl in Room 303."

"While you were hiding behind the shower curtain," she said, and the trace of a smile appeared on her lips. "Just like Polonius, except you didn't get stabbed. And you recognized my voice, Bernie. That's sweet."

"You got dressed in a hurry," I said. "You didn't waste time unmaking the bed, so you didn't have to waste more time making it. Carl got the letters from the shelf where he'd stashed them, and he gave them to you and you got out of there. Now I can't be dead certain you wouldn't have had time to cab up to my place, meet Karen, and stick a knife in her, but why the hell would you want to? You already had the letters and you were home free."

"That's right."

"And what did you care about her, anyway? And how would you know about the knife in her purse?"

"Carl could have mentioned the knife," Erica Darby said. "Who knows what kind of pillow talk they had?"

"But I didn't," Carl said. "I never even mentioned Karen's name. We were in Karen's room when we, uh, made love, because that's where the letters were. But I didn't tell Alice whose room it was."

"You told me it belonged to a permanent resident who was out on the Coast doing a guest shot in a sitcom," she said, "so you knew the letters would be safe there, and we wouldn't be disturbed."

"Let's get back to Karen Kassenmeier," I said. "What did you tell her about the letters?"

"I didn't tell her anything. She told me they were missing from her purse, and I told her the same person must have taken them as killed Miss Landau."

"This was after she realized she hadn't done it herself with the Scotch tape dispenser."

"Right."

"And what did she decide to do?"

"Well, she decided the letters were gone," he said, "and there was no sense crying over spilled milk, or spilled blood, either. At least she had the rubies. Then she went to her room and the rubies were gone, and I just couldn't believe it. She thought maybe I took them, because who else knew they were there? But I hadn't known where they were, and I couldn't say if they'd been there when I was in the room leaving the letters in the closet. But I didn't say that, because she didn't know about the letters in the closet."

"No."

"And then she decided you had them."

"The letters?"

"No, the rubies. You were a burglar, she said, and the rubies were stolen from a locked hotel room, so of course you were the logical suspect. Anyway, she heard that you had them. I don't know who told her."

"It wasn't me," Isis said. "I never met the woman, and I wouldn't have said anything to her anyway."

"And she knew where you lived," Carl went on. "She told me she was going to make one last try for the rubies, and if that didn't work she'd catch the first flight she could get to Kansas City. It was late at night when she told me all this, and she went out, and I immediately called Alice and we went to her room, because I knew she'd be away for at least a couple of hours."

"And she never came back," I said. "Somebody met her at my apartment, probably after luring her there in the first place. Somebody who could open the door for her, because she couldn't do it herself. Karen was a pretty good thief, but she didn't have burglar skills."

"Who did?" Ray wondered. "There's a lot of doors openin' an' closin' in this story, Bern, but so far the only person with burglar skills is you. An' you wouldn't need 'em to open your own door."

"That's true," I agreed. "And neither would the person who killed Karen Kassenmeier."

"You know who it is?"

"Yes," I said. "I know who it is."

"Well, you'd better tell us," Carolyn piped up, "because I for one haven't got a goddam clue. I followed most of what you've said so far, Bern, although it's pretty complicated. But I can't see how anybody could have done it. Maybe Karen Kassenmeier killed Anthea Landau after all, and when she got to your apartment she had a fit of remorse and stabbed herself."

"And ate the knife?"

"What, it was gone? So somebody else came along before the body was discovered and thought it'd be just the thing for peeling apples. All right, somebody murdered her. But it couldn't have been anybody in this room, and I can't think of anybody else it could be, so—"

"It was somebody in this room," I said. "And I wish I didn't have to do this, Carolyn, but what choice have I got? It was the woman sitting next to you. It was Erica."

"A longstanding resentment," I said. "Maybe they were lovers whose affair ended badly. Maybe they both went after the same woman. Whatever the cause, Erica Darby hated Karen Kassenmeier, and she nursed that hatred over the years."

Erica looked at me. Her expression was hard to read, and she hadn't said a word since I'd named her as the killer. Maybe she remembered that Ray had Mirandized everybody in the room, albeit in a casual manner. Maybe she just didn't have anything to contribute.

"Erica wanted revenge," I went on, "and she was evidently familiar with the Sicilian maxim about revenge being a dish that's best eaten cold, because she let things cool off so completely that Kassenmeier didn't even know the resentment was still alive. She got in touch when she hit town, and she let her old friend know what brought her to town and where she was staying.

"And Erica came to the hotel the night Karen was going to make her move. I don't know how much she'd planned and how much she improvised on the spot, but she must have gotten to the lobby while Carl was away from the desk. She already knew what room Karen was going to hit, so all she had to do was grab a key from the board and go upstairs with it. She got to the sixth floor while Carl was downstairs demonstrating his medical training, and she went into Landau's room and found the scene as the two of them had left it—Landau in bed unconscious, a gun on the floor, and Karen's purse on a chair.

"Maybe Landau woke up and started making a fuss, and Erica had to shut her up. But I don't think the old lady ever opened her eyes. I think Erica saw her lying there, and she remembered the knife her old friend always carried and got it from the purse, wrapping her hand in a handkerchief so only Karen's prints would be on it. And then she stuck it in Landau's chest and left it there.

"Then she left the hotel and called the police. They were already on their way when Carl called them after Isis reported her encounter with me in the hallway. That's how they got there so fast. Erica figured that would do it—Karen Kassenmeier, a known thief who was handy with a knife, was right there on the premises, and her knife with her prints on it was planted in the victim's chest, and her purse was a few yards away. The cops would be on Kassenmeier like buzzards on roadkill, and if she got a good lawyer she might see the sidewalk again in twenty years or so. If she got a bad one she could figure on life without parole, or a needle in her arm.

"What you didn't figure on," I said to Erica, "was that Carl would get to the room before the cops did. By the time they got there, there was no knife in the corpse, no purse on the chair, and nothing that would lead anybody to your old friend Karen. But she wasn't exactly sitting pretty, either. She didn't have the letters that had brought her to New York in the first place, and the jewelry she'd picked up along the way had somehow gotten out of her grasp.

"But that wasn't enough for you. You told her Carolyn had let something slip—you knew I had the rubies, and I might even have the letters, too. And you knew exactly where in my apartment I had hidden them.

"You had her wait at your apartment. You went out for dinner, went home to Carolyn's place instead of your own, and slipped out as soon as Carolyn was sound asleep. Then you dropped by your place to pick up Kassenmeier and the two of you went up to Seventy-first and West End. Once the two of you were inside my apartment, you just waited for your opportunity—first to get the knife from her handbag, then to use it on her the way you'd used it on Anthea Landau. This time your victim was conscious, so it wasn't quite as easy. The two of you made enough noise to get my neighbor Mrs. Hesch's attention, but not enough to make her call the cops right away. Then you let yourself out and went home."

"How'd they get in?" It was the uniformed cop, and he seemed interested now. "You said Kassenmeier didn't have burglar's tools. Is this dame a burglar?"

"Not that I know of."

"So how'd she get in?"

"She had a key," I said. "Carolyn's my best friend. We have keys to each other's apartment and place of business. She used her bookstore key the other day to feed my cat."

"And she gave the key to this dame?"

"The dame's name is Erica," I said. "Erica Darby, and you'll want to get it right when you write up the arrest for double homicide. She took Carolyn out for a night on the town, and for once she didn't show any concern about the way Carolyn was drinking. In fact she encouraged it."

"It was supposed to be a celebration," Carolyn said.

"Earlier, she'd shown some uncharacteristic interest in me. Asked you where I lived, and other questions about me. So she knew the address, and she knew you had keys, and she made sure you had enough to drink and enough, uh . . ."

"Stimulation," Carolyn supplied. "And I passed out and slept like I'd been clubbed. Then what? How did she know where to find the keys?"

"Where do you keep them?"

"On a hook on the bulletin board next to the front door."

"And what does the little tag on the key ring say?"

"Bernie's Keys," she said. "I guess they wouldn't be too hard to find."

"What about the doorman?" the cop demanded. "You got twenty-four-hour doorman service in your building, don't you?"

"Twenty-hour service is more like it," I said. "They don't always man their post every minute of the shift, and sometimes they doze off. But even if he was on the spot and wide awake, so what? Two well-dressed middle-class white women? Getting out of a cab and walking into the lobby together like they belong there?"

"In like Flynn," the cop said.

"Exactly. Then Erica closes the door on Kassenmeier's corpse, locks up, cabs back down to Arbor Court, and puts my keys back on the hook where she found them. She would have taken your keys, too, so she could get back in, and she puts them back, too. Then she goes home and sleeps the sleep of the unjust."

"And that's that?"

"That's that," I said. "End of story. She killed two people because one of them did something a long time ago that really pissed her off. I suppose the DA'll find out what it is by the time the case gets to court, but I kind of like the fact that we don't know. It makes the whole thing seem as senseless as it was."

"It's quite a story," Erica said.

"I'm proud of it," I admitted. "There are probably a few un-dotted *i*'s and uncrossed *t*'s in it, but it stands up."

"The only thing I'm going to say," she said, "is that there's not a shred of proof for anything you've said."

"I thought you'd say that. It's funny, but innocent people don't start hollering about lack of proof. They just say they didn't do it. But the fact of the matter is that there's plenty of proof, and there'll be more when the police start looking. There'll be people who know of your history with Karen Kassenmeier, for example. The cabbie who drove you and Karen to my place will probably remember you, once pictures of the two of you get shown around. Someone will turn up who saw you in the hotel on the night of Anthea Landau's murder, and I wouldn't be surprised if the police find your fingerprints, once they've got a set for comparison and know what they're looking for.

"Meanwhile, of course, there's the knife."

"What knife?"

"The one you used to kill two people, the stiletto with the four-inch blade. What do you want to bet it's in your apartment?"

"That is absolute nonsense."

"I have a hunch that's where the cops'll find it," I said. "Soaking in a bowl of Clorox, right on the counter under the Virginia Slims calendar. I guess that's to get rid of the blood traces, and that's not a bad idea, but why not ditch the knife altogether? Throw it down a storm sewer, say, or drop it in a trash can?" I looked at her. "A souvenir? Well, I guess it's bet-ter than the kind Jeffrey Dahmer kept, but it still strikes me as a risky thing to hang on to."

"There's no knife in my apartment."

"I guess I was misinformed. What did you do with the knife, then?"

"I never . . . How do you know there's a Virginia Slims calendar in my kitchen?"

"Carolyn must have mentioned the great picture of Martina."

"You bastard! You planted the knife. But—"

"But how did I get in?"

"I *know* how you got in. You're a burglar. But where did you get the knife? It can't be the same knife. It's a different knife. You planted a different knife in my apartment!"

"If you think about it," I said, "you'll figure out what everybody else in the room already realizes. There's only one way you could know that."

"You have the right to remain silent," Ray Kirschmann intoned. He'd said all this before, to the whole room, but now he was saying it to her, and the boy in blue was fastening handcuffs to her wrists. He had already moved over to her side while I was running it all down for them, and he had plenty of room, because Carolyn had been drawing away.

Then the two cops led her out of the room, and the door swung shut behind them.

TWENTY-THREE

I have to say the fresh air was welcome. Isis Gauthier's room was larger than the one I'd had, and it was a help having the window open, but all the same it got a little close in there. A little cross-ventilation didn't hurt a bit.

Even so, the room seemed to be holding its collective breath while the door was open. When it swung closed and clicked shut, the energy in the room picked up.

"Well," Hilliard Moffett said, running a hand through his mop of curls. "I'm glad that's out of the way."

"You said it," Lester Eddington said.

"It took long enough," Victor Harkness said, "but it's done, and the wretched woman's gone, and we can get on with it."

"Wait a minute," I said. "A very complicated series of events just got sorted out, and a murderer exposed and brought to justice. And you think that was just something to get out of the way?"

"It's not why we're here," Moffett said.

"It's why I summoned you all here," I said. "In case you were wondering."

"But it's not why we're here," Lester Eddington said. "It's why you're here, and it may be why that woman—Erica?"

"Erica," Carolyn said.

"It may be why she was here, and quite clearly it's why the police were here. But several of us are here because of the letters."

"Ah," I said. "The letters."

"From Gulliver Fairborn to his agent, Anthea Landau."

"*Those* letters," I said.

"The last we heard," Moffett said, with a nod toward Alice, "*she* had them."

"But not for long," Alice said.

"Now whose fault was that? You called to tell me you'd shredded and burned the letters. They were gone, you assured me, and you'd already notified Fairborn, and he was relieved. And you were on your way home to Virginia. In fact you had to cut our conversation short so you could catch a plane." I gave her my best sidelong look. "Another fib, Alice?"

"You'd already put yourself in jeopardy on my account," she said, "getting arrested and having to spend the night in jail. And I didn't want you to keep on looking for something you wouldn't be able to find. So I told, yes, another white lie to put you at ease and keep you out of harm's way."

"That was considerate," I said. "And I have to say it worked. I haven't been locked up since."

"But then you stole the letters from me," she said. "Didn't you?"

"I had a phone number for you," I said, "even if you never seemed to be there to answer it. Ray came up with an address to go with it, and I packed up my picks and probes and did what I do best."

"And you have them?" Moffett demanded.

"He must," Alice said, "because I'm sure I don't." She shook her head sadly. "If I'd just had a chance to copy them," she said, "I wouldn't care what happened to them. I was planning to do that right away, but I decided there was no hurry, and I might as well take time and read them through first. Then I could have them copied, and after that I could destroy the originals."

"My God," Victor Harkness said. "That's . . . that's vandalism!"

"You wouldn't have done that," I said. "You'd have found a way to sell them to one of these gentlemen."

She was about to protest, then shrugged instead. "Maybe," she said. "I don't have them anymore, so what difference does it make?"

"Let's get down to it." Moffett looked more like a bulldog than ever, and one sensed his bite was as bad as his bark. "Who gets them?"

"All I need are copies," Lester Eddington said. "As long as I'm given the opportunity to purchase a set of photocopies at a reasonable price, I don't care which of the other two gentlemen winds up with the originals."

"And the same goes for me," Alice said, and everyone turned to stare at her. "Well, I still have a book to write," she said, "and a story to tell, and the letters aren't indispensable, but it certainly wouldn't hurt to have them. And I'd pay a reasonable fee, too, the same as Mr. Eddington. In fact there's no reason we couldn't each have a set, without harming the originals or lessening their value in any way."

"That's up to the owner," Moffett said. "And after I've acquired the letters I'll decide who may receive copies."

"I must have missed something," Isis said. "When did you get to be the owner?"

"As soon as this formality is concluded," he told her, "that's precisely what I'll be. I'm in a position to outbid anyone else here, and that's what I intend to do. You're running this little auction, Mr. Rhodenbarr, so why don't we get on with it?"

"Just a moment," Victor Harkness said. "You may have deep pockets, sir, but Sotheby's has legal standing. Title to these letters remains with Miss Anthea Landau, and becomes a part of her estate upon her death. Our agreement with her is binding upon her estate. While we'll happily pay a substantial finder's fee to expedite matters, we'll certainly not stand idly by while someone with no right, title, or interest in the property seeks to transfer it to somebody else."

"Sue me," Moffett suggested.

"We're prepared to."

"Or save us both some aggravation and come to terms with me here and now. There's no reason I can't write out two checks, one to Rhodenbarr and one to Sotheby's. And when I say checks, it's a manner of speaking. It could just as easily be cash, more than enough to cover the commission your firm could expect to make on the sale."

"That's most irregular. I don't think my people would approve."

"I won't tell them if you don't," Moffett said. "In which case the cash could go wherever you wanted it to go, couldn't it?"

Harkness managed to look shocked and attracted at the same time. It would have been interesting to see which way he jumped, but it had already been a long evening. I raised a hand and signaled, and I didn't have to do it twice.

"I say," Marty Gilmartin said, clearing his throat. "It's not my place to say anything, as letters are out of my purview, but aren't you fellows getting a little ahead of yourselves?"

Someone asked him what he meant.

"You're fighting over some letters," he said, "that may or may not exist, and may or may not be in our friend's possession. Shouldn't you check the hypothesis before leaping to the conclusion?"

"A good point," Moffett said. "If you've got those letters with you, Rhodenbarr, now's the time for you to give us a look at them."

"And if you haven't," Harkness said, "this might be a good time to go get them."

I reached into my breast pocket, drew out the sheet of purple paper I'd showed them earlier. This time I unfolded it and handed it to Marty. "I brought a sample," I said. "Read this, why don't you?"

He put on a pair of reading glasses and peered through them. " 'Dear Anthea,' " he read. " 'I still haven't received the check for the sale of Italian rights. Tell them I was planning on stocking up on spaghetti, so the money'll all come back to them. Meanwhile they're sitting around playing bocce and sipping cappuccino with my money, and I don't like it. In high dudgeon, Gully.' "

"Let me see that," Moffett and Eddington said as one, and clustered around Marty.

"It's his signature," Moffett said. "I'd know it anywhere."

"So would I," said Eddington. "I should—I've seen it often enough. And I couldn't swear to it, but that looks like the same Royal portable he was using during those years. The top of the small *e* is filled, and the *g* strikes a little high."

"I'll take that," I said, and did.

"That's a genuine letter," Moffett said, "and I'm willing to believe you have the rest in a safe place. So let's get down to cases. What do you want?"

"You've all told me what you want," I said, "and now you want to know what I want."

"Well?"

"What no one seems to care about," I said, "is what Gulliver Fairborn might want."

"He's not here," Moffett said, "so we can't ask him. Get to the point, man."

"In any event," Harkness said, "he's not an interested party."

"Oh? It seems to me he's the most interested party of all. He wrote the letters."

"But they ceased belonging to him the minute he dropped them in the mail. He retains the copyright, but the actual letters are legally the property of the recipient."

"I know."

"Then what he wants or doesn't want is immaterial."

"Not to me," I said. "I didn't get into this mess for money. Believe me, there are easier ways to turn a dishonest dollar. I wanted to do something nice for a man who wrote a book that changed my life."

"Get to the point, man."

"All right," I said. I had been moving closer to the fireplace. I looked up at Elvis, who looked back at me. It was silly, I know, but I got the feeling the King approved of what I was going to do.

So I reached over the top of the fire screen and slipped the letter on through. "There," I said. "Alice, you said you burned the letters. Well, let's say you did. And let's say that was the only one that escaped. Now it can join the others."

They were a little slow off the mark, but once they got moving they didn't waste time shoving me aside and yanking the screen out of the way. The letter they'd all just examined was on top of the dying fire, and as they watched it burst into flame.

It was a pretty sight, that sheet of purple paper burning brightly atop a heap of half-burned logs and glowing ashes. And as they stared at it they saw other scraps of purple paper, the charred remnants of all the other sheets that had been burning up while we'd been learning who killed their lawful owner.

"My God," Victor Harkness said.

"An irreplaceable treasure," Moffett said. "Unique material, and now it's lost forever. You rotten son of a bitch."

"You've just stolen something from future generations of scholars," Lester Eddington said. "I hope you're happy."

"You've broken the law," Harkness said. "We could press charges, you know, on behalf of the Landau estate. Criminal mischief, wanton destruction of property . . ."

"Laws were made to be broken," I said, "and you might have trouble making those charges stick. But what choice did I have? How much choice did any of us have?"

Isis asked me what I meant.

"Well, we're all obsessed, aren't we? Alice is obsessed with her book, and Eddington's obsessed with his studies. Moffett is obsessed with his collection. Harkness is obsessed with doing his job. And look at Erica Darby. She was obsessed with revenge. Look where that led."

"And you, Bern?"

I looked at Carolyn, then at everybody else. "I may be a criminal," I said, "but that doesn't make me a bad person. It sounds corny, but I was obsessed with doing the right thing."

Silence greeted this remark, a profound and all-embracing silence, and it held until I took the fireplace poker and stirred the ashes. Little scraps of purple paper that had managed to be incompletely consumed came into contact with glowing embers and at once were burning brightly, if briefly. The sight brought a gasp to some of the people watching. The scraps were too small to be worth saving, but it was still somehow shocking to see them disappear altogether.

"That's it," I said. "The party's over. Unless you fellows want to stick around. How's the room service here? Carl, can we call downstairs and order drinks?"

He shook his head.

"Then that's it," I said. "Thanks for coming, everybody. You're free to go now."

The three wise men, Harkness and Moffett and Eddington, left in a body; they'd been opponents a few minutes ago, but now they were drawn together for the moment by their mutual hatred of me. Carl Pillsbury hung around for a few minutes, trying to figure out some way to save his job. If he lost that, he demanded, what would he do for a place to live? Isis told him he could go someplace else and start over.

"And let your hair go gray," she advised him. "You'd look terribly distingué."

"Do you really think so?"

"Oh, there's no question," she said. "You're an attractive man, but with gray hair you'd be irresistible."

I guess he believed her. He was, after all, an actor. He brightened considerably, said goodbye to everybody, and went out the door.

Alice was next, pausing just long enough to assure me that I was a son of a bitch, no question about it, but she had to admire my dedication to my principles. "So that makes you a principled son of a bitch," she said. "And who knows? Maybe you'll wind up in my memoirs."

She swept out with a flourish, and when she was gone I took the jewelry case out of my trouser pocket and lifted the top. Isis picked up the necklace, opened the catch, and refastened it around her throat. She got a compact from her purse and checked her reflection in the mirror, then called Carolyn over to show her.

"Beautiful," Carolyn said.

"But you know," Isis said, "I'm not sure I'd ever feel quite the same wearing them. Two women were killed, not *over* these jewels exactly, but *around* them. Do you know what I mean?"

"I guess so," Carolyn said.

"So," she said, and took the necklace off and returned it to the case. I closed the case, and she took it from me and handed it to Marty. "I hope Cynthia Considine enjoys them."

"She'll never look as lovely as you," Marty said. "With or without rubies, my dear."

"That's sweet," Isis said, waiting.

He didn't keep her waiting long. He opened the jewelry case to see the rubies for himself—and who could blame him, after everything that had gone on already that evening? Then he put it in a pocket, and from another pocket he drew out a thick envelope and held it out to Isis.

She said, "Twenty?"

"Twenty-five," he said. "I persuaded John to be a little more generous."

"That's so sweet," she said, and kissed him on the cheek, then took the envelope and put it in her purse. "Diamonds are allegedly a girl's best friend, and I suppose you could make a similar case for rubies, but in the uncertain life of an actress they both take a backseat to cash. One has to be practical, doesn't one?"

"Absolutely."

"But you're not practical, Bernie. You're a burglar, so you have a dark side, but your dark side has a light side of its own, doesn't it? I suspected as much when I heard you took a bear to your room. A burglar with a teddy bear!"

"Well," I said.

"And then you gave up a small fortune to do a favor for a man you never even met. You stole my rubies and gave them back, and you're not making a dime on the deal, are you?"

"I'm not a very good businessman," I admitted. "I don't do all that well at the bookshop, either."

"I think you do just fine," she said warmly. "You're quite the fellow, Bernie Rhodenbarr. Quite the fellow."

And she shook my hand, and held it a little longer than you might have expected.

TWENTY-FOUR

Some days later I was in the bookstore, tossing balls of paper—white, not purple—for Raffles. He looked bored with the enterprise, but kept up his end out of loyalty. Then the door opened, and it was Alice Cottrell.

"You really have them," she said. "Or do you? This wasn't just a ruse to get me down here, was it?"

"Not at all," I said, "but while we're on the subject of ruses, suppose you show me the money."

"First show me yours, Bernie."

I shook my head. "Carl didn't get the money first, and look what happened to him. All I'm getting is the same two grand you promised him, and until I have it in hand I'm not showing you a thing."

"I suppose I deserve that," she said, and took a sheaf of bills from her purse. They were hundreds, and there were twenty of them. I know because I counted.

I found a home for them in my wallet and drew a manila envelope from under the counter. It was not unlike the one that had been at various times in Karen Kassenmeier's purse, in the closet of Room 303 at the Paddington, and in Alice's own East Side apartment. I opened it and drew out a stack of papers similar to that original envelope's contents. These were plain white paper, however, like the balls I'd been throwing for Raffles.

She grabbed the stack, paged through it. "Here's the last one you burned," she said. " 'In high dudgeon, Gully.' It sounds like a London suburb, doesn't it? 'Where do you live?' 'In High Dudgeon, just a stone's throw from . . .' from where?"

"Boardham," I suggested.

"Perfect. You could say Gully Fairborn spends a lot of time in High Dudgeon. Bernie, I don't know how to thank you."

"You paid me."

"You went through a lot for two thousand dollars. You know, that's not all I promised Carl."

"I know."

"Did you really recognize my voice when you were hiding in the bathroom? I spoke very quietly, and I barely said a word."

"What I recognized didn't involve a lot of words."

"You could probably hear those sounds again, you know."

"Oh?"

"If you played your cards right."

"I'll call you," I said.

"Have you got my number?"

"You could say that," I said.

Within the hour the door opened again, and this time it was a gawky guy wearing a tweed jacket over a plaid shirt. It was Lester Eddington, and I didn't ask him for cash in advance. I handed him an envelope a lot like the one I'd handed Alice Cottrell, and he smiled apologetically as he withdrew its contents and had a careful look at them.

"One can't be too careful," he said. "I'd only had a look at one letter, and it was clearly authentic, but . . ." He frowned, nodded, clucked, and muttered to himself, looking up owlishly at last. "This is a gold mine," he said. "It would have been absolutely tragic to have lost these."

"That's why I made a copy first."

"And thank God you did," he said fervently. "I shouldn't say it, but I'm just as glad the originals are gone. I don't need to worry about someone else using this material before I do."

"And you won't use it in Fairborn's lifetime."

"Absolutely not. I won't publish a word until he's not around to object. Or to bring suit."

This time he was the one who counted the money, and there was a little more of it—a mixture of fifties and hundreds running to a total of three thousand dollars. I thought how hard he must have worked for that money, and it made me consider giving it back to him. And I did what I always do with thoughts like that. I squelched it mercilessly.

"You'll be listed in the acknowledgments," he said, "but I won't specify what assistance you provided."

"Well," I said, "you can't be too careful."

Victor Harkness turned up in a suit and tie, and carrying a great-looking briefcase. It looked as though it cost the better part of a grand, but for all I knew it was a knockoff like the ones the Senegalese had tried to get me to carry. I mean, how can you tell?

I had a customer—an older fellow with a beret and a silver beard—so I led Harkness to the back room and got a nine-by-twelve manila envelope from the file cabinet. He took a seat and opened the envelope, drawing out a few dozen sheets of purple paper.

"Excellent," he said.

"There's one missing," I said. "The one I had to burn to convince the others that I'd destroyed the lot."

"The one about bocce and cappuccino?"

"And high dudgeon," I said. "Everything else is here."

"The firm is deeply grateful," he said, "as am I. Our commission is the least of it. We'd announced that we were going to be offering these letters, and we'd look a little foolish if we were unable to do so."

"We wouldn't want that."

"Certainly not. But there's also the incalculable loss to literary history, and the dollars-and-cents loss to the worthy charities who are the beneficiaries of Anthea Landau's estate. I'm only sorry they won't know how much they owe a certain antiquarian bookseller."

"I'll let the credit go," I said.

"And take the cash, eh?" He opened the briefcase, drew out a bank envelope. "Five thousand dollars, as agreed. I trust you'll find this satisfactory."

A little after twelve I picked up lunch at the deli and took it over to the Poodle Factory, and a little after one I walked out the door and turned left instead of right. I took another left at the corner of Broadway and walked to a coffee shop two blocks uptown. Hilliard Moffett was waiting for me in a booth at the back. I slid in opposite him and laid—surprise—a manila envelope on the table.

He'd already eaten, and all I wanted was a cup of coffee. While I waited for it to cool he examined the envelope's contents with the care one would expect. He used a pocket magnifier and he took his time, and when he had concluded his examination he sat up straight in his seat and damn well glowed. He was a collector, and right in front of him was something to collect, and that was all it took to turn him positively radiant.

"When you burned that letter," he said, "my heart sank. And when you drew the screen aside and showed all the other letters, letters that had turned to ash while you were establishing that one miserable woman had murdered two equally miserable women, I thought I was going to die of heartbreak."

"I knew I was going to cause you some anguish," I said, "but I didn't know it would be that bad."

"But you didn't burn them after all."

"I had to make it look that way," I said, "or I'd never have been able to turn them over to you. Sotheby's had a legitimate claim, and Victor Harkness wasn't going to lie down and roll over just because you offered to scratch his stomach. But now that he's convinced the letters are gone . . ."

"He'll never know otherwise," Moffett vowed. "No one will know about these, no scholars will ever secure access to them. I'll cherish them in private."

"You'll have to." I leaned forward, lowered my voice. "I heard a rumor," I said, "that Sotheby's will be offering a group of letters, allegedly from Fairborn to Landau."

His eyes bulged slightly. "These letters?"

"Hardly. The same number, give or take a few, but different contents. Also on purple paper, and authentic-looking, but . . ."

"You're saying they're fakes, Rhodenbarr?"

"They'd have to be, wouldn't they? I can't say what I heard or where I heard it, but I gather they're damned good fakes. You'll want to look at them when they go on view, I would think."

"Absolutely."

"You might even want to buy them," I said, "Even if you're sure they're fakes, if the price is right. Because—"

"Because then my ownership of the Fairborn-Landau correspondence becomes a matter of record, and I can display what I want when and where I want. Good thinking, Rhodenbarr. Good thinking indeed. I'm paying you a lot of money, but I have to say you earned it."

"Speaking of which . . ."

He nodded and started reaching into pockets and coming out with envelopes.

"Well, well, well," Ray Kirschmann said. "If my eyes was sore I swear you'd be a sight for 'em. Good to see you, Bern."

"Always a pleasure, Ray."

"So how'd it go? You see them people?"

"I did."

"An' you did a little business?"

"That too."

"What I wish," he said, "is I coulda been there to see the looks on their faces when they saw their pipe dreams go up in smoke. Why are you lookin' at me like that, Bern?"

"Pipe dreams always go up in smoke," I said. "Never mind. It was something to see, I'll grant you that."

"You show 'em a letter on purple paper, you burn it, they see you burned a shitload of other purple paper, an' what are they gonna think? But all you did was get some purple paper an' burn it, along with one real letter to make it look good."

"It seems to have worked," I allowed.

"Then you sold 'em," he said. "An' we're partners, right?"

"Even Steven," I said, and handed him an envelope.

At six o'clock Henry helped me with the bargain table. I hung the CLOSED sign in the window and turned the lock, and the two of us went in the back room and sat down. I sighed, thinking what a long and busy day it had been, and how I could use a drink right about now. And Henry—I'll go on calling him that, if it's all the same to you—Henry drew a silver flask from the breast pocket of his jacket. I found a couple of glasses that were as clean as they needed to be, and he poured us a pair of straight shots.

I drank mine down and said no to a refill. "All done," I said. "And I have to say it went well."

"Thanks to you, Bernie."

"No, thanks to you," I said. "Typing out fifty phony letters and signing them, then starting over again and typing out fifty completely different letters and signing those."

"It was fun."

"All the same, it must have been work."

"That was part of the fun. It was a challenge, I'll grant you that. But it was so much easier than writing a novel. There was no plot, there was no continuity, there was no requirement but that the letters sound like me, and what could be easier than that?"

"I suppose."

"I had the most fun with that awful Alice, knowing that she'd be paying money for copies of letters that would only blacken her reputation. 'Dear Anthea, I'm having no end of aggravation with an annoying little poseur named Alice Cottrell, of whom you may have heard, due to the appalling bad judgment of *The New Yorker*. She manages the neat trick of being at once precocious and retarded, while having the adhesive properties of a barnacle. She's so pathetic one hates to hurt her, but so whining and physically unappealing one would like to gas her.' Let's see her paraphrase *that* for her fucking memoir."

"I made sure it was in the batch I had photocopied."

"Good."

"And you don't mind that all these people have letters of yours? Eddington? Moffett? And whoever buys the ones Sotheby's will be offering?"

He shook his head. "Let them enjoy themselves," he said. "They won't be looking over my shoulder and reading my private thoughts. They'll be enthralled by some fiction I spun out for the specific purpose of enthralling 'em. They'll be all wrapped up in an epistolary novel and they won't even know it."

"You're getting a kick out of the whole thing, aren't you?"

"I haven't had this much fun in years," he said, and treated himself to another short one. "I've had trouble writing lately, you know. I think this happy chore may have broken right through my writer's block. I can't wait to get back to work."

"That's great."

"It is," he said, "and the only sad part is parting. Sweet sorrow, according to Shakespeare, and I'd say he nailed that one good. I'm all checked out of the Paddington, Bernie, and I've got a plane to catch. I consider you a genuine friend, but you know the kind of life I lead. The odds are we'll never cross paths again."

"You never know."

"True enough. And maybe I'll drop a line."

"I'll look for a purple envelope," I said. "And burn it as soon as I finish reading it. But you're forgetting something."

"What?"

I handed him an envelope. "Put it someplace safe," I said. "There's thirty thousand dollars in there."

"That's too much."

"Our deal was fifty-fifty, remember? I got two thousand from Alice, three thousand from Eddington, five thousand from Victor Harkness, and fifty thousand dollars from Hilliard Moffett of Bellingham, Washington. That adds up to sixty thousand bucks, and half of that is thirty, and that's what you get."

"You took all the risk, Bernie."

"And you did all the work, and a deal's a deal, and you can use the dough. So put it someplace safe and watch out for pickpockets."

TWENTY-FIVE

I don't know, Bern," Carolyn said. "I'm confused."

"Well, there's a lot of that going around," I said. "I think I might have picked up a touch of it myself."

"I know it's 'Feed a cold and starve a fever,' or else it's the other way around, but neither one of them applies here. What do you do with confusion?"

"You could always try drowning it."

"Now that's an idea," she said, and waved desperately for Maxine, who sometimes took a long time to get our order. "Hi, Max," she said, when the dear girl showed up. "Let me have a double scotch, and don't even think about bringing any of that mouthwash to this table. Bern, what about you? You still drinking rye?"

"I think I've had my last taste of rye for a while," I said. "Scotch for me too, Maxine."

"Henry went home, huh, Bern?"

"Henry hasn't really got a home," I said, "so how could he go there? But yes, he's moved on. I saw him for the first time without his silver beard. Well, unless you count the times I saw him in the Paddington lobby, when he was just an anonymous gent reading a magazine. This afternoon he went into the john at the store and came out clean-shaven, with his beard all wrapped up in tissue paper. He said he'd grow a real one if only it would come in that color."

"He could always dye it."

We talked about Carl, and how people said they could always tell a dye job, the same as they could always tell when a guy was wearing a toupee. But all that meant, we agreed, was that you could tell a bad dye job, or an obvious toupee. And we asked each other why it was that it was all right for a woman to dye her hair, or get a little surgical help hiding time's ravages, but that it was somehow Not The Thing for a man to do so.

"Or makeup," I said. "Speaking of which, I see you're not wearing any. And I like your haircut."

"It's the way I always wear it, Bern. I've been wearing it this way as long as we've known each other."

"Until recently," I said.

"That was a phase I was going through," she said, "and I'm through it, and the hell with it. My fingernails don't look short to me now. They just look like my fingernails."

"And I like your shirt," I said. "What is it, L. L. Bean?"

"So?"

"Their stuff holds up," I said, "and plaid's always in style, isn't it?"

She gave me a look. "I know I look dykier than usual," she said, "and I don't give a rat's ass. I'm reacting, okay? Overcompensating. I'll get over it. Meanwhile, Bern, I'm still confused, and I'm not talking wardrobe."

"What's confusing you?"

"The knife."

"Which knife? The one Erica used to kill both victims, or the one the police found in her apartment?"

"Then it wasn't the same knife."

"How could it be? She took it with her, and she must have

had the sense to get rid of it. I went into one of the few remaining stores on Times Square that hasn't died of Disneyfication and bought a knife to plant in her apartment."

"I figured you did, Bern. And you left it soaking in Clorox to account for the lack of bloodstains. But how did you know what kind of knife to get? Carl said it was a stiletto with pearl trim, but you had already been in and out of Erica's apartment by then. Did you have a little talk with him earlier?"

I shook my head. "I was just guessing."

"You were just guessing? And you just intuitively bought a knife that was a perfect match for the murder weapon?"

"It wasn't a perfect match," I said. "It wasn't even all that close. It was your basic generic Times Square switchblade, with a blade a little longer than the murder weapon. It didn't have a stiletto-type hilt, and the sides were black, not pearl."

"Oh."

"But it was a knife the approximate size and shape of the one used to kill the two women, and it was soaking in a bowl of bleach in Erica's kitchen, and I figured it would be hard for her to explain. What's she going to say? 'That's not the knife I used! My knife was trimmed in mother-of-pearl!' "

" 'I'd never in my life use such a butch knife!' I see what you mean."

"I just wanted to shake her up," I said, "and get her so she didn't feel in control of the situation."

"Well, it worked. Bern, I was sleeping with a murderer. I'd say 'murderess,' but that's sexist, isn't it?"

"Whatever."

"Whichever word you use," she said, "that's what I was doing. And I never suspected a thing. I knew she was over the top, especially that last night, when we picked up those two meteorologists and then rained on their parade." She shuddered, then reached gratefully for her drink. "It still shakes me up to think of it," she said. "But that's not what I'm confused about."

"Oh?"

"You burned up Gulliver Fairborn's letters in the fireplace in Isis's room," she said. "Everybody saw you do it."

"Right."

"Except all they actually saw," she said, "was one letter that they'd had a chance to examine get fed to the flames. And they saw the burnt fragments of a lot of other letters on purple paper. But you didn't burn the letters after all."

"Well, you already knew that," I reminded her. "You bought the purple paper and typed out a batch of dummy letters for me, remember?"

"I'm not about to forget the lazy dog," she said, "or the rabid brown fox. I typed 'em up and you burned 'em."

"Right."

"Meanwhile, Henry got to work writing fake letters. I still think of him as Henry, Bern."

"So do I," I said. "But he wasn't writing fake letters, because they were genuine enough. He's Gulliver Fairborn, so any letter he writes is a real Gulliver Fairborn letter."

"I don't see how you can call them genuine, Bern."

"Well, how about fictional? Not genuine, maybe, but not fake, either."

"Okay. He went to work writing fictional letters. Then you took the fictional letters and made photocopies."

"Of one set," I said. "He fabricated—"

"That's good, 'fabricated.' I like that."

"—two sets of letters, and I took one set to Kinko's, call it the A set, and ran two sets of copies."

"For Lester Eddington and Alice Cottrell."

I nodded. "I didn't bother to tell either of them that the other was also getting a copy," I said. "One of those little white lies of omission."

"Alice would probably call it a fib of omission, Bern."

"She might. Anyway, the A set was the one I gave to Victor Harkness. That way, if Eddington or Alice should happen to show up when Sotheby's offers the lot for viewing, they'll see a set of originals that are a perfect match for their copies. And they'll have one thing the Sotheby's set doesn't."

"What's that, Bern?"

"A photocopy of the letter everybody saw me burn, the one from High Dudgeon. Proof positive that the photocopies were made before the letters were burned."

"How'd you manage that?"

"Well, it wasn't all that hard. I copied the letter that afternoon, before we all got together in Isis Gauthier's room."

"Oh, right."

I sampled my drink. "The other set of letters," I said, "the B set, went to Hilliard Moffett, and I didn't make any photocopies of that one. So he's got a unique item, and it's only fair, because he paid five times as much as the other three people combined. But look how he'll treasure what he's got. I'd call it money well spent."

"You would? That's where I really get confused, Bern."

"What's so confusing?"

"What's confusing," she said, "is how all this money changes hands, and you come out with nothing to show for it. Did you make anything on the rubies?"

"I made a friend," I said, "and I returned a favor. The favor was Marty's. He bailed me out, which is one of the nicest things anybody ever did for me, and I managed to do him a favor in return. Cynthia Considine has her necklace and earrings back, and John Considine's enjoying married life, at least until the next hot-looking actress comes along. Isis doesn't have the earrings, but she's got a nest egg that's immune to whatever impact synthetic stones may have on the price of rubies. And Marty enjoyed a brief fling with Isis and came out of it with good feelings all around."

"That's the favor. Who's the new friend?"

"Isis," I said. "We got off to a bad start when I ran into her in the hallway, and it got worse when she found out I stole her rubies, but during the showdown scene in her room the other night I came off a lot better in her eyes."

"Plus she liked that you had a bear."

"And one that matched her outfit, too. I've got a date with her tomorrow night, and if all goes well she'll get to see Paddington up close."

"Where?"

"In my apartment," I said. "That's where he lives these days. I suppose I could have returned him and asked for my deposit back, but I decided I'd rather keep the little guy. So that's something else I got out of the deal, Carolyn. I returned a favor, made a new friend, and acquired a teddy bear."

"And your new friend gets to meet the bear tomorrow night. Maybe she'll get to hear Mel Tormé, too."

"One can but hope," I said.

"All of that's great," she said, "but what about money? Isis Gauthier got money, Henry aka Gulliver Fairborn got money . . ."

"And don't forget Ray."

"He got money, too?"

"We had a deal, remember? Even Steven."

"Go through the numbers for me, Bern."

"Alice paid two thousand dollars," I said, "and Lester Eddington paid three, which was a little better than his original offer of covering the tab at the copy shop. And Victor Harkness paid five grand on behalf of Sotheby's."

"And Hilliard Moffett shelled out fifty K."

"That's right."

"Two and three is five and five is ten and fifty is sixty. Sixty thousand dollars?"

"It's amazing you can do that without pencil and paper."

"And you gave Henry . . ."

"Half. Thirty thousand."

"And then you went fifty-fifty with Ray?"

"That was our deal."

"Half of what you had left after Henry got his share, right?"

I shook my head. "Ray didn't know about Henry," I said, "beyond the fact that this dapper old guy was hanging around the shop a lot and even spelled me once or twice behind the counter. As far as Ray knew, there was only one set of letters, and it was written twenty years ago by some famous author he never heard of. I faked burning the letters, then sold photocopies to two people and gave the originals to a third. So I couldn't tell him I'd paid out thirty thousand dollars to Henry. It would only have confused him."

"So instead you gave the other thirty thousand to him? And wound up with nothing?"

"I never expected anything," I pointed out. "Alice flimflammed me, telling me we were doing this big favor for Gulliver Fairborn, but it turned out to be true. I did manage to do him a big favor."

"So you've got a nice warm fuzzy feeling in the pit of your stomach," she said. "And outside of that you've got zilch."

"Well," I said, "not exactly zilch."

"How come?"

"Ray only knew about one set of letters," I said, "so it would have confused him even further to bring up the second set. I gave him half of the ten grand I got from Alice and Eddington and Sotheby's, and I didn't deduct anything for expenses, not even the cost of making copies. He got exactly five thousand dollars, and he seemed very happy with it, and I figure that's about as even as Steven has to get."

"So you wound up with . . ."

"Twenty-five thousand dollars," I said, "which is not the biggest possible payoff for the kind of high-risk work I put in, but it's a far cry from zilch. I have to sell a lot of books to net twenty-five large."

"I have to wash a lot of dogs. It's not a fortune, but you're right, it's way more than zilch. You know what? It's the same amount Isis got."

"You're right," I agreed. "One more thing we've got in common."

"Mel Tormé, start warming up your tonsils. Bern, you've got something else."

"I do?"

"The letters."

"What letters?"

"The real letters, Bern. The original originals, the ones Karen Kassenmeier stole from Anthea Landau and Carl Pillsbury took from Karen Kassenmeier's purse and gave to Alice Cottrell and you stole from her apartment and pretended to burn but didn't."

"Oh," I said. "Those letters."

"Well?"

"Well what?"

"You've got them, don't you? Nobody else does, and they didn't go in the fire."

"Henry thinks they did. He doesn't know you typed up a dummy set for me to burn."

"And you kept them." She grinned. "Another souvenir, Bern? Like the Mondrian in your apartment, that everybody assumes is a fake, but you and I know is the real deal? Like the copy of *The Big Sleep* in your personal library, the one Raymond Chandler inscribed to Dashiell Hammett, that nobody can ever know exists?"

"They'd be in that class," I said. "I couldn't sell them, couldn't even show them to anybody. But I could have the pleasure of possession, the same as I have with the book and the painting. But I couldn't do it."

"What do you mean, Bern?"

"I don't suppose there's any way Henry would ever find out," I said, "and I'll probably never see him again, but I'd know, and it would bother me. He thought those letters were destroyed, and he'd be unhappy to know that they weren't. He'd feel betrayed." I frowned. "If he's never going to find out, does it still constitute betrayal? I don't know. All I can say is it bothered me. If I had a working fireplace I'd have burned them."

"So what are you gonna do?"

"I already did it. Did you know there are companies in New York that'll rent you a shredder?"

"I'm not surprised. There are companies in New York that'll rent you an elephant. You rented a shredder?"

"They delivered it yesterday," I said, "and last night I fed it the Fairborn-Landau letters a sheet at a time. One of Alice's fibs was that she shredded the letters and burned what came out of the shredder, but there was no need. All the king's horses and all the king's men couldn't have reconstituted those fragments. I bundled them up and dropped them down the compactor chute."

"So the letters no longer exist."

"Not in a readable form, no."

"But you read them before you shredded them, right?"

"I was going to," I said.

"And?"

"And I decided against it," I said. "I decided it would be a violation of privacy."

"You violate people's privacy all the time," she said. "Bern, you break into their houses and go through their drawers and closets, and when you find something you like you take it home with you. Reading some old letters seems pretty minor by comparison."

"I know," I said, "but this is Gulliver Fairborn, Carolyn. This is the man who wrote *Nobody's Baby*."

"And that book changed your life."

"It did," I said. "And I figured I owed him something."